PREGNANCY COUNTDOWN
Linda Randall Wisdom

HARLEQUIN®

TORONTO • NEW YORK • LONDON
AMSTERDAM • PARIS • SYDNEY • HAMBURG
STOCKHOLM • ATHENS • TOKYO • MILAN • MADRID
PRAGUE • WARSAW • BUDAPEST • AUCKLAND

In memory of Frances Gesswein, my very own Grammy Fran.
While you weren't my biological grandmother, you were
the grandmother of my heart who probably encouraged your
"red-haired granddaughter's" rebellious spirit a little too much at
times. I cherish the times we had together and I miss you very much.

And many thanks to Arlea Johnson
for her husband and the dead coffeemaker story.

ISBN 0-373-16991-4

PREGNANCY COUNTDOWN

Copyright © 2003 by Words by Wisdom.

Visit us at www.eHarlequin.com

Printed in U.S.A.

ABOUT THE AUTHOR

Linda Randall Wisdom is a California author who loves movies, books and animals of all kinds. She also has a great sense of humor, which is reflected in her books.

Books by Linda Randall Wisdom

HARLEQUIN AMERICAN ROMANCE

Don't miss any of our special offers. Write to us at the following address for information on our newest releases.

Harlequin Reader Service
U.S.: 3010 Walden Ave., P.O. Box 1325, Buffalo, NY 14269
Canadian: P.O. Box 609, Fort Erie, Ont. L2A 5X3

Dear Reader,

The first time a friend tried these brownies she said they were better than sex. Naturally, this is something we tend not to say to men. Poor babies just wouldn't understand that there are times when chocolate is extremely important to our well-being!

BETTER THAN SEX BROWNIES
aka Texas Brownies

2 cups flour
2 cups sugar
$1/2$ cup margarine
$1/2$ cup shortening
1 cup strong brewed coffee or water (I use flavored coffee such as french vanilla or Bordeaux coffee.)
$1/4$ cup cocoa
$1/2$ cup buttermilk
2 eggs
1 tsp baking soda
1 tsp vanilla

Frosting

$1/2$ cup margarine
2 tbsp cocoa
$1/4$ cup milk
3 $1/2$ cups powdered sugar
1 tsp vanilla

Combine flour and sugar. In heavy pan combine margarine, shortening, coffee or water and cocoa. Stir and heat to boiling. Pour boiling mixture over the flour and sugar in the large bowl. Add the buttermilk, eggs, baking soda and vanilla. Mix well using wooden spoon or high speed on mixer. Pour into well-buttered 17" x $1/2$" x 11" jelly roll pan. Bake at 400°F for 20 minutes or until brownies are done in center.

While brownies bake, prepare the frosting. In pan combine margarine, cocoa and milk. Heat to boiling, stirring constantly. Mix in powdered sugar and add vanilla; stir until smooth. Pour warm frosting over brownies as soon as you take them out of oven. If you want thicker frosting, add half again, or double the ingredients.

Enjoy!

Chapter One

Nora Summers thought about how the day was meant to be spent. She would have been dressed in a lovely lilac gown with a circlet of flowers on her head. She would have been watching her best friend get married. She would have spent the afternoon eating cake, drinking champagne and dancing. She would have joined her friends in trying to catch the bridal bouquet and she would have cried happy tears as she watched her best friend and her new husband leave on their honeymoon.

Instead, today she bid a last goodbye to her beloved grandmother.

Nora's flight home was delayed for almost six hours. The airport was quiet as the cranky passengers disembarked.

"I'll be home soon," she murmured to herself as she trudged up the corridor toward the terminal interior. "I will be in my very lovely soft bed where I will indulge in lots of sleep."

She moved past people waiting for the arrivals. She stopped short when a familiar figure straightened up from a leaning position against a pillar and walked toward her.

Nora decided she was dreaming. Men wearing tuxedos weren't a normal sight at airports at 1:00 a.m. Especially not this particular man whose wardrobe consisted of blinding Hawaiian-print shirts and shorts or jeans.

"Hey, Nora." His smile was dazzling against his tanned skin. He reached out and took her carry-on bag from her, then switched it to his left hand while circling her waist with his right. He kissed her gently on the forehead.

She wrapped her arms around him. She felt the strength of his body under his clothing. There was comfort in the familiar lime scent mingled with the warm aroma of his skin. Hints of different perfumes were added to the mix. She guessed Mark had been a very popular guy at the wedding.

"Mark, what are you doing here?" She was tired enough to feel bewildered by his unexpected appearance.

"Ginna mentioned what time your flight was due in," he explained as they walked through the terminal. "I thought you might appreciate a ride home."

"I do appreciate it," she admitted. "But my flight was delayed for almost six hours. You haven't been here all that time, have you?"

"Funny thing about airport terminals. They're loaded with coffee kiosks and bars with wide-screen televisions."

Nora shook her head trying to dislodge the fuzz clinging to her brain. Weariness was making it difficult for her to think clearly.

"Where are your baggage-claim tickets?" Mark asked.

"I only have my carry-on." She gestured to the bag he held in his hand.

"How did you manage that? When Ginna goes away for more than a day she requires at least two suitcases."

"I only needed a black dress," Nora said dully. She was tired enough to take a nearby chair, curl up in it and go to sleep.

Mark squeezed her shoulder, offering silent comfort as they walked toward the entrance.

"I'm impressed." She looked him over from head to toe. "What threats were used to get you into formal wear?"

He moved off a couple paces. He spread his arms out wide and cocked one hip in a fashion-model's pose.

"Like it? It was my wedding gift to Gin. Plus she said if I showed up at her wedding wearing my favorite shirt she'd personally burn every piece of clothing in my closet. Since she'd been in a pretty crazy mood the past few weeks, not to mention she always backs up her threats, I wasn't taking any chances.''

Nora nodded. She knew her friend would have done exactly that. "She'd invite everyone over for a barbecue and marshmallow roast.''

Mark winced. ''Yeah, she does have that cruel streak.'' He again flashed a smile that weakened many a woman's knees, including Nora's once upon a time.

They were silent as they exited the terminal and headed for the parking lot.

Mark stopped at an elegant-looking Jaguar sedan and unlocked the passenger door for Nora before going around back to open the trunk and set her carry-on bag inside.

''Your father let you take one of his cars?'' She slid onto the buttery-soft leather seat.

''He said you should be picked up in style. I won't tell you what he said will happen if I get so much as a microscopic scratch on it,'' he added ruefully as he slid onto the driver's seat.

Nora smiled. She knew Lou Walker, Mark's father, only too well. The older man was an expert in the art of restoring classic automobiles. His family liked teasing him that he treated his vehicles like beloved children. She didn't doubt that Lou demanded nothing less than a blood vow that Mark would protect the Jaguar with his life.

The engine purred like a satisfied kitten as Mark drove out of the parking lot.

''I won't be offended if you want to nap on the way home.'' Within moments, he was driving onto the freeway that boasted more than moderate traffic even at the late hour. ''I can imagine you're exhausted with all that flight delay.''

She smiled her thanks and leaned back against the headrest.

In no time, the gentle glide of the car lulled her into a light doze. Mark glanced at her a couple times as he drove down the freeway.

He'd always thought Nora was one of the most beautiful women he'd ever known. Tonight was the first time he'd ever seen her looking weary and dejected. Her skin was pale and her emerald-green eyes weren't flashing their usual fire. Even her copper-penny hair had lost its luster. She looked like a woman who'd lost an important part of her world. Which he knew she had.

Nora and her grandmother had been close. The elderly woman had raised her after Nora's father abandoned his family, and her mother retreated into herself. She never talked about it much, but Mark guessed that she wasn't more than five or six when it happened. Nora had been helping his sister, Ginna, plan her wedding when she'd received word her grandmother was dying. Nora had immediately flown to Seattle and remained with her grandmother until the end. Mark had been looking forward to dancing with Nora at the reception, but it wasn't to be. While Ginna had recited her wedding vows to Zach, Nora had attended her grandmother's funeral.

All it took was Ginna's mention that Nora was returning that evening for Mark to suggest he pick her up. His reason being, after the week she'd had, Nora shouldn't have to worry about finding transportation home.

Nora and Mark had dated for a few months a couple of years ago. The only description he could give to their relationship then was stormy. He recalled times she'd appeared insecure, which he couldn't understand since he'd never given her a reason to doubt his fidelity. His father had raised his sons to revere the opposite sex, and if there was one thing Mark was good at, it was revering women. To this day, he didn't know the exact reason why Nora had broken up with him.

"NORA. Nora," The male voice whispered her name. "Hey, you've arrived at your castle, Sleeping Beauty."

Her lids felt leaden as she strained to lift them. "I don't think I can move. Could you just wave a wand and pop me into my bed?"

Mark chuckled as he climbed out of the car. "Sorry, I left my wand at home. Besides, with my luck, you'd end up in a parallel universe." He walked around to the passenger door and opened it. "Let's just try it one step at a time, shall we?" He took her hand and helped her out. He gazed at the house, frowning. "Has anyone been staying there while you were gone?"

"Just dust bunnies." She looked in the same direction. "Oh, the lights. I put a few lamps on timers so it wouldn't look as if the place was deserted."

"Good idea." Mark left her long enough to pull her bag out of the car's trunk.

He was on her heels as she entered the house.

"Thank you for picking me up," she said, reaching for her carry-on.

"Wait a minute." He set the bag down. "You don't think I'm going to leave without checking the closets and under the bed, do you?"

Nora laughed. "Everything is fine, I'm sure of it."

"I don't see the Brumb anywhere around."

"I wouldn't have left Brumby alone this long. He's staying at the Canine Castle," she said, explaining her dog's absence.

"Ah." Mark nodded. "Five-star facilities for the discriminating canine. Since he isn't around to keep the place safe, I consider it my duty to ensure everything's all right." He wandered toward the back of the house.

Nora walked into the family room and set her purse down on a table. She could hear doors opening and closing. She was grateful she'd picked up her clothes before she left for Seattle. Looking around the room, she felt as if she should be doing something, but had no idea what.

Inside, she felt numb. All she wanted was to be left alone so she could lie down and give in to tears. Again.

"All's safe," Mark announced, coming into the room.

Nora managed a brief smile although she felt as if her lips were ready to fall apart along with the rest of her.

"Thank you again for picking me up." She none too subtly herded him toward the front door.

He held up his hand in a stop position. "One more thing. I'll be right back." He walked outside.

"Mark!" Her protest was ignored as he walked swiftly down the front walk.

She stood in the open doorway and watched him take something out of the car. He returned carrying a small pink box.

"Ginna asked me to give you this," he told her, handing her the box.

Nora held the box in one hand and opened it with the other. A soft gasp escaped her lips as she stared at a slice of white cake decorated with delicate lilac flowers. She knew the filling was tart lemon and the frosting rich enough to send anyone into immediate sugar shock. She, Ginna and Cathy, Ginna's mother, had sampled more than their share of wedding cakes before the final decision was made. She blinked rapidly to keep the tears at bay. It didn't work. She looked up.

"This is so sweet of her," she whispered.

"Aw, Nora, don't cry," Mark pleaded, getting that panicked look all men get when facing a tearful woman. "I'm no good with tears." He took the box out of her hand before she dropped it, and gently pushed her toward the family room.

He set the bag on the coffee table and turned to face her.

"You treat injured people for a living. Some of them must cry," she sniffed. Her face crumbled with fresh tears.

"Yeah, but I don't know them." He reached out and pulled her into his arms. He bestowed awkward pats on her back while looking as if he was ready to run at any minute.

"I'm sorry," she sobbed into his jacket. "Maybe I'm just tired. It's been a traumatic week."

"Hey," he said gently, now softly rubbing her back. "You've had a lot going on. Ginna told me she wanted to go with you and you told her no. Maybe you should have let her so you wouldn't have been alone."

"And have her postpone her wedding? No, I wanted her to go ahead. There was nothing she could have done in Seattle. Besides, think of the commute from Newport Beach. She had a wedding to attend, since she was the guest of honor." She tried for a bit of humor, but the stark look of misery in her eyes belied it. The last thing she would have done was ruin her best friend's wedding.

"There is definitely something she could have done. She would have been with you," Mark pointed out.

Nora shook her head but said nothing. She wrapped her arms around his waist. It had been a long time since she'd been in a man's arms. She'd forgotten how good it felt. All week she'd run on sheer nerves and coffee. She'd sat there and watched her grandmother's spirit leave her. Now she felt as if a big piece of herself had gone missing. Growing up, she'd only had her grandmother to count on when her father left her and her mother. Then her own mother had mentally abandoned her daughter. With her grandmother gone, Nora was now truly alone.

All of a sudden she knew just what she needed.

"Please stay, Mark. I don't want to be alone tonight," she whispered against his shirtfront. When she felt his body tense, she started to pull back. "I'm sorry. I'm tired. I don't know why—" Her words were cut off by the swift descent of his mouth on hers.

NORA'S DREAM involved lying in front of a cozy fire. She felt so comfortable that she thought about stretching out under her lovely soft blanket to keep this comfy feeling.

She smiled as the heat wrapped itself around her. Then her sleepy mind realized something touching her wasn't all soft and fluffy and comfy. In fact, it felt pretty firm. And male.

Her eyes flew open.

She wasn't lying in front of a fire. Yes, there was a soft fluffy blanket, but it was draped down around her ankles. The warmth she was experiencing had to do with something more than any flames. A gentle rumble resembling a snore sounded in her ear while a hand settled in a warm possessive position over her breast. She didn't miss that she hadn't bothered putting on a nightgown last night. An equally naked male body was lying spoon-fashion against her back. Then she noticed the male body was definitely aroused, and that had her memory replaying everything in living color.

Oh my God! What have I done?

Nora's first instinct was to jump out of bed and put as much distance between her and temptation as she could. Her second instinct was to snuggle back against the human furnace that was keeping her so warm and toasty. Perhaps give a couple of wiggles to wake the rest of him up. Or maybe she'd just try to breathe, because she was positive all the air had left her lungs.

For now she settled for holding her breath. She stealthily made her way out of bed without waking her companion. She crept into the bathroom and carefully closed the door behind her.

She flipped the light switch and winced as the bright light poured down on her. Perhaps checking herself in the mirror wasn't such a good idea. She moaned softly as she leaned across the counter to get a closer look at herself.

Her hair looked as if it had been through a wind tunnel, while her cheeks were much too rosy for someone who must have had maybe a good half hour's sleep for what remained of last night.

This wasn't the mirrored reflection of a woman who was on the verge of a full-blown panic attack. Her eyes sparkled with brilliant emerald lights, her normally pale skin was flushed with color and, if she wasn't mistaken, there was the slightest hint of a satisfied smile curving her lips.

"Oh my God," she moaned again. "I look like a woman who spent last night making the kind of wild incredible love that you only read about in books." She noted how languid her movements were as she stretched her arms over her head. She stared at her reflection again, leaning over the counter until her nose almost touched the glass.

"It's not as if I picked up a stranger in a bar and brought him back home for incredible sex. It's not as if I've just had a one-night stand," she whispered to her image. "All right, it was a one-night stand because this can't happen again." A whimper escaped her lips. "Oh my God, I had sex with my best friend's brother," she whispered to her image. "I had heart-stopping, mind-blowing, wild, crazy lovemaking that deserved nothing less than a triple-X rating."

More strangled whimpers left Nora's lips. She braced her hands against the sink edge, feeling light-headed as she tried to concentrate on regulating her labored breathing.

She straightened up and pushed her hair away from her face.

Nothing but an application of shampoo and conditioner would help her tangled tresses.

She took the quickest shower in history, all the while praying Mark wouldn't wake up and decide to join her. After last night, she wasn't sure she could resist him.

Last night.

A heated tingling started way down in the pit of her stomach at a memory that was sending some very real pictures to her mind. All in incredibly living color complete with sound effects.

She moaned and quickly twisted the knob to cold. It took a lot of willpower not to shriek as the icy water rained down on her head.

"It was temporary insanity. It was temporary insanity." She turned the four words into her personal mantra.

By the time her body temperature equaled that of the South Pole, Nora felt prepared to face the day.

And Mark.

MARK WOKE UP feeling as if he'd conquered the world, and it had nothing to do with the comfortable bed he was lying in.

He rolled over hoping to find a warm and willing Nora lying beside him, but no such luck.

He settled for lying back and thinking about the previous night.

He'd only planned on picking Nora up at the airport and depositing her safely at home. He was lucky enough to still have both sets of grandparents, so the idea of losing a loved one was foreign to him. But he'd figured that Nora would be feeling pretty low when she got back. The least he could do was make sure she didn't have to go home alone.

What he hadn't expected was to have her in his arms and later find himself in her bed.

When they had dated, their relationship hadn't moved to the intimate stage. Not that he hadn't tried. But instead of charming his way into her bed, he had found himself out in the cold.

To this day he still wasn't sure why Nora had broken up

with him. If that hadn't been bad enough, she had tripled the action by doing it on Valentine's Day.

Since that day, Nora had treated him as if he were a carrier of the worst kind of plague. At one point he'd even gone so far as to ask Ginna why Nora had broken up with him. All his sister had done was give him one of those haughty sniffs she did so well and inform him that if he wanted to know that badly, he'd have to ask Nora directly. Since she hadn't been returning his phone calls, that hadn't been an option for him.

That had been two years ago and he still hadn't found the nerve to ask Nora what caused the breakup.

He'd been stunned when she told him she didn't want to be alone last night. At first he'd kissed her as an attempt to comfort her. The last thing he would have done was take advantage of a woman who was vulnerable, but dammit, she'd felt so good and so right in his arms. Then when she'd asked him to make love to her, he couldn't think of anything else but banishing the shadows from her eyes. Calling what they'd shared mind-blowing was an understatement. If he hadn't woken up in Nora's bed, he would have been convinced it had been nothing more than a hot fantasy dream.

He was in the midst of remembering every incredible minute, when the door opened and Nora breezed in.

She looked more animated than she had when he'd picked her up at the airport. Her copper-penny hair was piled up into one of those complicated twists secured by a tortoiseshell clip. He was disappointed that she was covered up by a deep emerald-green plush robe that fell to her toes. He preferred seeing her bare skin flushed with desire. But he'd settle for the coffee cup she held in her hands.

"Good morning," she greeted him with a bright smile and a light kiss on the mouth. She stepped back before he could deepen it. She handed him the cup. The rich aroma of coffee tempted his nostrils. "There's a razor and clean towels in the bathroom," she informed him. "I'll have breakfast ready by the time you're done." She smiled at him again before she exited the room.

"I would have been willing to sacrifice myself as the main

course," he told the closed door. Since she didn't return, he settled for climbing out of bed and walking into the bathroom, where he found his tuxedo hanging neatly on the back of the door. The last he remembered, his jacket had been abandoned somewhere in the hallway and the pants tossed on the floor just before they fell onto the bed.

Mark turned on the shower and tested the temperature before stepping into the cubicle. He surveyed the array of shower-gel bottles lining the shelf.

"I can either smell like a sugar cookie, fudge brownie or key lime pie," he murmured. "Whatever happened to plain old vanilla?" He finally settled on key lime pie, thinking it would be similar to the lime-scented shaving foam he used. He soon discovered it wasn't even close.

It wasn't Mark's first time in a woman's bathroom, but it was the first time he'd been in Nora's. Deciding he had the time, he did a little exploring. A closet revealed a colorful supply of towels in tangerine, turquoise, lime and lemon colors. The bath towels were oversize, the dimensions perfect for a man. He wondered how many men had showered in her bathroom. He quickly decided it wasn't something he wanted to think about.

Once he finished, he towel dried his hair and worked to make himself as presentable as a morning-after visitor could be.

Mark left his jacket in the bathroom as he followed his nose to the kitchen. The homey aroma of food cooking sent his appetite level up several notches.

Damn, if he didn't feel like the man of the house going in to have breakfast with the woman of the house. He stopped abruptly. Now where had that come from?

Who knew?

Nora felt her pulse rate start to speed up as sultry images again invaded her mind.

Mark's family liked to tease him that he never moved any faster than he had to. Last night, Nora had learned that was very true. The man knew how to draw lovemaking out until she'd been gasping and crying out for him to put her out of her misery. He had ignored her pleas, and when he finally did release her, she felt as if she'd been shot out into space among the stars.

She was positive she still hadn't come down.

Nora concentrated on putting last night in a logical perspective. It wasn't working. She didn't want to call last night a mistake, but the word was blinking in bold red letters inside her head. She feared making love with Mark was the first step down a path she didn't dare travel. She told herself she could make it easy. She could blame the event on unsettled emotions. She'd been grappling with mind-numbing grief that had evolved into the need to connect with another living being. Mark holding her last night had fed that need.

She tried to tell herself that it could have happened with whomever had been holding her last night, but Nora had never been a good liar.

Come on, Nora, call it what it was. A one-night stand.

Sure it was. The earth spun around, the stars fell down around us. I'm still in shock.

Making love was different with Mark. They shared a past, even if that past hadn't included their being lovers. After they broke up, she'd told herself it was easier *because* they hadn't been lovers. That had been because she wasn't completely sure of Mark. For a man who'd been given more than the usual allotment of charm, he'd never provided her with any reason to distrust him. But she had always felt it could happen at any time. Mark had only to flash one of those devastating smiles of his and women fell all over him. Literally.

Nora never stopped to think that it was her own insecurity that pushed her away from Mark. That what her father had done to the family had remained in the back of her mind and affected any chance of Nora finding love because she was afraid she would be left behind the way her mother had been. She never stopped to think that the breakup might have been her fault, not Mark's. Nora couldn't live with the fear that one day, Mark might be tempted to leave.

"Something smells good."

She whipped around so fast the small pitcher she was holding slipped from her fingers. Only Mark's quick reflexes kept it from shattering on the floor. He set the jug on the counter.

"Pancakes?" He eyed the golden-brown circles on the hot griddle.

"Sourdough pancakes," she explained, picking up a plate. "What with my being gone a while, I didn't have too many supplies in the house, but I did have my sourdough starter and I had some freeze-dried eggs to use along with some sausage from the freezer. I'm surprised I had as much in there as I did." She nodded toward the coffee pot. "There's juice in the refrigerator if you want any. Glasses are in the cabinet."

"Want some?"

Been there, done that.

She banished her mocking private voice to the far reaches of her brain. The man was merely inquiring if she wanted orange juice.

"Yes, thank you." She slowly poured more of the pancake batter onto the griddle. At least she could hold on to her composure on the outside.

It wasn't the first time a man had spent the night in her bed. Although, for many months, the only male who had been there was Brumby, her beloved bulldog.

A few minutes later she handed Mark a plate heaped high with pancakes, sausage and a couple of scrambled eggs. The look of bliss on his face rivaled Brumby's when he was given a beef bone.

"Tell me about the wedding," she requested when she sat down across from him.

"The usual. Everyone was dressed up like grown-ups, Zach looked as if he was ready to pass out at any moment, Ginna looked gorgeous," Mark replied. "The only hitch was the nephew-to-be, Trey, taking his ring-bearer duties too seriously. When big brother Jeff untied the ribbons to give the rings to Zach, the little guy pretty much threw a fit. He said loud and clear that he was to protect the rings and Jeff couldn't have them. Trey's sister, Emma, told him to shut up and stop acting like a baby. That broke up any solemnity the service had."

Nora smiled at the idea of Zach's twins adding a few surprises to the ceremony. "Who caught the bouquet?"

"Our aunt Minnie pretty much trampled the competition," he replied. "Six marriages and she's still hopeful she'll eventually get it right. I give her credit for perseverance."

"And the garter?" She referred to the custom of the groom tossing the bride's garter over his shoulder toward the single men. A custom that revealed who the next groom would be.

Mark studied his pancakes as if they held the secrets of the universe. "No one interesting, although Aunt Minnie wanted to participate. Dad and Gramps told her no way."

Nora arched an eyebrow. Her smile grew in proportion with her glee as she easily figured out who the lucky recipient was.

"You caught the garter?"

"It was a conspiracy. I had no plans on standing out there with the other idiots," he said. "At the last minute, Jeff and Brian pushed me out into the front of the group, and just like the Red Sea the group parted so the garter was literally thrown in my face." His expression boded ill for his two older brothers.

"You should have known you'd be the next target. Your dad said he hopes Nikki waits until she's forty before she gets married," Nora reminded him, speaking of his youngest sister.

"Nikki has no desire to get married until she's out of medical school. It's Aunt Minnie who needs watching. The reception had barely started before she had husband number seven narrowed down to three victims." He leaned back in his chair and spoke, emphasizing his words with eloquent gestures.

Nora's smile widened into a genuine one as she listened to Mark's stories about friends and relatives celebrating his sister's special day. He described each incident so well that she felt as if she were right there with him.

But she also knew she had to consider last night a one-night stand even though that kind of experience wasn't her style. The last thing she needed was to get caught up with Mark Walker again. It hurt too much when she'd broken up with him. After making love, she feared that not only her heart, but her soul, wouldn't recover if she got involved with him a second time.

She'd put all the blame on herself for last night. She was hurting and vulnerable and he was there.

There was no reason for it to happen again, no matter how much her tingling body argued with her at just the memory of what had flared up between them.

No reason at all.

Chapter Two

"I really appreciate you fitting me in, Nora," Lucie Donner said, settling back in the soft-cushioned salon chair.

"You sounded so urgent on the phone I was afraid you were going to walk in here with purple hair." Nora smiled at Ginna's new sister-in-law.

"After everything that's gone on, that would be a plus," Lucie laughed.

"That's right, you lost part of your house. What's happening with that?" She ran a brush through Lucie's hair then ran her fingers through the shoulder-length strands.

"You haven't lived until you come home and discover an airplane engine has dropped into your home office at ten o'clock in the morning," she confided. "Talk about a shock."

"And?" she prodded.

"And I realized that ordinarily I would have been sitting in there, except I had a parent-teacher conference with Nick's teachers that morning. I've decided it's time to make some changes. I sold the house."

"You're moving? I thought it was being rebuilt for you after the accident."

"Accident is an understatement," Lucie chuckled. "Almost half my house was flattened after that jet engine fell through the roof. I didn't even want to consider going back there. I'd mentioned selling it to a neighbor and he wanted to buy it for his son and daughter-in-law and rebuild the house to his own specs. He offered me a great price and I took it. I'm hoping that moving to a new area will give Nick a new chance. I swear, it was getting to the point where I thought I'd have to seduce a judge just to keep my baby boy out of jail,'' she said.

"I thought he was doing much better.'' Nora mentally cataloged highlight shades and which ones would do best for Lucie.

"Oh, he is. I haven't received a call from the school for almost three weeks. That's pretty much a record for him. But I never drop my guard,'' she chuckled, half turning. She froze. *"Ohmigod!"* She grasped Nora's arm. "Is that who I think it is?''

Nora smiled. She easily guessed which client Lucie was staring at. She pressed her hands on Lucie's shoulders, keeping her turned to the mirror. "Yes, it is. Try not to drool.''

"Drool would be the least of my problems. I once seriously thought about moving to Australia because of that man. Look at his smile!''

Nora chuckled as the object of their conversation turned toward them, smiled and winked.

"Now I can die happy,'' Lucie sighed. "Right after you turn me into a blonde.''

"And we want this because…?''

Lucie's smile dimmed. "We want this because I've come to realize life is much too short. Just the idea of having that engine come so close to wiping me out started me thinking about my priorities. I realized a majority of my outside contacts consist of being the helper mom at Nick's school, chaperoning his class's field trips, and being a voice over the phone when someone is booking a trip. Other than occasional recharge days here at the spa, I haven't done much for myself. I don't mean that I hate being known as Nick's mother or Zach's sister or even so-and-so's travel agent. But, there are days when I'd like someone to think of me as Lucie, Wild Woman.''

"Well, Wild Woman, you don't have to be blond to change your life. Besides, going totally blond wouldn't suit your coloring,'' Nora explained. "What if we intensify your highlights? That won't be as drastic.''

Lucie stared in the mirror at her reflection. "Whatever you think best."

"Carte blanche. I love it." Nora combed her fingers through the other woman's hair. "Don't worry. You'll look great when I finish."

She brightened. "Maybe the new me will tempt the sexy Australian."

Nora chuckled. "Oh, honey, stand in line."

Two hours later, Lucie surveyed her new image. Shades of dark blond, gold and copper added more light to her hair. Nora had trimmed a few inches off the ends, giving her a more casual look.

"I like it," Lucie said. "Now to buy some new clothes to go with the new image."

"Are you sure Nick can handle having a sexy mom?" Nora teased.

"If I can handle that sky-high IQ of his, he can handle this." She quickly stroked dark coral lip gloss across her lips. "Yep, just what I needed."

"You'll be beating the men off with a stick," Nora predicted.

Her face lit up. "You know, that wouldn't be so bad."

After Lucie left, Nora glanced at the empty station that belonged to Ginna. She missed having her best friend there. Then she mentally reminded herself that Ginna knew her only too well. The last thing Nora wanted her friend to hear was that Nora had slept with her brother.

Even if a tiny voice deep inside reminded her that sleep hadn't been exactly high on their list that night.

"HEY, buddy, Magnum called. He wants his shirt back!"

Mark rolled his eyes at the reference to the famed television private detective operating out of Hawaii.

"Ha, ha, very funny. I never heard that one before," he said with perfect deadpan delivery. He opened his locker door and pulled out a navy blue polo shirt with the fire department's insignia embroidered on the upper left-hand corner of the chest. He hung up his short-sleeved shirt on a hook inside the locker.

He didn't care what anyone else thought. The shirt with swaying palm trees and hula girls dancing under the trees across the white cotton fabric was one of his favorites. He tossed his well-worn khaki shorts into his locker after pulling out navy twill pants that finished his uniform, identifying him as a paramedic.

"I hate to think where you find those shirts," his older brother Jeff said as he also changed into his uniform. His locker door slammed shut with a metallic clang. "I worry about you, baby brother. I'm thinking in forty or fifty years you're going to be one of those little old men with the knobby knees, eye-blinding plaid Bermuda shorts, black socks and sandals who'll be chasing sweet young things."

"As to that horrifying little-old-man picture you drew, there's no way I'd steal that pleasure from you, big brother. Don't worry, Jeff, I'm leaving that up to you and Brian." Mark clapped him on the back. "I can see it now. You two will be wearing shirts that match Abby's and Gail's dresses," he said, referring to his brothers' wives. "You'll all take cruises together and play shuffleboard and bingo. Maybe you two will even go wild playing a few hands of canasta. Lights out at nine," he snickered. "You'll be real party animals."

"Grandma would whomp you upside the head if she heard you describe her lifestyle that way," Brian, Mark's other older brother, warned. "That woman can party all three of us combined under the table and you know it. That's why Gramps quit traveling with her. He couldn't keep up with her."

"I thought Theo had agreed to go on that Alaskan cruise with Martha and her bridge club," Eric, one of the brothers' friends and co-workers, commented as he walked past them.

"Grandma said Gramps could stay home, which makes him happy since he doesn't like cruises. But he didn't like it when she told him he cramps her style," Jeff replied.

"She is the grade-A party animal," Eric agreed. His head whipped up when a piercing signal echoed over the speaker system. "Time to roll!"

Mark and Brian exchanged telling looks as they heard information about a multivehicle traffic accident. They knew their skills as paramedics would be needed.

At the station, Mark was known as the party animal. If there was a practical joke played, he was most likely behind it. He was the one to plan any celebration. But when it came to his work as a paramedic, he was all business. Anyone who was familiar with the lighter side of the man would not recognize his more serious demeanor.

The two brothers climbed into their EMT truck and rolled out with the fire engines. Their day was just beginning and it was promising to be a long one.

MARK COULDN'T STOP thinking about Nora. He was convinced his fingertips could still feel her silky skin. He even imagined her subtle scent was imprinted on him. He could feel the touch of her lips on his mouth, his jaw, his shoulder and just about everywhere else on his body.

He remembered once reading about a fever in the blood.

That's how he thought of her. She was a fever that never let up.

So if they had something that good, why hadn't she returned any of his calls in the past couple of weeks?

No wonder he was parked outside her house at six o'clock in the evening.

He hadn't realized before just how isolated Nora's house was. While its location on the end of the street was ideal for privacy, the nearest house was set some distance away with a small park in between. He frowned at the open grassy area set between Nora's house and her neighbor's. Most of the area was set up with a variety of playground equipment. He thought it was a nice little neighborhood park where mothers could take their kids for playtime. But he didn't like it for Nora's sake. With evening coming on quickly and the old-fashioned–style streetlights spaced far apart, he felt she was too vulnerable to a home-invasion robbery.

"Why did she pick a house that doesn't offer very much protection?" he muttered, sitting slouched behind the steering wheel. "Any pervert could sit out here watching her." He didn't stop to think that anyone might view him as the kind of unwanted intruder he was visualizing.

Finally realizing it might not be a good idea for him to just hang around there, Mark switched on the truck engine with the intention of leaving. He was getting ready to pull away from the curb when he noticed a light turn on by the front door. The door opened and a tan-and-white bulldog walked out. He slowly made his way down the front walk in a bowlegged waddle while Nora stepped out onto the porch. She leaned against the front post and watched her dog walk across the street and over to Mark's truck. He stopped by the front tire and awkwardly lifted his leg.

"Damn dog," Mark muttered, throwing open the door and climbing out. He scowled at the damp spot on his front tire. The dog looked up at him and gave a canine grunt.

"Are you lost?" Nora called out with a mocking tilt to her lips.

"I just happened to be in the neighborhood," he said, offering her one of his patented killer smiles while inside he winced at the use of an old line that hadn't lost any of its idiocy over the years. Judging from her set expression, it wasn't working. He forced himself not to flinch when Brumby attached himself to his leg. "Ah, would you call off your dog, please?"

Nora's gaze shifted downward to her dog then back up to meet Mark's eyes. "Brumby has a mind of his own."

"And that was a fact I'd happily put in the back of my mind." Mark shifted from one leg to the other. Damn! He hadn't felt this awkward since fourth grade, when he'd asked Julie Chambers to sit with him at the class picnic. She had turned him down flat and elected to sit with Ryan Miller instead. Payback had come in the form of a nice juicy-looking lizard showing up inside Julie's hamburger. The teacher had had no trouble nabbing the culprit. And Mark had suffered detention after school for three weeks. He hadn't minded. It had been worth it.

"Can I come in?"

He didn't miss the indecision shadowing Nora's eyes before she finally gave a brief nod. She called out to her dog and waited as the bulldog lumbered back up the walkway. Brumby rotated his head just enough to look back at Mark with a gaze that was suspicious at best.

"I was invited," he informed the dog as he followed Nora into the house.

"One of my neighbors called me to say there was a strange man lurking across the street from my house. She was ready to call the police, but I informed her you were fairly harmless," she told him as she made her way to the rear of the house. "Of course, if you'd rather have the police hauling you in I can call her back and tell her to feel free to make the call. She loves nothing better than to call in anyone she considers a pervert. You'd make her day."

"Gee, thanks for saving my dignity. Such as it is." He found himself walking carefully as Brumby still tried to keep himself plastered against Mark's leg.

Nora eyed his shirt covered with swaying palm trees and hula girls. "Have you ever had a parrot try to built a nest on you?"

"Not lately."

Mark sniffed. If he wasn't mistaken, he could smell cinnamon and a few other scents that could only add up to one thing, cookies fresh from the oven. He closed his mouth before he embarrassed himself by drooling. There was no hiding his hopeful expression.

Nora sighed. "I suppose you want some of my cookies."

He opened his mouth, ready to throw out one of his infamous lines loaded with innuendo. Luckily for him he closed it in time.

Nora glared at him as if she knew exactly what he was thinking.

"Yes, please," he said meekly, shifting over to lean against the counter. He watched her place several good-size cookies on a plate. She opened the refrigerator door and pulled out a carton of milk. A filled glass soon followed the plate to the table. A soft snuffling sound attracted her attention. "No cookies," she told her dog in a firm voice. "The vet said you have to lose five pounds."

A rumbling response from the bulldog told them his opinion

of the diet. He settled back awkwardly on his haunches. His tongue lolled happily as he gazed up at his mistress with adoring chocolate-brown eyes.

Nora didn't miss that a pair of sizzling blue eyes were also watching her. Except, instead of adoration, she saw something more fundamental in his stare. Her first instinct was to look away, so she forced herself to return his steady gaze. She wasn't about to let Mark know he left her feeling unsettled.

Without taking his eyes off her, Mark pulled the chair out on the other side of the table. When Nora settled herself in it, he carefully pushed it forward before walking around to the opposite chair and sitting down. He picked up a cookie.

"Oatmeal?" he questioned. She nodded. "Please tell me these don't have raisins in them."

"I firmly believe oatmeal cookies should only come with chocolate chips," Nora told him, aware of his extreme dislike for the tiny wrinkled fruit.

He bit into one and groaned with delight. "Still warm," he muttered, taking a second bite. "Damn, these are good!" He paused. "Please don't tell my mom I said that or I'll never get any cookies out of her again."

"You're safe. It's your mother's recipe," she replied.

Mark polished off the rest of the cookies in record time. He cast a beseeching look in Nora's direction.

"Brumby begs a lot more eloquently." She carried the plate over to the counter and put a few more cookies on it then dug a dog biscuit out of a box and tossed it in Brumby's direction. The dog's jaws promptly parted long enough to catch the biscuit before snapping shut. A low rumble of satisfaction sounded deep in his throat after he finished his treat. He looked up with hopeful eyes.

"You are so pathetic," she sighed as she tossed him another biscuit.

"Spoiled is more like it," Mark muttered then grabbed his plate before she could take it away from him. "Well loved," he amended.

"You're as pitiful as the dog." She used a spatula to place the rest of the cookies on a cooling rack. When she finished, she turned around. "Care to tell me the real reason you're here?"

"I wanted to make sure that you were all right."

That wasn't the answer she had expected.

"I'm fine," she said shortly.

Mark didn't take his eyes off her. "After—"

"We had sex, Mark," she said flatly. "No promises were made, no declarations given, no strings attached. Let me make this perfectly clear to you. I haven't been sitting by the phone in hopes you'd call. I didn't expect you to show up with flowers and candy and spouting love poems. It was just one night, Mark," she said in a voice that sounded forceful. "I needed some comforting that night. It was nothing more." She ignored his wince at her blunt word choice. She mentally put his expression down to a fragile male ego. Not that what she said might matter to him. That *she* might matter to him.

Mark leaned back against his chair, one arm draped along the back.

"Don't ignore the truth, Nora. We had more than a one-night stand," he said softly.

"I was grieving for a beloved relative," she stated just as softly. "I was vulnerable."

"Don't try to say I took advantage of you."

"I'm not saying that!" She paused and took a deep breath. "You're off the hook, Mark."

He shot to his feet so fast his chair fell backward onto the floor.

He blew up at her. "Off the hook? Who the hell said I thought something that ridiculous? Dammit, Nora! Can't a guy just stop by to see a woman? Can't he come over to see how she's doing when she's been through a rough time without her thinking the worst of him?"

"Are you saying you came by here without an ulterior motive?" She smiled when she saw the guilty flicker in his eyes.

Bingo!

"I was worried about you."

His simple statement doused the fury still roaring inside her like a cold shower. Nora collapsed against the counter. Her hands gripped the edge so tightly the knuckles turned white from the strain.

"I'm fine," she managed to say eventually but not convincingly.

"No, you're not."

She laughed. "Are you calling me a liar?"

"Only someone who's lying to herself." He walked over to her and gently pried one of her hands away from the counter's edge. His thumb gently caressed the inside of her wrist in a manner that wasn't the least bit intimate. "Pulse a little too fast. Pupils reacted a little quickly. Shallow breaths," he recited. He smiled at her look of surprise. "Honey, you forget I'm a trained paramedic. I can recognize the signs of full-blown panic a mile away."

She snatched her hand back. "I am perfectly calm." That wasn't panic in her voice, was it? She hadn't counted on her emotions getting the best of her. "Dammit, Mark! Why are you here? We had a nice night, but that's all it was. Afterward, you were supposed to go your way while I went mine. You weren't supposed to return to the scene of the crime!"

He looked affronted. "I don't recall doing anything illegal." He screwed up his face in thought. "Well, maybe in some states people could consider that one thing…" He paused with a meaningful look.

"Stop it!" She didn't care that his wince meant her shriek was less than pleasant to his eardrums. "Stop the jokes. Stop the 'I wanted to know you were all right' idiocy. Just stop it all!" She blinked furiously to keep the tears from falling. She was positive that at that moment she downright hated the man. The last thing she wanted was for him to see her cry. She took a deep breath to settle herself down and waited for Mark to crack one of the many jokes that resided in his memory bank. She was certain that he could come up with one that would fit the occasion.

Instead, he stood there and calmly looked at her as if she hadn't just screamed at him. Silence stretched between them like a taut wire.

Mark moved a step forward. He lifted his hand to cup her

cheek. She resisted the urge to lean into his touch. She closed her eyes against the tumultuous feelings welling up inside her.

"Please go," she whispered, keeping her eyes closed.

"You don't want me to go, Nora." His breath was a warm caress against her forehead.

"Yes, I do."

"Then open your eyes, look directly at me and tell me to go," Mark murmured.

Her lips parted slightly. Whatever she was about to say was swallowed up by Mark capturing her mouth with his own.

A dizzying sensation she'd only experienced once before returned in full force. She gripped his shoulders as her knees gave way and the world spun crazily around her. She tasted the rich flavor of chocolate on his tongue, felt the hardness of his body against her. For one wild moment she wanted to crawl inside his body and just plain feel.

"Do you really want me to go, Nora?" he murmured against her ear.

She dragged her senses to the surface as her lips formed the word *yes*.

"No," came out instead as she drew his mouth back to hers.

Mark didn't need to be reminded where Nora's bedroom was. Nor did he have to be forcibly dragged to the back of the house. He kicked the door shut and danced Nora toward the bed.

Nora was left awash in sheer sensation as she reveled in Mark.

A faint scent of lime was on his cheeks, the taste of chocolate on his tongue and the sound of seduction as he whispered in her ear.

Clothing fell to the carpet a piece at a time. Sheets rustled their own story as they dropped onto the bed.

She arched up under his touch as he reacquainted himself with every inch of her body. Lightning zigzagged through her body as he pressed his mouth against her nipple and gently suckled. As if he wasn't making her crazy enough, he started moving farther down, dropping soft kisses along the way.

"Mark!" she wailed, blindly reaching for him. She was greedy for all he could give her.

"Just wait. It will get better," he promised, pausing long enough to drop a kiss on her belly button before moving farther downward.

Nora threw back her head as she laughed. The sound that emerged was thin and high-pitched.

"Promises, promises. Ah!" she gasped as his forefinger brushed against the ultrasensitive nub of flesh.

She felt shock waves course through her as his fingertips brushed it again. Before she had a chance to recover, she felt his warm breath. After that, she knew nothing as she rode each cresting wave. Even then, Mark didn't allow her to catch her breath before he moved up and over her.

"Open your eyes, Nora," he ordered. His hips rested comfortably against her as if they were made to be together.

Except she noticed they *weren't* exactly together. Not that there was any hesitation on his part. There was no doubt he was *very* interested. She could feel the proof against her. She didn't want him merely nuzzling against her, she wanted him *inside* her.

"Mark!" She wiggled her hips against him.

"Look at me!"

She opened her eyes and looked up into eyes that were such a bright color, she felt as if she were drowning in a white-hot blaze of blue. Her hands had been gripping his shoulders. Now they reached up and cupped his face.

"Show me the world, Mark," she murmured, bathing his lower lip with the tip of her tongue.

His smile flashed white as he bent his head to kiss her deeply at the same time as he thrust into her. Her hips arched up at the same time.

Mark not only showed Nora the world, he flew with her into the outer reaches of the cosmos.

Chapter Three

"Something is going on and I want to know what it is," Ginna insisted.

Nora buried her nose in the newspaper. She couldn't believe it. Her friend had been in the salon for barely ten minutes and she already sensed something. If Nora hadn't had a full day booked she would have stayed home no matter how much she wanted to see Ginna.

"Did you know scientists found a dinosaur egg in an ice cave and they were able to successfully hatch it?" Nora reported in a bright voice. "And everyone thought those movies were fiction." She gave an unladylike little snort.

"Nora!" The paper was snatched out of her hands. "You always make fun of those papers."

She looked up with guileless eyes. "Do you mind? I'm studying for my next appointment. Mrs. Crockett loves to discuss the latest tabloid headlines. This way I can hold my own in the conversation."

Ginna lowered her voice. "Mrs. Crockett also believes little green men visit her once a month and on Arbor Day. They go out for brunch and come back to her house for bridge."

"That's because they love her lemon tea cakes."

Ginna dropped into the chair beside Nora. The women were relaxing in the well-appointed break room set up for the employees of the Steppin' Out Hair Salon and Day Spa.

When Ginna had walked inside the salon that morning she'd gone over to Nora, studied her face and hugged her hard.

"You better tell me what is going on," she'd whispered in her friend's ear just before she released her.

Nora had been able to avoid any private conversation with Ginna all morning thanks to a heavy schedule. Zach showed up to kidnap Ginna for lunch. Now she was back with a little too-pleased brightness to her smile and stalking Nora with single-minded intent.

Nora's time was up. She carefully folded the paper and set it down.

"Let's see. You had a beautiful wedding and an even more beautiful honeymoon. You have a husband who adores you and two stepchildren who are absolute dolls. I am happy that you've found your true love in Zach, I really am. Yes, I'm a little envious, but I know you understand and forgive me for that envy."

"You've been through a lot in the last month, sweetie. I saw your sorrow and I wished I could have been with you. But what I see in your eyes now isn't all grief," Ginna murmured. "I see confusion in there too and I don't think it has anything to do with your grandmother's death. Does it?"

Nora took a deep breath. She should have known Ginna's sharp eye would pick up on her unsettled emotions.

Since the morning she'd woken up beside Mark again, she'd asked herself why she'd invited him back into her bed. She knew she couldn't blame him. He'd taken his cues from her. She couldn't lie to herself that she didn't know what she was doing. Because she did know what she was doing and it was eating her up inside.

Making love with Mark transcended anything she'd ever experienced before. The two nights she'd spent with him were a pure sensual joy she could easily find herself addicted to. It had been a month and she still recalled every moment they spent together.

She was already addicted to that joy and craved more. Except that meant adding Mark to the equation. That was a dangerous combination.

"I miss Grammy Fran. I miss our nightly talks on the phone, her visits down here every Thanksgiving through Christmas and my visits up there every summer. I miss her advice," Nora replied. "But I feel her spirit with me all the time and that helps. That's probably what you see."

Ginna leaned forward, propping her chin in her cupped palm as she stared at her friend. Nora resisted the urge to fidget under her piercing gaze. She'd forgotten Ginna's eyes were the same brilliant-blue color as Mark's. All the Walker family shared the identical eye color.

Except, while Ginna's examined her with a disconcerting thoroughness, Mark's eyes seduced her.

"Anyone I know?" Ginna asked softly.

Some kind of temporary insanity tempted me to make love with your brother, not just one night but two. The man is a genius in bed. He had me practically screaming with pleasure. Is that what you wanted to know?

"Nora, Mrs. Crockett is here." A tall willowy woman in her early twenties seemed to float through the doorway. An off-the-shoulder peasant-style blouse in a creamy white topped a handkerchief hem skirt in the same color. Decorative embroidery in reds, yellows and greens highlighted a color that would have normally been boring at best. Black hair was skimmed back from an oval face that could have easily graced an antique cameo. Tan leather strappy sandals graced narrow arched feet with toes tinted the same red as the embroidery in her skirt and blouse. An equally narrow waist was cinched with a soft leather belt.

"Thank you, Paige," Nora said, grateful for the interruption.

"She is so different from Renee," Ginna commented, mentioning the receptionist who had worked at the front desk until just before Ginna's wedding.

Nora nodded. "Paige is twenty-three and a graduate of Vassar who's trying to decide what to do with her life. Her father is a producer at Warner Bros. and her mother designs jewelry that starts at five figures and she's a close friend of the spa's owner, CeCe. Paige's ancestry goes back five generations in this state. Her great-great-grandfather was a senator and an aunt a couple generations back was in the Ziegfeld Follies. The woman later married a railroad magnate," Nora replied. "CeCe said Paige needed to find her true self and she would be able to do it here. She's a real sweetheart, to boot."

"Good thing I snagged Zach before he got a look at Miss Way-Too-Good-To-Be-True," Ginna said dryly. "Otherwise, I would have had to kill him to make sure he didn't talk to her."

"I doubt that would have happened. He was hooked from the first second he saw you. He even admitted it."

Ginna grinned. "Yeah, I did look really good that day." She waved her hands at Nora. "All right, escape to your client. I'll corner you later and find out what's happened while I was gone." She heaved a theatrical sigh. "It's not fair. I go away for a few weeks and I miss out on all the fun."

"Somehow I doubt you thought about any of us while you were gone," Nora teased as she fled.

For the next hour, Nora was relieved only to have to listen to her beloved client's stories about past alien abduction.

"I know you think I'm cuckoo, dear, but I don't mind." Mrs. Crockett patted Nora's hand after Nora finished styling her snowy-white hair. "My friends certainly think that, although they're nice enough not to say so out loud. I appreciate you being so sweet and listening to me prattle on."

"You don't prattle. You use such vivid imagery when you tell me about your adventures, I think you should write about them," Nora urged her. "There are magazines out there that would publish your stories."

Mrs. Crockett's eyes twinkled merrily. "Actually, I have written a few tales," she admitted in her whispery-soft voice. "In fact, I would love it if you would read one of my little stories." She dug into her briefcase-size black purse and pulled out several sheets of paper.

Nora took them from her. "I'm flattered you're asking me," she said honestly.

"You don't have to be kind with your critique, dear." The elderly woman patted her arm. "But I would be interested in your response."

"I'll read it before I see you next week," Nora promised.

She watched the elderly woman walk toward the front of the salon where an equally elderly man sat on one of the soft-cushioned couches. His wrinkled face lit up in a smile as she approached him. The two walked out together, arm in arm.

"I thought Mrs. Crockett was a widow," Ginna commented, following the direction of Nora's gaze.

"She is. That's Harold, her boyfriend," she explained. "She told me she likes to call him her boyfriend because he makes her feel seventeen again. It seems they were high-school sweethearts, had a fight back then and they broke up. They didn't run into each other again until a few years ago. Both spouses are gone and they decided to give it one more try."

"How adorable! Did she ever say what the fight was about?"

Nora chuckled. "He wanted them to be intimate, she told him no. Sixty years later, they're living together. She said she hasn't told her mother she's living in sin. The woman would be horrified."

"You mean her mother's still alive?"

"She's ninety-eight and going strong. She lives in Leisure World in Laguna Niguel."

"And now Mrs. Crockett is writing stories about her alien visitors?" Ginna eyed the papers with curiosity.

Nora nodded as she held up the papers. "For the past sixty years they've met for brunch at one of the hotels in Newport Beach. She's never said which one."

"Since your next appointment is here and I have a free hour, may I read the story?" Ginna's glance focused on the papers.

Nora handed them to her. "Don't tell me the ending."

As she worked that afternoon, Nora found herself looking toward the front every now and then. Did she expect Mark to walk through the door and declare that she was the only one for him? Was that why she'd spent the past few nights picking up her phone every now and then to make sure it was working? Or looking out the window every time Brumby gave one of his rumbling barks? She was furious with herself for these feelings of expectation.

After all, she was the one who'd told him that what they had was nothing more than sex. She didn't want any ties between them. She didn't want to expect more and have him fail her somewhere down the road. She had pretty much told him she would prefer he didn't come back.

"I am such a hypocrite," she muttered to herself as she stood in the supply room selecting hair color.

"Nora!" Ginna ran into the room. The papers Nora had given her were in her hand.

Nora turned and noticed her friend's high color. "What's wrong?"

Ginna carefully folded the papers in half then half again. "I suggest you stand in a cold shower when you read this."

"What?"

Ginna laughed. "Trust me, Nora. This stuff is so hot it's downright sizzling. Mrs. Crockett didn't just write about her alien visitors, she wrote about their sexual practices. This makes the *Kama Sutra* sound like a grade-school textbook."

"Their *what?*"

Ginna nodded. Her blue eyes danced with laughter. "We aren't talking about little green men here either. We're talking about guys with huge orange—" She gulped. "I can't go on. The thing is, she writes an incredibly believable story. It doesn't read like a joke." She lowered her voice. "It reads like the truth."

Nora took the papers from her and tucked them into her skirt pocket. "No offense, Gin, but I think you honeymooned a little too hard."

"After I read her story I wanted to call up Zach and tell him to be ready, because I was going to jump his bones big-time when I get home," Ginna admitted as she walked back to the door. "If she gives you any more stories, I want to read them!"

Nora shook her head in disbelief. "Oh yes, the woman had way too much honeymoon," she muttered under her breath.

"HEADS UP, little brother."

Mark looked up at Jeff, who held out a can of beer. He accepted the icy can. "I just finished three straight games of dodgeball with twenty million kids. I'm discovering I'm getting

too old for those games." They were at their parents' house
for the family weekend barbecue.

"You volunteered to be their first target," Jeff reminded
him. He dropped into the patio chair next to him. "So who are
you looking for?"

"Your hot-stuff wife. Who else?" Not for anything was he
going to admit who he was really looking for.

Mark knew Nora had a standing invitation to attend the
weekend barbecues and any other party thrown by the Walkers.
She'd still shown up once in a while even after they had broken
up.

It wasn't until today that Mark realized Nora hadn't been
out here for some time. For the past couple of years, he'd been
able to put her out of his mind. Mainly because it was easier
that way rather than constantly wondering what went wrong
between them. It was only after the first time they made love
that he'd found himself looking for her. Not that he asked about
her. Privacy about one's love life wasn't an option in the Walker family. If he asked about Nora, his mother would want to
know if they were dating again. There was no way he'd admit
they'd slept together. Cathy Walker would be making noises
that it was time for her baby boy to get married. Then Jeff and
Brian would join in on the chorus…and Ginna. Hell, Ginna
would just plain make his life miserable. She'd done more than
her share of that right after he and Nora broke up.

He'd always felt Ginna's accusations about his being a
scuzzball were unfounded. After all, he'd been the injured party
in the relationship. All he knew was that they'd gone out for
the evening, at some point she had turned a little surly, and by
the end of the night she had told him not to call her anymore.
When he'd demanded a reason, all she'd said was that she
finally saw him for what he was and she didn't like it. When
he'd asked her exactly what she meant, she'd coldly informed
him that he, of all people, ought to know. He'd left her house
confused, angry and just plain hurt. He had called her, wanting
to know what went wrong, and she had refused to even speak
to him. Finally, he'd pushed his hurt deep down inside and
went looking for any woman who would assure him he was

still a stud. He'd never admitted that his mega-dating spree hadn't helped one bit.

To this day, he still had no idea what he supposedly did wrong that night. And he still wanted to know.

Come to think of it, he'd add to that interrogation by asking Nora why she pretty much threw him out of her house that second morning. Some hostess she'd been. The last time, she didn't even offer him coffee.

"Like hell you're looking for my wife," Jeff said amiably, stretching his legs out in front of him. "Admit it. Abby terrifies you."

"Yeah, she does have that scary quality, but that doesn't mean I don't like looking at her. Your wife is one hot-looking babe. *Ow!*" He clapped his hands on top of his head where he'd just been delivered a painful thump.

"Ingrate," Abby Walker informed her brother-in-law with a shark's smile. She stepped around him and dropped into her husband's lap. She looped her arm around Jeff's neck as she studied Mark. "No wonder you can't keep a girlfriend. You always look like a fugitive from a Jimmy Buffet concert."

"I give you a compliment and this is what I get in return?" Mark grumbled.

"Be grateful you didn't get worse." Abby stared him down.

"Fine, you're an old crone."

Which everyone knew was untrue. Not when Abby was blessed with California-blonde good looks. As a mother of three small children, she should have looked tired and worn out. Instead, she was the picture of energy and health in a pair of pink floral-print capris and a solid-pink tank top that bared her flat midriff. Her sun-golden blond hair was pulled back in a complicated braid he knew Ginna had created that morning. At the moment, Abby looked more like a college cheerleader than a thirty-something mom of three young children who kept her constantly running.

Until recently, Mark hadn't bothered to consider how lucky his older brother was. Now he looked at Jeff and saw more than a guy who had lost his freedom on his wedding day. Now he saw the father of twin girls and a boy who was starting to walk, a loving husband to a woman who was drop-dead beautiful. He remembered when his brother seemed to have a girlfriend for every day of the week. Then Abby flew into Jeff's life with hurricane force and Mark's big bad brother had fallen like a ton of bricks for the energetic blonde.

Mark watched Brian on the other side of the yard talking to their dad. Brian had been something of a party animal too. Then Nikki, their baby sister, put Brian's picture and personal information on the Steppin' Out's Blind Date Central bulletin board and Dr. Gail Douglas chose him to accompany her to a dinner. Instead, they were carjacked, kidnapped, dumped in the middle of nowhere, caught in a rainstorm and, after spending the night in an abandoned house, almost arrested for trespassing.

Gail was an uptight, no-nonsense pediatrician and Brian was a laid-back, easygoing guy. Who knew they'd end up together along with a baby girl conceived on that memorable night?

Mark suddenly felt a tightening in his throat as he looked around at his family that seemed to be growing at a steady rate.

His oldest brother had the kind of family Norman Rockwell painted.

His other brother was well on his way to having Hallmark's idea of a perfect family.

One sister was now married with two stepchildren who fit right in with the Walker clan.

His parents and grandparents were perfect examples for their children.

Then there was Mark and Nikki. He knew his younger sister was safe from family hopes of her getting married since she was premed and had long years in medical school ahead of her.

Mark was in his thirties and his family expected him to start adding to the Walker family tree.

He didn't think that was possible. Not that he thought he couldn't have children. Just that he wasn't sure his adding to the Walker population was a good idea.

Mark was convinced that when the fatherhood gene was passed out to the Walker brothers, he was off somewhere else.

He made a great uncle and knew it was a job he could easily handle. He just couldn't see himself as a dad 24-7.

"*Mark!*"

He jumped. "*What?*" He glared at his sister-in-law. He was positive Abby's shout just took out an eardrum. "Are you trying to make me deaf?"

She rolled her eyes. "As if! You were already impervious to your surroundings."

"Impervious. Wow, the kids teach you that ten-dollar word? Storybooks have come a long way since we were kids." He pretended to cower under her look of outrage.

"You know, I really pity the woman who ends up with you," Abby told him.

Mark looked to his brother for moral support, but Jeff's broad grin told him he'd find no sympathy there. He leaned forward and pushed himself out of the chair.

"You are an evil woman," he told Abby with as much dignity as a man wearing a wild fuchsia and green flowered shirt and baggy stone-colored cargo shorts could give. He walked away with her laughter ringing in his ears. He didn't mind. He knew he would get even with her later on. Abby and Ginna giving him a bad time was nothing new to him.

Mark didn't have to go far to find someone to talk to.

He hung out at his parents' house on most of his free weekends, as did many of his friends. They brought their wives or girlfriends and treated the place like a second home the way Cathy and Lou Walker liked. Mark couldn't remember the last time he had brought a date with him.

This was the first time he'd spent time looking for Nora. And the first time it really mattered that she wasn't there.

Chapter Four

Nora couldn't remember the last time she had felt so terrible. For all she knew, she had never felt this bad before. If she had the strength she'd beg someone to put her out of her misery.

She sat on her bathroom floor with her back against the wall and held a wet washcloth against her forehead.

A faint snuffling sound came from her left as a cold nose pushed against her leg.

"Oh, Brumby, I feel horrible," she moaned, keeping her eyes closed. She was afraid if she opened them her stomach would resume its acrobatics. She wasn't used to getting sick just by looking at her bathroom tile.

She'd woken up that morning feeling as if her stomach was turning itself inside out. She'd spent the next hour in the bathroom and vowed never to get takeout at that new Chinese restaurant again. By the time her stomach settled down she'd vowed never again to eat Chinese food, period. The following hour, she was starving. By then, she'd even felt well enough to fix herself a big breakfast and eat every bite. Afterward, she took Brumby for a long walk, which pleased the bulldog to no end since he loved nothing more than patrolling the neighborhood.

That afternoon she'd settled down on the couch with a book and had fallen asleep before reading three pages. The activity wasn't a usual occurrence for her, but it seemed like a good idea at the time.

When Nora woke up a couple of hours later, the open windows invited in the rich aroma of steaks cooking on a grill at a neighbor's house. Her stomach rolled over as if she'd just stumbled off the fastest roller coaster in the world. She barely made it to the bathroom in time.

Thirty minutes later, she was still in the bathroom because she was afraid of straying too far. She feared she was in for a repeat of that morning. Which meant it wasn't last night's Chinese food. Then she remembered several people at the salon had come down with a nasty flu virus.

"How could I catch the flu?" she mumbled. "I take just about every vitamin I can imagine." She smiled at the dog's muffled snore. Her smile took a downturn and her voice turned to a groan when she heard the doorbell chime. "The last thing I want right now is company!"

Nora remained seated on the floor. Whoever was at the door could assume she wasn't home and leave. Even Brumby didn't stir. Except the melodic summons didn't stop, it turned downright annoying. She knew that only occurred if someone was keeping a finger on the button. She didn't care. She wasn't budging.

"Come on, Nora! I know you're home. You better answer before I call 911!"

Nora muttered a curse that was very unladylike.

"What is *he* doing here? There's no reason for him to be here," she muttered, slowly rising to her feet. For a second, the world swayed around her. Nora held on to the sink until everything settled into place.

She paused to see if her stomach would give her the excuse she needed to ignore the doorbell. The traitorous part of her body decided to behave. She caught a glimpse of herself in the mirror. Skin white as paper. Eyes dark and sunken in her face. Her hair was sticking out every which way. She couldn't look any worse if she tried.

"Talk about scary. This is good. One look at me and the man will run for the hills," she observed.

"Nora?" Mark's voice sounded panicked as it floated through the front window. He started pounding on the door.

"I mean it. If you don't come to the door I'm calling the cops."

"Not if I call them first," she said under her breath as she slowly walked down the hallway.

"If you don't open this door in five seconds, I'm calling my mom!" he shouted the ultimate threat. "Do you really want her coming out here? You know she will."

Nora groaned. The last thing she needed was Mark's mother showing up at her door. Cathy Walker would do just that if Mark called her to say Nora wasn't well. Nora loved the woman dearly, but she didn't need anyone fussing over her. She took a deep breath and headed for the door.

"You are such a mama's boy." She threw open the door. "Go away." Having given her command, she started to close the door, but Mark gripped it tightly and held fast. "Mark!" She tried pushing again, but he easily moved her to one side and stepped inside.

"What happened to you?" he demanded, walking past her. "You look like hell."

"Thank you so much for that heartfelt compliment. Now that I've scared you into Halloween, would you please leave?" She swung the door open in hopes he would get the message. The last thing she wanted was company. While she had at first thought it was a good idea that Mark see her at her worst, she now realized she didn't want him seeing her when she looked less than human.

Mark held up two plastic grocery bags in one hand. He used his foot to gently move Brumby away from his leg.

"Mom was sorry you didn't come out for the barbecue. She asked me to drop some of the food off to you," he explained. "There's some of her potato salad, some of Abby's chocolate cake, not that I'd recommend it, but Abby stuck it in. There're also slices of tri-tip roast and some rolls if you want to make sandwiches."

As the aromas wafted upward to her nose, Nora could feel her stomach start to roll over again. She swallowed convulsively. The last thing she wanted was to become sick in front of Mark. If that happened, he would not only refuse to leave, he'd probably call his mother, to boot! If she thought Mark was difficult to get rid of, Cathy would be downright impossible, because she would insist on staying until she was certain Nora was all right. Nora would feel much better if Mark would just leave her alone.

Except Nora knew she was lying to herself.

The idea of a man taking time to stop by as a favor for his mother and not put off by a woman who looked like something dragged out of one of the hiding places where Brumby kept his precious toys, was charming. She didn't want Mark to be charming!

She looked at Mark. She wanted to reach out for him. To ask him to take her in his arms and tell her she was going to be all right. That he'd make it all better. She blinked rapidly for fear she'd completely disgrace herself and break down in tears.

"I'll have to call Cathy and thank her for her thoughtfulness. It was very nice of you to drop the food off, so sorry you have to leave," she said, her voice husky.

She should have known that Mark would ignore her. He walked past her and disappeared into the kitchen. She could hear the rustle of the bags as he set them on the counter and her refrigerator door open, then close as he put the perishable food away. She was ready to march in there and demand to know what was taking him so long, when he returned with Brumby following fast on his heels.

"I hope you don't mind that I tossed Brumb a small piece of the tri tip. Hey, are you sick?" he asked. He reached forward to press the back of his hand against her forehead. She reared back. He stepped forward again and this time succeeded in touching her.

"It's a toss up between the Chinese food I had last night or the beginning of the flu, which I'm certain you wouldn't want to catch." She suddenly felt weak in the knees. She wasn't sure if it was because she'd been sick a good part of the day or because of Mark's proximity. She wanted him to go before she broke down and begged him to stay. When had she turned so indecisive? She used to know her own mind and stick to it.

Now all she seemed to do was argue with herself as to what she should do.

Mark was bad for her. He was the kind of man she didn't need in her life. Which was why, deep down, she'd actually been pleased to see him at the door. Not that she'd ever admit it.

"I'm a trained paramedic, Nora," he gently reminded her. "You do feel a little warm. You have a thermometer around so we could double-check?"

Nora blinked back the tears that threatened to fall. She told herself he was only concerned about her because he needed to do the right thing.

"I don't need anyone to check up on me. I don't need my temperature taken, Mark. I just need to get some sleep. But I can't do that until you go." She feared she sounded as desperate as she felt.

Mark looked surprised by her curt tone.

"Nora, if it is the flu, you need to be checked out. Let me call someone." His voice softened. "I can call Gail. I'm sure she'd come over to examine you."

Nora laughed softly. "I think you've forgotten something. Gail's a pediatrician and I'm not five years old."

"That doesn't matter. She's still a doctor," he persisted. "She can still tell you if it's the flu or something more serious."

"It's not the flu. Something I ate disagreed with me. That's all. All I need is something to settle my stomach and some quiet time. Both of which I'll have once you're gone," she said pointedly.

He didn't move. "If you start feeling worse, will you call me?"

Nora edged him toward the door. "Yes, I will call you," she lied.

He looked at her searchingly. "No, you won't," he said finally. "I wish you'd let me into your thoughts, Nora. I don't know why you won't believe it, but I do care what happens to you." He leaned forward, kissed her on the forehead and walked out the door. "And I mean it, Nora. If you need something, call me no matter what time it is. I'm off for the next few days."

"All right," she lied, knowing it was the only way he'd leave.

Mark looked skeptical. His expression let her know that the small smile on her lips and her impassive gaze was an assurance that didn't ring quite true.

"Try to eat something," he said.

"I will," she replied, mentally urging him out the door.

Thankfully, this time he heard her silent plea and headed the rest of the way to the door. The minute he was on the other side of the threshold, she flashed him one last smile of dismissal.

Nora had barely closed the door after Mark when she felt the familiar upheaval in her stomach. She clapped her hands over her mouth and ran to the bathroom with faithful Brumby toddling after her. She didn't think about Mark any further.

A couple of hours later, after a bowl of chicken noodle soup, which she always considered one of her comfort foods, she curled up in bed. A favorite movie on TV provided background noise that mingled with Brumby's rumbling snores.

When the telephone rang, she reached over to pick up the handset.

"Hello?"

"Nora, it's Mark. I wanted to make sure you were okay."

You should have known he would call to check on you. Mark may have been a wild boy at times, but he was also a caring one shot through her mind. She was rocked by a familiar voice echoing inside her head.

"I'm much better, thank you. Proof it had to have been something I ate," she replied.

"You looked pretty pale earlier," he pointed out. "Even if you feel better now, it doesn't mean you might not have the flu."

"Most redheads are pale. That's why we have the hair to make up for it." She pushed her pillow behind her as she sat up.

"That's what your grandmother used to say."

"You remembered that? You only saw her, what, two or three times?" she said, surprised.

"Hey, don't sound so surprised," he chuckled. "Your Grammy Fran reminded me a lot of my grandma. She always spoke her mind, let you know where you stood with her and she was a lady who fully enjoyed her life. Who wouldn't remember someone that special?"

Nora couldn't keep the tears back. She felt a strange tug down deep in her stomach along with a soft ache in her heart. The need for Mark to hold her in his arms was strong.

"She once said your shirts were so loud she'd never need a hearing aid around you." She pressed her fingertips against her lips, unsurprised to find them trembling. She took a deep breath. "Mark, I have to go. Good night and thank you for calling." She pushed the disconnect button and set the handset down. She picked it back up and shut off the ringer. She curled up under the covers and closed her eyes. A moment later, she took further precautions by pulling her second pillow over her head.

Nora couldn't remember experiencing a more miserable night. By the time she fell into a decent sleep, Brumby was uttering throaty growls and pawing at the doggie door that Nora kept locked at night because the neighbor's cat liked to make late-night visits.

The next morning, after spending most of the day before in bed, she felt more human and even hungry.

As she cooked breakfast, thoughts raced through her head. Too many questions and not enough answers. If she and Mark had made love when they were seeing each other, would she have been so quick to break it off with him?

"There's no guarantee we would have stayed together," she told herself as she slid behind the wheel of her lime-green Volkswagen Beetle. "Mark liked to party too much. I didn't. And then, I convinced myself that I was the damper on the relationship and I dated way too many guys to prove I could be a wild woman. All I got out of it was a case of dating overload." She looked both ways before zipping onto the busy highway that paralleled the beach.

It may have been mid-September, but the weather was more like June. She wished she'd lowered the convertible top before she left the house so she could have enjoyed the morning sun the way so many Californians did that day.

Nora parked in the grocery's parking lot and walked swiftly toward the store. Her steps faltered momentarily when she saw a tall figure wearing a colorful shirt. Then the man turned and she realized it wasn't Mark.

"What's wrong with me?" she muttered, picking up her pace. "The sex wasn't that good."

Liar.

"Shut up," she ordered the voice inside her head.

Come on, Nora, the man did things to you that had you tied in knots. Admit it. You never had anything as good as what you had those nights. The man was fantastic.

"There's nothing worse than a mouthy conscience." Nora blithely ignored a woman's startled glance in her direction as she snagged a shopping cart and headed for the produce department.

Ordinarily, she would have treated her trip to the grocery store with the same enthusiasm she greeted a trip to the dentist. She'd been known to pick up a week's worth of groceries in ten minutes flat. Today was different. She first picked up a latte at the coffee bar. Then she took her time strolling up and down each aisle as if she were a world explorer on a quest. By the time she finished her shopping, she not only had everything that was on her list but a great deal more than she'd normally eat in a month. A stop at the dry cleaners, the drugstore, and she finished up her errands with shopping for new toys for Brumby at a popular pet superstore.

"Pig ears for my baby," she announced, carrying bags into the house. Brumby made his way toward his mistress, drool dripping from his jowls. He accepted his favorite treat with a canine grunt of thanks and waddled off to his favorite spot where he could enjoy it in peace.

As Nora put away her groceries, she had an unsettling thought. She'd bought enough food to feed two or more. Anyone coming in would think she was expecting company.

Company such as Mark, who's always been known for his large appetite; in more ways than one.

She grimly stifled the crowing voice in her head.

"It's to make up for those days I felt as if I couldn't even drink water," she told herself.

That night, Nora cooked herself a huge meal and savored every bite. The following morning, she woke up convinced she was going to die.

"Please tell me you have an opening this morning," she begged her doctor's receptionist when she called to see if she could get a last-minute appointment. She promised to be there promptly at ten when she was told they would squeeze her in.

Nora showed up ahead of time, and when ushered into an examination room, she answered questions, gave the requisite samples and impatiently waited for the doctor to come in and tell her what was wrong with her.

"So you've had an upset tummy that won't go away, have you?" her doctor said, smiling at her when he stepped into the room.

"Which is really nothing more than the flu, right? Or are you going to tell me it's something worse? Okay, give it to me in twenty-five words or less," Nora said, bracing herself to hear the worst.

Her doctor smiled. "I can do better than that, Nora. I can give it to you in two words. You're pregnant."

Chapter Five

Nora's sense of the world tilted dangerously. If she hadn't been sitting down, she would have fallen to the floor.

"Ah, no, that's not possible," she protested, even as the logical part of her brain kicked into high gear. Dates circled on her calendar that had gone by without incident was the loudest reminder. "I'm on the Pill," she stated as if that said it all.

Dr. Averick smiled warmly. "It's not only possible, Nora, but very true. It can happen even when you're on the Pill. All the symptoms you've been experiencing should have been your first warning. I'm sure you probably thought they were side effects to all you've gone through lately, but that's not the case here. Besides, tests don't lie," he said gently. "I'd say you're about six weeks along."

Six weeks. The night Mark came over to her house and she cried on his shoulder. The second time she invited him into her bed. And she had forgotten to take her pills when she was in Seattle and for about a week or so after she got back.

She pressed her fingertips against her temples. It did nothing to cease the voice in her head. She closed her eyes as the softest of whimpers escaped her lips.

Nora opened her eyes when a warm touch landed on her wrist. Dr. Averick's fingers lay lightly against her skin.

"Am I to gather you and the father are no longer together?"

She smiled at his less-than-subtle probing. The man had been her doctor since she'd arrived in the Newport Beach area more than ten years ago. Here, she'd been afraid she might have something more serious than the flu. In a way, it was more serious. She just found out her flu would last another eight months.

"Not exactly. He's my best friend's brother and, ah, he's part of a large family," she said lamely, afraid she wasn't making much sense. "He has lots of nieces and nephews." She swallowed then whimpered. "Excuse me, but I think I'm going to be sick."

Ten minutes later, Nora felt better after the doctor prescribed medication he assured her was safe for the baby and would calm her nausea. Armed with samples of prenatal vitamins and a prescription for the nausea, she left the office. Her head was still spinning and the sensation had nothing to do with nausea.

Nora was grateful she'd cleared her schedule that day. She knew there was no way she could return to the salon and Ginna's sharp eyes. The woman would have the truth out of her within minutes. Nora didn't want to think what Ginna's reaction would be. She wanted to wait on that conversation until she was more comfortable with it herself.

She recalled it wasn't so long ago that Ginna thought she was pregnant by Zach. A total surprise since Ginna was convinced she couldn't have children. It took Gail interpreting an old medical report to explain that it wasn't Ginna's fault there were no children during her first marriage, but an allergy to her husband's semen that caused her to reject every wiggly sperm that tried to do its job. It had turned out Ginna wasn't pregnant, but it had given her the courage to go to Zach and make things right. Now Ginna was married to a man who loved her with all his heart and had two adorable stepchildren who loved her just as much.

And now Nora was going to have her best friend's brother's baby.

"Stay tuned for our next emotionally packed episode of 'There's Something About Nora'," she muttered as she drove out of the parking lot. "She let her hormones take control and oh boy, they went wild." She suddenly wondered if she'd be able to fit inside her car eight months from now. *"Oh my God! I'm going to be a mother!"*

Nora had no idea how she made it home in one piece. Since the afternoon had turned chilly, she changed into forest-green leggings and a baggy black-and-green-striped sweater that hung down past her thighs.

"It will probably be a snug fit before I know it," she said wryly as she slipped on her tennis shoes.

Brumby uttered growling barks when she picked up his leash.

"Yes, we're going to your very favorite place," she told him, fastening the leash to his collar. She tucked her house key and wallet in her waist pack along with two small bottles of water, one for her and one for Brumby. She headed for the door with an eager Brumby pulling on his leash.

Nora liked that her house was only a few blocks away from the dog park. What Brumby couldn't do in speed, he could make up in enthusiasm at the sight of other dogs. Some days, she took him to the little park next to her house. His next favorite activity was sprawling on the grass and watching the kids play on the swings and the other equipment. Not to mention he graciously accepted all the attention the kids lavished on him.

At the dog park, Brumby greeted a few dogs he knew then happily followed his mistress toward one corner of the park. Nora sat cross-legged on the grass while the bulldog plopped down beside her. He panted heavily as he surveyed the park in search of friends, old and new.

"I have news for you, Brumby," Nora began. His ears pricked up at the sound of his name. "We're going to have a new addition to the family. Not a puppy," she swiftly assured him. "A baby. There's going to be a little boy or girl for you to play with although not like Theodore Train Engine or Sam the School Bus." She mentioned two of his favorite toys that made appropriate noises when he bit down on them.

Brumby looked up at her and made sounds that she hoped meant "Congratulations" and not "No way am I sharing my toys!"

"Now I just have to figure out how to tell Mark. Not right away, of course. I have to get used to the idea myself first." She suddenly groaned. "Oh no! Everyone is going to jump all over this piece of news. Another Walker brother turns into a surprise daddy. First Jeff, then Brian and now Mark." She buried her face in her hands. "He'll never live this down." Tears that threatened to fall were halted when Brumby scrambled up onto her knees in his attempt to offer her doggie kisses. She hugged him tightly as he continued to lick her face. "We'll do fine, sweetie. Once I figure out how I'm going to handle all this."

An hour in the park of playing Keep Away with Brumby cleared Nora's mind and raised her spirits. She was still smiling during their walk back to the house. Her smile wobbled a bit when she saw a familiar truck parked in her driveway and an equally familiar figure seated on her front steps. He stood up as she and Brumby approached him. The dog woofed a couple of times and strained at the leash. Nora dropped it as he waddled toward Mark.

"You must be feeling better," Mark greeted her.

"Just something I ate." She almost choked on her lie.

He frowned. "Ginna said you haven't been feeling good lately. That has to be more than just something you ate."

"I've learned what foods to avoid. Why are you here, Mark?"

He looked away and mumbled something.

Nora felt tired and not in the mood to act nice. Not to mention, she was afraid he would just look at her and guess her secret. Mark might not be a doctor, but he was a paramedic. He had told stories of his delivering babies that weren't going to wait to reach the hospital. She hoped it didn't mean he could diagnose pregnancy by just looking at a person.

"What did you say?"

He turned back and kept his eyes trained on her face as he said, "I said I wanted to make sure you were all right." There was no doubt of his sincerity. She didn't want him caring about her. She wanted him to go on with his life the way she planned to go on with hers. She knew after their breakup he'd gone on with his life with the help of a public relations assistant named Daisy who worked at a local advertising firm. After Daisy came Kate, then Joanna. Nora wouldn't be surprised if he worked his way through the alphabet. She was proud of herself for not once asking Ginna about Mark. That didn't stop Ginna from occasionally dropping comments about her brother's social life. Nora had always been grateful Ginna had never asked Nora her reason for breaking up with Mark. Nora had never admitted just how much it hurt to realize Mark was just like her father. The last thing she wanted was to be with a man whose eyes wandered too much.

She refused to re-create her mother's life. Nora thought she was safe because marriage had never been brought up when they dated.

She walked over to the steps and sat down beside him. He shifted his body so that he was facing her. Brumby ambled up to plop down between them. He groaned happily when Mark scratched him behind the ears.

"Mark, you don't need to be the good guy here," she said softly. "I told you that first morning that I wouldn't be the clinging vine or expect anything from you. No strings. You're safe." She was surprised by the slight frown creasing his forehead.

"And you told me the same thing the second time around. You're not a one-night stand, Nora."

"No, I'm a two-night stand," she said slowly and deliberately, not missing his wince at her blunt choice of words. "You happened to be there when I was feeling vulnerable. I didn't wake up hoping for bouquets of roses and impassioned declarations."

"Some would say you're protesting too much." He stood up and held out his hand. She placed hers in it and he pulled her up. He didn't let go of her hand as he started down the driveway toward his truck. A sharp-edged whistle had Brumby on their heels.

"What are you doing?" She tried to hang back, but he was having none of it.

"I'm taking you out to dinner. I bet you haven't had a decent meal in days."

"I have so." She couldn't believe he'd guessed her lunch was a container of orange-crème yogurt. It seemed to be the only thing her touchy stomach could handle. At least the doctor's news had cleared up that mystery. She watched him pick up her dog and put him in the back seat. "Last I heard, dogs weren't allowed in restaurants."

"They are if you go to Syd's Place where dogs are welcome on their patio," he told her.

"Mark!" She tried digging in her heels but didn't get very far. Plus, he already had her dog in the truck. He gave her an ungentlemanly push up into the passenger seat. As if he guessed she still might try to bolt, he reached over her and pulled the seat belt across her chest and fastened it.

"I have plenty of food in my refrigerator," she argued.

"You've cooked for me twice. Since cooking isn't one of my better skills, I'll take you out." He jumped into the driver's seat and started up the engine. The Rolling Stones immediately filled the cab. He quickly turned down the volume.

"Brumby will drool all over your clean seats." Nora tried another argument.

"As long as he's not toxic, I'm not worried." He stretched his arm along the back of the seat as he half turned while backing down the driveway. "I hope you're hungry. Wednesday is chili night at Syd's."

"Just don't give Brumby any," Nora warned.

"You can pick something from the dog menu."

She knew it was time to give up. For some reason, Mark was determined to take her out to dinner, so she may as well let him. A tiny smile touched her lips. She *was* hungry and she *was* eating for two.

Though the light was dim, Mark didn't miss Nora's smile. At least she had stopped arguing with him. Damn, the dog was drooling all over the back seat! He tightened his jaw and concentrated on the road.

"How do you know Syd's Place? You don't have a dog," Nora pointed out.

"Brian mentioned that he and Gail go there a lot since they can take their dog," he replied. "Seems the baby loves the beach. They like to stop there to eat before heading home."

Nora saw the comparison between Mark and Brian much too clearly. She didn't expect any impassioned declaration of love from Mark or an insistence on doing the right thing. It wasn't his style. It was a well-known fact he didn't like to be tied down.

She knew how he would react as well as she knew how his family would react. His parents, Cathy and Lou, would welcome a new grandchild and his grandmother and grandfather, Theo and Martha, would boast about the newest great-grandchild.

She knew her baby would have the joy of a large family. Something Nora hadn't had as a child. She knew she wouldn't keep the baby from them. The older Walker clan was never happier than when they spent the day together with family and friends.

She gave herself a mental shake. She was looking ahead to perhaps a year from now. She needed to concentrate on getting through dinner without divulging news she was still trying to get used to.

Look at this evening as a positive echoed inside her head in a voice that sounded way too much like Grammy Fran's. *The two of you made a baby. Be friends if you can't be anything else.*

Nora looked out the window at the colorful buildings that housed surf shops next door to art galleries and swimsuit boutiques.

A wooden sign weathered by the salt air with multicolored letters announced they had arrived at Syd's Place. Mark found a spot near the eatery and helped Nora out of the truck. He picked up Brumby and kept hold of his leash as the dog eagerly explored the bowls of plants set outside a florist's.

"No way, guy." Mark reined him in. "You water those plants, they'll make you buy them."

"His allowance couldn't cover buying a flower petal from there," Nora said.

Mark studied the shop's exterior, white with dark green accents. Green window boxes filled with colorful blooms highlighted a display window that showed off an elegant crystal vase holding a rose in a delicate shade of peach. Tiny fairies hung from the ceiling looking as if they were flying around the vase.

"Mom loves stuff like that," he commented.

"Christmas will be here before you know it." Nora smiled slyly.

He didn't miss her smile. "What do you know about that vase that I don't?"

"The cost. Twelve hundred dollars and that's without the rose."

Mark tried to say something but air was caught in his chest and he started choking. Nora reached over and helpfully slapped him on the back.

"You're joking, right?" he wheezed.

She shook her head. "The shop caters to those who want Italian crystal for their vases, flowers flown in from all over the world, and who are willing to pay for it."

"Good thing Syd's Place lets us lowly paramedics in." Mark held the door open for Nora.

"Hello, sexy!" a yellow-nape Amazon parrot sang out as they walked through the door. He let out a piercing wolf whistle that had Nora laughing.

"Hello, Syd," she greeted the bird who fluffed his feathers and wolf whistled again.

"Hey, Nora." A man wearing white jeans and a brightly colored tropical print shirt smiled at her then looked past her. "Mark! Haven't seen you here in some time." He picked up two menus and a bone-shaped sheet.

"Hey, Ryan, I like the shirt." Mark grinned as Nora rolled her eyes.

"Yeah, and I get to wear mine to work." The restaurant owner grinned back. He led them outside to the patio and seated them at a table that overlooked the beach. There was only one other couple out there with a haughty-looking Pekinese seated sedately by a chair. Brumby uttered a soft woof. The dog didn't respond.

Mark leaned down to speak in the bulldog's ear. "She's not your style, Brumb. A lady like that is high maintenance. Look at that silky fur. Can you imagine the grooming costs alone? Not to mention doggie perfume, manicures and pedicures. Trust me, you can do much better."

Nora accepted the menu Ryan handed her along with the bone-shaped menu listing the canine cuisine the restaurant offered.

"You're giving him dating advice?" She arched an eyebrow at Mark.

"I know these high-maintenance women. They'd rather look in the mirror than talk to you."

"Hey, guys," a young woman wearing white shorts and a snug-fitting bright coral cotton T-shirt greeted them with a warm smile. The badge pinned to her shirt proclaimed her name was Cyn. She set a metal bowl filled with water in front of Brumby. "Hey, Brumby." She gave him a scratch between the ears. "How about you two? Do you want a drink before dinner? Can I start you out with some of our potato skins, our onion-ring tower or fried zucchini?"

Mark looked at Nora inquiringly. "What do you think?"

"Any and all sounds good to me," she replied, feeling hungrier by the minute.

"You two want to share the sampler platter?" the waitress asked.

"Bring it on, gorgeous," Mark agreed. "Nora, do you want to share a bottle of wine?" he asked.

Nora shook her head. "Not tonight. I'll have the passion fruit iced tea, Cyn," she told the waitress.

"Regular iced tea for me," Mark said.

"Got it." Cyn turned on the patio heater set next to their table and bounced off to place their order.

Mark returned to studying the menu.

Nora had one eye on her menu and another eye on Mark. She knew his brown hair owed its deceptively casual look to Ginna's mastery with scissors, but the cotton shirt covered with hula dancers, his baggy khaki shorts and battered running shoes with no socks was pure Mark.

He leaned forward, focusing his blue eyes on her. "Tell me the truth, Nora."

She froze. He couldn't have guessed, could he? Was the word *pregnant* branded on her forehead?

"That depends," she said warily.

"So all you've had was a stomach bug, wasn't it? I know there's been one going around for about the past month."

She was grateful she wasn't drinking her water when he spoke, because she knew water would have been sprayed all over him.

"You're right, Mark. It was a nasty stomach bug," she admitted, tamping down the impulse to laugh hysterically. "I saw the doctor this morning and he said I'm fine."

"Good. It's not something to mess around with."

"Definitely," she said gravely. "You don't have to, you know."

He looked puzzled. "Don't have to what?"

"Worry about me. I've taken care of myself for some time now, Mark."

"You've had a lot going on lately. Your immune system was probably low."

Not to you.

She kept a bland smile pasted on her lips.

"Oh good!" she said cheerfully when a large platter filled with potato skins, onion rings, garlic bread and fried zucchini was placed in the middle of the table.

"And a special appetizer for you, Brumby," Cyn said, bending down and offering him a dog biscuit. The bulldog took it from her and plopped down to enjoy his treat.

"Hey, Cyn, you might want to bring a second platter for me. The way Nora's looking at it, I might not get any food," Mark kidded, watching Nora pile her plate high with some of everything. "Handsome guy like me needs to keep my strength up."

"As if you'd run fast if a woman was chasing you," Cyn teased.

"I'd have to run some, so she wouldn't think I was easy."
He grinned.

Nora's stomach took a nosedive as she watched and listened
to Mark's banter with Cyn. Logically, she knew he was just
being himself, but memories of nights spent huddled in her bed
hearing raised voices from another room were too strong.

"Why do you have to humiliate me?" her mother would cry.

"How did I humiliate you this time?" Her father always
made it seem as if their arguments were more her mother's
fault. That what she saw was nothing more than a figment of
her imagination.

*"You know very well what you did! The cocktail waitress
was practically sitting in your lap because you were flirting
with her. She gave you her phone number, didn't she?"*

"You're talking nonsense, Jan, like you always do."

*"It's not nonsense. We can't go anywhere without you flirt-
ing with a waitress or the hostess or even the tour guide the
day we took Nora to the aquarium. Why do you have to make
a mockery of our marriage?"*

*"Tell me something, Jan? How can you make a mockery of
something that's already a big joke?"*

"That's not fair! Don't you know how much I love you?"

*"And there's the problem, because I sure don't love you. In
fact, I don't think I ever have."*

By then, young Nora would pull her pillow over her head
so she wouldn't have to hear her mother's voice grow more
strident, almost hysterical, and her father's voice turn colder
and uncaring. Those nights, she'd always fallen asleep with
tears making their way down her cheeks. She'd grown to hate
when her parents went out, because their return meant arguments. Until the night her father left and didn't bother coming
back.

"Nora? Do you know what you want, or would you like
Cyn to come back in a few minutes?"

She pulled herself back to the present and looked at Mark.
Judging by the expression on his face, he'd asked her the question more than once. She dredged up a smile that she hoped
looked convincing.

"Sorry, I guess I was off in another world," she murmured. She handed Cyn her menu. "I think I'll have seasoned popcorn shrimp, zesty seasoned fries and salad with blue cheese dressing. Brumby will have the canine burger."

"I'll have the five-alarm chili and corn bread," he told Cyn. The minute the waitress left them, Mark turned back to Nora. "Are you sure you're all right? We don't have to stay if you're not feeling good."

Oh, I'm feeling fine considering I found out I'm pregnant by you. She swallowed the bit of hysterical laughter that threatened to crawl up her throat. "I'm feeling fine." To give credence to her lie, she picked up a potato skin and brought it to her lips. Each bite felt like a stone going down her throat, but she was determined to carry it off. The way her mother had all those times.

Mark watched Nora take dainty nibbles out of her appetizer. He could feel a tug down deep. For a moment he felt as if she were nibbling on his skin the way she had that night six weeks ago. All he had to do was touch his shoulder and he could recall her mouth on his skin, her teeth biting down gently then her tongue soothing the area. He imagined he could feel her apricot-glossed mouth on him again. He picked up his iced tea and almost drained the glass. He looked up and smiled his thanks when Cyn stopped by the table to refill it.

He put down his feelings to the sunset highlighting Nora's delicate skin, giving her an extra glow as if she'd been washed with gold and copper. Her shoulder-length copper-penny hair was swept up in loose curls and secured on top of her head with a tortoiseshell comb. Tiny stars hung from her ears, winking gold in the waning light. Her pendant matched her earrings.

She was the opposite of his sister, yet the two women were the best of friends.

While Ginna was tall and willowy, with the Walker trademark brilliant-blue eyes and dark brown hair, Nora was petite with hair the color of fire and eyes like rare emeralds. She was like a woodland nymph. He mentally gave himself a shake. He'd had no idea there was even one poetic word in his vocabulary.

She looked at him with those emerald-colored eyes wide and questioning. Just as she hadn't heard him earlier, he hadn't heard her this time.

"Sorry." He smiled. "Guess I wandered into that world you were visiting before."

"The way you were holding your onion ring, I thought something might have been wrong with it."

He shook his head. He looked down at his hand. He'd been so engrossed in admiring Nora, he hadn't realized he'd picked up the food. He ate it before he lost himself in memories again.

He'd only planned to stop by her house to make sure she was okay. When he'd seen Ginna a couple of days ago for a haircut, she'd mentioned that Nora had been keeping a short schedule lately. That she hadn't been feeling well. He didn't think Nora had mentioned their nights together or Ginna would surely have mentioned it. At the very least, he would have been missing an ear. Ginna took her friendships seriously. If anyone hurt one of her friends, she was ready to defend that person. If she knew Mark and Nora had made love, she would have automatically branded Mark the villain and taken action in a way that would have hurt. A lot.

There was an excellent reason why he intended to make sure his sister never found out he'd spent the night with Nora. Twice.

He liked living.

Chapter Six

"That was wonderful." Nora sighed, mopping up the last bit of chocolate-fudge cake, French-vanilla ice cream and rich hot-fudge sauce.

"Are you sure you don't want a second dessert?" Mark asked. He looked a little stunned. While Nora drooled over the dessert tray, he'd asked for a coffee for himself.

She glanced toward the dessert tray. "I admit the white-chocolate raspberry cheesecake is calling my name, but I don't think there's any room."

"For a little thing, you can sure pack it away." Mark dug out his wallet and laid his credit card on the tray.

"I think I'm making up for lost time. I haven't eaten too much the past few days. I guess my appetite decided to return tonight. Thank you for dinner." She smiled. "Brumby also thanks you."

"Yeah, he cleaned his plate too." He looked down at the bulldog who was happily chewing on a rawhide stick Cyn had given him for his dessert. He was glad to see Nora relaxed. Before dinner, he would have sworn she'd actually looked sad. It wasn't until their meal arrived that he could see color return to her cheeks and the lost expression leave her eyes. It didn't stop him from wondering what had brought it about. He also found himself reluctant to end the evening. "Feel like taking a walk to work off dinner?"

"I probably would have to be rolled out of here." She laughed. "But I'm game."

Mark kept hold of Brumby's leash in one hand and Nora's hand in the other as they made their way down a set of wooden stairs that led to the beach.

"Wait a second." Nora tugged on his hand to bring him to a stop. She braced herself against his arm as she slipped off her tennis shoes. "Nothing worse than sand in my shoes."

"Good idea." He quickly took off his own socks and shoes.

As they walked, he gazed toward the pier lit up like a Christmas tree. Laughter and screams could be heard from the carnival-style rides and arcade games set along the pier.

"Want to check out the midway?"

Nora followed the direction of his gaze. "After all I ate, I'd be afraid the pier would collapse if I stepped foot on it."

"I guess Brumby wouldn't like the Tilt-A-Whirl, would he?"

"His stomach wouldn't like it and I can imagine you wouldn't like the results."

A woof from the object of their discussion reminded them they weren't moving. Mark chuckled and started off again.

"Demanding, isn't he?"

"Always."

"Tell me something, why the name Brumby? Why did you choose a bulldog?" he asked. "I'd think you'd want something cute and fluffy."

"I wasn't even looking for a dog when I got Brumby. Although, I guess you'd have to say he chose me," she said simply. "The people who had him didn't want him anymore. They wanted the typical cute and cuddly puppy instead of a bulldog that had his own agenda most of the time. I took one look at him, saw my college psychology instructor's face, and from then on he was Brumby and I was his." At the sound of his name, the bulldog skidded to a stop and looked up.

"I didn't know that," he murmured, realizing it was something he should have known. They had dated for some time and it wasn't as if he didn't already know the dog.

"When you were around Brumby, you were too busy trying

to keep him away from your legs," she reminded him with laughter coloring her voice.

"How could I forget? Persistent devil that he is."

"Brumby might have a face only a boxer's mother would love. The fighter, not the dog, but he has lots of love to give and I can't imagine having anyone else around," Nora said.

As if guessing he was the object of their conversation, the bulldog looked up with an adoring gaze. He uttered a soft woof and started waddling off, giving Mark no choice but to follow.

It wasn't long before they passed the brightly lit pier and the night's darkness enveloped them. Only the faint sounds from the pier's midway and the sounds of the waves brushing the sand reached them. They stopped when they reached a small outcropping of rocks. Nora sat down on a rock and pulled her knees up to her chest.

"I came down here for the first time when I was in college," she said in a soft voice. "It was spring break and three of us decided we didn't want to spend it in Seattle. We drove down here, found the beach and just soaked up the sun. And boys." A faint smile touched her lips. "After spring break, my friends went back to Seattle, but I stayed here. I worked as a waitress while trying to figure out what to do with my life. I saw an ad for a cosmetology school and saw it as a way to be in business for myself. I thought I could cut hair a couple of days a week and spend the rest of the time on the beach."

"Isn't that what you do now?" he teased her.

She shook her head. "Not even close. I discovered it was more than a means to a end, CeCe hired me and the rest is history." She threw her arms out for dramatic effect.

At the moment she threw out her arms, Mark stepped into them and kissed her.

Without thinking, she circled her arms around his neck and kissed him back. His lips were firm as they molded themselves to her mouth. When her lips parted, his tongue slid inside and curled around her tongue. She tasted the rich flavor from the coffee he drank and the darker flavor that was all Mark. With her eyes closed, mental pictures of what they could be doing turned sensuous and downright hot.

It would be so easy to melt into his embrace. To allow it go a little further. She ached for his touch. She hungered for his hands to reach under her sweater and find her bare skin. All she would have to do is say the right words or make the right motions and she knew he would do just that.

Wait a minute. Isn't that how she had gotten in the situation she was presently in?

Sanity hit like an ice-cold shower.

Stunned by the thought, Nora reared back. She moved so quickly, she overbalanced and would have fallen sideways if Mark hadn't held on to her.

"What's wrong?" he asked, stunned by her sudden rebuff.

"This is so wrong!" she blurted out, batting at his hands.

He still stood close enough to her that she could see the tightening in his features.

"Don't worry, I get the message." He dropped his hands.

"We shouldn't be doing this," she insisted, sliding her butt back up the rock.

"You sure acted like we should be doing this and more." She wasn't sure if he was angry or just plain frustrated.

She pushed him away from her as she climbed off the rock. She started to stalk away then remembered he had brought her there. She kept her back to him, her arms wrapped around herself as if she was cold.

"I'm sorry if you thought I was asking you to kiss me."

Mark walked over to her and gently placed his hands on her shoulders. He almost flinched when he felt her tense up under his touch.

"No, I should be the one to apologize. I guess I thought we were doing the romantic angle. You know what I mean. Moonlight, the beach, romantic music in the air."

"Romantic music?" She cocked an eyebrow. "You call that romantic music?" She gestured behind them.

"Maybe you don't think it's romantic, but I bet there's someone out there who thinks 'Oops, I Did It Again' is romantic," he defended his description.

"Only if you're fourteen." She tried taking Brumby's leash from him, but Mark held on tight. The dog looked up. His head swiveled from one to the other as if to say, "Make up your mind!"

"Come on, I'll take you home." He reached for her hand, but she sidestepped him. After what had happened, it wasn't surprising that their walk back to the stairs by Syd's Place didn't take as long as their walk out to the rocks.

Once he was in the truck, Brumby stretched out across the back seat and promptly fell asleep. His rumbling snores soon filled the interior.

"I wasn't trying to be difficult," Nora said after Mark pulled into her driveway and stopped. She unbuckled her seat belt and half turned to face him. "It's just…" She paused. "Just that things have changed between us."

"Sex does that," he agreed.

She gave a quick nod of the head.

"Mom and Dad are having a barbecue for Ginna and Zach in a couple of weeks. They're hoping you'll come," he said.

"I'll see," was all she said. She climbed out of the truck and opened the back door for Brumby, easily lifting him down to the ground. "You don't need to get down," she told Mark.

"And risk Mom's wrath because I didn't do the gentlemanly thing?" He opened his door and climbed out.

"I promise not to tell her." She leaned down and gathered the end of Brumby's leash. The dog strained at his lead as he investigated shrubbery planted along the side of the driveway.

"Trust me, she'll know. She knows everything." Mark walked up to the door with her. "She can just look at me and know I wasn't a gentleman. Then I get the sad motherly smile of disappointment that's a hell of a lot more traumatic than any lecture she can deliver. Growing up, we were always more scared of her than Dad. Dad might lay down the law, but Mom knew how to make us feel as if we'd really let her down." He waited as she unlocked the door and stepped inside. "Will you at least think about coming? You know Ginna will want you there."

She hesitated before slowly nodding. "I'll think about it. Again, thank you for dinner." She held on to the door, ready to close it.

"You're welcome." He smiled. "Good night, Nora. Now let me hear your dead bolt click and then I'll get out of your hair." The minute he heard the sound of the dead bolt, he stepped down and walked back to his truck.

Nora stood near the front window and watched Mark drive away.

If she hadn't accepted his dinner invitation then the walk on the beach that smacked of romance, he wouldn't have tried to kiss her. If he hadn't tried to kiss her, she wouldn't have nearly fallen off the rock in an attempt to avoid it. If he hadn't been his charming self in the restaurant, she wouldn't have been reminded of the two people she tried so hard to keep in a small box locked deep within her mind. And be reminded of exactly why she broke up with Mark.

The minute his truck disappeared down the street, Nora moved away from the window. She suddenly felt very tired. While the hour wasn't late, she felt as if she'd been up for days. As she walked toward the kitchen, Brumby walked ahead of her and squeezed himself through the doggie door that led to the backyard.

Nora rummaged through the refrigerator and pulled out a bottle of lime-flavored sparkling water.

"No caffeine for a while." She mentally bid *adieu* to the morning coffee that she considered the magic potion guaranteed to turn her human. She sadly realized she would have to tough it out for the next seven and a half months. "At least the doctor didn't say I had to give up chocolate, too," she murmured, pouring the sparkling water into an ice-filled glass.

Nora stood at the sink and looked out the window, watching Brumby wander around the backyard. He wanted to make sure no one had intruded on his territory while he was gone.

For a brief moment, it wasn't dark outside, with the bulldog barely visible. Instead, it was a bright sunny day, flowers blooming everywhere. On the edge of the patio was a playpen with a brown-haired baby boy working his way up the side to hold on to the bars so he could reach out to Brumby who looked as if he wasn't sure just what he was supposed to do with the tiny human. What disconcerted Nora was the figure standing next to the baby. Mark looked all too comfortable in the picture, as if he'd been there all along.

The picture before her mind's eye was so sharp it took a minute for her to realize it wasn't real. She blinked and shook her head to clear her head of the vision. A clacking noise alerted her to Brumby coming back into the house.

"How about an early night?" she asked the dog.

The fact that she was going to bed with her dog instead of a good-looking man wasn't lost on her. But she refused to worry about it.

It wasn't the first time.

"HAPPY BIRTHDAY, Rick!" Mark held up his beer bottle in a toast. "Thanks for giving us reason to celebrate."

"Until next month when it's Eric's birthday," Rick pointed out, holding up his own bottle along with the five other men present at the country-western bar to celebrate a friend, and co-worker's, birthday.

"Whatever works," Jeff touched his beer bottle to the others held up for the toast. He took a long drink then reached for another slice of pizza.

"Hey, Mark, you've got some admirers," Brian commented.

"Huh?" He looked blankly at his brother.

"Two little blondes at the bar are giving you the eye," Brian said.

"They're not looking at him, they're looking at me," Rick boasted. "Two blondes for my birthday sounds like the perfect present."

"Nah, they're checking out Mark." Eric grinned. "You giving them the patented Walker charm, Mark?"

"Giving who?" He looked blankly across the table at his friend.

"Aren't you listening to us? There's two cute blondes at the bar," Eric repeated. "One in red and the other one in blue."

Mark shrugged. "I didn't notice," he said, not bothering to look in that direction.

The other men first looked at Mark then looked at each other.

"Something is gravely wrong here, gentlemen," Brian intoned in a somber voice. "It looks like my babe-magnet brother is at death's door."

"He must be at death's door since he hasn't bothered even looking at those cute blondes," Jeff took up the conversation. "There has to be a reason for this absence of interest in the opposite sex. Anyone have any ideas?" he appealed to his friends.

"Terminal illness?" was one suggestion.

"Temporary blindness?"

"A bad case of indigestion?"

"A woman?"

"A woman?" Jeff hooted. "Baby brother hooking up with just one woman? No way." He leaned forward, using his hands to make his point. "Who are you seeing now? The last one I remember is Kim."

"We broke up three months ago," Mark said, shifting uncomfortably under his friends' avid regard.

"That's right. You're dating Paula, the flight attendant, now. Are you bringing her to the barbecue at Mom and Dad's?" Brian asked.

"I haven't seen Patti in a while," he admitted.

Each man slowly turned to stare at him.

"Paula, not Patti," Brian reminded him.

Mark shrugged as if his giving the wrong name wasn't of any importance.

"You're saying you're not seeing anyone right now?" Rick asked as if he couldn't believe his ears.

"I didn't realize there's a law that says I have to date," Mark said sarcastically.

"Where you're concerned there is," Terry, one of the other EMTs, said. "Do you realize your exploits are better than anything we can watch on TV? So if you're not dating Paula, there must be someone new and you're not willing to share the news. Who've you got stashed away? Does she have a sister?"

"Cousin?"

"Young aunt?"

All the men laughed and kept pressing Mark for answers, but he wasn't having any of it. He was so engrossed fending off the questions, he didn't notice the silent communication flying between Jeff and Brian.

Mark wasn't about to admit he was so busy thinking about Nora that he not only didn't notice other women, he didn't mind his suddenly dateless nights.

He was still haunted by Nora. Except now all he had was the memory of her in his arms, the smell of her perfume and the warmth of her smile.

He wasn't about to tell even his friends that only one woman mattered to him. He felt as if he was following the same path as his brothers, and damn, how terrifying that feeling was.

Mark picked up his beer bottle and drank deeply then reached for another slice of pizza. "We should have had them put candles on this," he joked.

"Hey, Mark, since you're not interested in the blondes, you won't mind if Rick and I see if they'll settle for us, will you?" Terry asked.

"I'd be careful of the one on the right. She looks like she could eat you up and spit you out," Mark warned.

"Maybe once you tell her you're a fireman, she'll just melt into your arms," Brian kidded.

Terry grinned and flashed him an obscene gesture as he pushed back his chair and headed for the bar. Rick followed him.

"Are you sure you're not sick or have some strange rash you don't want to talk about?" Jeff asked Mark.

"Yeah, little brother, you turning down a gorgeous woman isn't normal," Brian added.

"None of the above. I'm just taking a breather," he told them.

Mark flashed them a grin he hoped would convince his brothers enough to lay off him for a while until he could come up with a better reason.

Right now, the only woman that interested him was one who didn't want anything to do with him unless he could find a way to convince her to give him a second chance.

He realized he was at a point where he might need the help he'd dreaded asking for before.

"I've got to make a phone call," he announced, pushing back his chair and reaching for his cell phone that was hooked on his belt.

"A woman?" Eric asked.

"Is there any other kind?" He winked before heading for the door and outside where he hoped he'd have enough privacy for his call.

He walked to the side of the building and punched in a number. Two rings and a woman answered.

"Did I ever tell you you're my favorite mother?"

NORA WAS GOING to get through this morning if it killed her. And it just might.

She was on her third packet of crackers and fourth glass of Diet 7-UP and it wasn't even ten o'clock. Her hopes her stomach would settle down were long gone.

"Are you all right?" Ginna stopped her when she returned to her station.

"Remind me not to eat Thai food late at night," Nora lied, pasting a credible smile on her lips.

Ginna didn't look convinced. She placed the back of her hand against Nora's forehead.

"Ginna!" She wiggled away.

"You don't have a fever," she said, peering closely at her. "But you do look pale. Are you feeling faint?"

"All I'm feeling is the aftereffects of eating very spicy food," Nora replied.

"I hope you don't have the flu. I don't want you to miss the party at Mom and Dad's this weekend."

"I'll have to see how I'll feel," Nora said, deciding it might be better if she acted a little weak until after the Walker party.

"You have to be better by then!" Ginna insisted. "I want you there. You used to come out all the time."

Until you and Mark broke up.

Could she do it? Could she go out there and act as if nothing happened? All right, she could do it, but could Mark do it? He was still leaving messages, asking her to call him. So far, she'd been able to hold off returning his calls.

"If I feel fine, I'll be there," she promised.

"Then please stay away from Thai food," Ginna pleaded.

Nora solemnly drew an X across her heart and held up her hand, palm out.

"Not even a noodle."

Ginna rolled her eyes as she walked away.

"Just for that I won't bring my killer brownies," Nora called after her.

"Yes, you will."

"Yeah, but I won't frost them," she added the additional threat that she already knew didn't hold an ounce of truth. Nora considered the frosting the best part of her fudgy brownies.

By the time Nora got home that evening, she found two messages on her answering machine. One she expected. What she didn't expect was the heavy artillery.

"Hi, it's Mark." She knew who it was the moment he said hi. "I thought I'd see if you'd like a ride out to Mom and Dad's for the barbecue on Sunday. No strings attached, I swear. Let me know, okay?"

"Nora, dear, it's Cathy Walker. We're giving a barbecue for Ginna and Zach this weekend. I hope you'll come. I'd love to see you. It's been a while. And don't forget to bring Brumby with you."

A woof caught Nora's attention. She looked down at her dog.

"I guess if you could have picked up the phone you would have told your auntie Cathy we'd be there, wouldn't you?" she asked the dog.

She took Brumby's woof to be a yes.

"All right, you can go too, but no begging goodies from the kids," she warned him. She picked up her phone and tapped out Mark's number. She was prepared to leave a message on his voice mail, when she heard him pick up.

"Hello?"

"Mark, it's Nora."

"Hi!" He was clearly surprised to hear from her. "Does this mean you're going to Mom and Dad's?"

"Your mother also called me." She cradled the handset between her shoulder and chin as she dug for a can of dog food and hooked it under the can opener. Brumby's nails clicked on the floor as he pranced back and forth eagerly awaiting his dinner.

"I knew bringing out the big guns would work." He sounded satisfied with himself. "No one ever turns down Mom."

"What if I still said no?"

"Then I would have called Gramps and Grandma. No way you could turn them down."

"Theo said he'd never forgive me for buying a German car," she reminded him.

"Which means he'll take advantage of your presence by pointing out what a mistake you made and try to talk you into buying an American car. He thinks you bought your Beetle on purpose just to rile him up. Besides, you know Gramps. There's nothing he loves more than the chance to make a point."

"Seems like there's some of that personality in his grandson," Nora said dryly. She spooned beef chunks in gravy into Brumby's dish and placed it on the floor. The bulldog immediately buried his face in his dinner.

With her dog's dinner out of the way, Nora rummaged through cabinets to find something for herself. She discovered once her morning and afternoon sickness left her that she was incredibly hungry. Right now she was convinced she could eat an entire cow.

"At least Dad's more subtle about it," Mark pointed out.

"True, he merely mourns that one of the great classic cars came from overseas." She winced as a can rolled out of her fingers and dropped onto the counter.

"What are you doing?"

"Fixing myself some dinner."

"Anything good?"

"I haven't done any shopping for the past few days, so it's more a matter of what I can find." She opened the refrigerator and studied its contents. Nothing looked good. She closed the door and then realized there was a pizza coupon slid under a bulldog-shaped magnet. Her mouth started watering at the idea of a roasted red-pepper-and-mushroom pizza with extra cheese. Maybe some spiced ground beef too. Her mind was spinning with the possibilities.

"Nora?" She immediately came back to earth.

"Sorry, I was still getting Brumby's dinner ready. Mark, I have to go." She needed to call the pizza place and have them deliver a large pizza. On second thought, she decided, an extra-large would be better.

"How about I pick you up around nine?"

"I'll see you then." She quickly disconnected and tapped out another set of numbers. "Hi, this is Nora Summers. I'd like to order an extra-large mushroom and roasted red-pepper pizza with extra cheese to be delivered. Oh, and a salad. And your cheese garlic bread." She figured the salad would be the healthy part of her meal.

What Nora didn't expect was that her favorite pizza toppings would keep her up half the night with heartburn.

"We need to have some ground rules here, kid," she muttered, tapping antacid tablets out of a bottle into her hand. She chewed them slowly. "The day will come when you'll love pizza, so why are you giving me a hard time already?" A cold wet nose nudged her bare leg. She looked down at her dog. "We have to train the little human right away, Brumby. I hope you're up to the job." His grumbling woof told her his opinion. He waddled back into the bedroom and waited for her to join him. Before she climbed in, she picked him up and placed him on the end of the bed. She fluffed her pillows behind her and reached for the book she'd been reading before she fell asleep earlier. Brumby made a tight circle several times before settling down, and immediately began snoring gently.

Nora sighed, wishing she could sleep as easily. But it seemed her dinner of pizza, salad and garlic bread wasn't about to let her even doze.

"If you try this with me when I eat chocolate, I swear you will have an eight o'clock curfew until you're at least thirty," she informed the tiny being nestled inside her.

If she didn't know better, she could have sworn she'd heard giggles.

MARK WISHED he was on duty that night. Maybe with the other guys around him he'd be able to sleep instead of lying in bed and staring at the ceiling for the past couple of hours. Restless beyond belief, he kicked off his covers and crossed his arms behind his head. Since he couldn't sleep, he replayed his conversation with Nora.

Normally, he spent as little time on the phone as he could manage. He was never one to spend hours on the phone talking to his latest lady. Tonight he wanted to keep on talking. He didn't want to lose that connection with Nora.

He thought that maybe he could have another chance with her. She'd claimed she didn't like him kissing her out there on the beach, but for a second her lips had clung to his. He sensed she'd wanted to kiss him back. So why hadn't she? She wasn't acting coy. If anything, she had seemed almost sad about the whole thing.

Which gave him more questions than answers.

Could he have hurt her so badly back then that she felt she had no choice but to break up with him?

Mark cast his mind back to that time. What had they done that evening? Where had they gone? All he could bring up from his memory bank was a mental picture of Nora's face as she told him she didn't want to see him anymore. What surprised him was how clear her face was in his mind's eye. Not just her face, but the memory of a lone tear trailing down her cheek.

"Damn!" He shot up in bed. Had she cried when she had broken up with him? He couldn't remember anything but his anger and frustration that out of the blue she had told him to stay out of her life and never call her again. After his discovery she'd changed her home telephone number, he'd done just that.

So, was the tear something he had conjured up now or had he deliberately ignored it back then?

He didn't think she'd forgiven him since then, but something must have changed. And not because of those two nights they'd spent together. He had felt something happening between them when they had gone to dinner at Syd's Place. Then it had seemed to disappear. Nora had retreated and he'd seen the animation leave her face and her expressive eyes. He had no idea why. As far as he could tell, nothing had happened out of the ordinary. Unable to just lie there any longer, Mark climbed out of bed deciding he'd be better off finding something on one of the sports channels to watch until he got tired. He barely took two steps before he tripped over something hard and unforgiving.

"Son of a bitch!" he swore, hopping up and down on one foot. He started to kick at whatever had tripped him up then had second thoughts. He hopped around it over to the bedroom light. He narrowed his eyes against the bright light as he stared down at the offender. "Where did the hammer come from?"

Then he looked around at his bedroom that looked as if a hurricane had blown through it. Clothes were tossed everywhere, a baseball bat rested against the chest of drawers, a baseball mitt on the floor next to it and his towel from that morning's shower tossed nearby.

He kept everything where it belonged at the station. At home, he seemed to keep everything where it didn't belong.

Mark winced as he viewed the devastation he called home.

"I've got to keep Mom away from here."

Chapter Seven

"Woof!"

"Yes, Brumby, you are going," Nora carefully wrapped plastic cling wrap over the large pan of brownies she had just finished frosting.

Brumby walked from the front door back to the kitchen, his nails clicking on the hardwood floors. In his own way, he knew something exciting was going to happen and he didn't want to be left out. He stuck close to Nora's heels, impeding her movements as she grabbed her toast out of the toaster the moment it popped up. Used to his insistence on not being ignored, she merely stepped over him as she moved around her kitchen. She poured honey on her toast and stuck it in her mouth, chewing furiously.

"Finally, something my stomach won't reject first thing in the morning."

Still nibbling on her toast, Nora headed back for her bedroom with Brumby still hot on her heels.

"Luckily, what to wear hasn't become difficult yet," she murmured, studying the contents of her closet. The day was warm, so she chose a pair of black-and-white-gingham capris and a loose-fitting black V-necked top with three-quarter-length sleeves. For color she added a trio of black, red and white plastic bangle bracelets and a braided necklace with the same three colors. She dug out a pair of black tennis shoes and slipped them on. She brushed her hair up into a loose knot and secured it with a clip. She kept her makeup minimal with a brush of mascara, a hint of dusty-rose blush and rose lip gloss.

She was just adding a bottle of sunblock to her tote bag when Brumby barked and ran as fast as his short legs would carry him to the front door a few seconds before the doorbell chimed.

"A man has to be very self-confident to wear a shirt like that," Nora proclaimed, studying the psychedelic colors and geometric shapes that adorned Mark's shirt. In contrast with the eye-jarring colors, his baggy cargo shorts were a sedate tan. She wasn't sure if his running shoes were supposed to be the off-white they were or just not washed lately. Or perhaps not ever washed.

He grinned. "Like it?" He spread his arms out and turned in a circle.

"I'd like it better if I was wearing sunglasses," she said dryly, handing him the large pan holding her brownies.

"Why would you want to share your brownies with those cretins?" he asked, also taking her tote bag from her while she held on to the end of Brumby's leash. She held what looked like a halter in her other hand.

"Those *cretins* are your family and friends," she pointed out as she locked the door.

"Exactly." He took her arm with his free hand and guided her out to his truck.

"Here's Brumby's harness for the seat belt." She handed him the harness. "I forgot this the last time."

Mark lifted Brumby into the back seat, slid the harness around the dog and clipped it to the seat belt. Then he set the container of brownies on the floor. After Nora settled herself in the passenger seat, they were ready to go.

"What was it like growing up in a large family?" she asked after Mark reached the freeway.

He looked surprised by her question.

"I guess the opposite of being the only child." He guessed the reason for her inquiry. "When you're little you always have someone to play with. Someone to blame if it looks like you are going to get in trouble. But you're also fair game when you're the youngest, which I was for some time before Nikki came along. Jeff and Brian used me for their personal target practice and Ginna bossed me around every chance she got,'' he chuckled.

She smiled, caught up in his story. ''Something tells me you made sure to get even with them.''

''Hell, yes. Jeff discovered his book report for *For Whom the Bell Tolls* somehow turned into *Horton Hears A Who*. Brian ended up with two dates to the homecoming dance and let's just say the next time Ginna gave her hair some highlights, they turned an interesting shade of powder blue.''

''You didn't do them all at once, did you?'' She wasn't sure whether to laugh or commiserate with her friend for having a devilish younger brother.

''Nope, I eked them out over the course of a few years. Those were just the more memorable of my little antics,'' he admitted.

''I can't imagine they let you get away with it,'' she said. ''Or did they leave the punishment up to your parents?''

''Dad always felt we should fight it out among ourselves as long as blood wasn't spilled. Mom pretty much felt the same. I had to type Jeff's correct book report, explain what I did to both girls and pay for Ginna's hair to be returned to the right color,'' Mark said. He cast her a sideways glance. ''Did you miss not having brothers and sisters?''

''Sometimes,'' she confessed. ''Then other times I decided it was for the best. Grammy Fran lived in a neighborhood with very few children in it. I got used to being on my own most of the time.''

Mark drummed his fingers against the steering wheel. ''We never talked about our childhoods all that much, did we?''

''No, we didn't. What I knew about your family came from Ginna,'' Nora replied.

He grinned, easily reading more into her statement than she let on. ''I can imagine what she said about me.''

''Pain in the butt was probably the politest description.''

''She must have been in a good mood that day.'' Mark quickly changed lanes and set the cruise control. ''Usually she refers to me in much more colorful terms.''

Nora half turned in her seat so she could face him. "I may have done a little paraphrasing. I'd hate to think I'd hurt your feelings."

"If you'd grown up with those three, you'd have to have a cast-iron self-esteem or go down in flames in no time. If you didn't have siblings to make your life miserable, what did you do?"

"Grammy Fran made sure I had as normal a childhood as possible. She had trunks of old clothes. When I was little we'd play dress-up and have afternoon tea. I helped bake cookies for bake sales at church. My grandmother sat on a lot of committees."

Mark was quiet for a moment. "Still, it must have been pretty lonely for you."

"It was sometimes," she agreed. "I was pretty shy back then, so I didn't mind that I didn't have a lot of friends." She touched his arm. "It wasn't as if I was a prisoner or something."

"You never said much about your parents."

"Not much to say about them," she said offhandedly. "They divorced when I was young. My father moved out of the state and started a new life and my mother didn't. Grammy Fran took over and she did her best to make sure I had a fairly normal childhood. I was better off than a lot of children." She hated herself for sounding so defensive. "How big a crowd is expected today?"

Mark's expression told her he knew she was deliberately changing the subject. She didn't care. She didn't want to talk about her grandmother. That wound was still tender. She especially didn't want to talk about her parents. Those memories she locked away long ago and she preferred to keep them filed away. It was bad enough a few had snuck out recently.

"The usual mob. Most of our crew and families," he replied, meaning co-workers from the fire station and family friends. He flipped the turn signal and headed down the freeway off-ramp. The strip malls and housing tracts soon turned into rural surroundings.

Nora looked out the window at horses grazing in one paddock with doe-eyed llamas strolling leisurely around their own grassy areas. Farther down was an emu ranch. A loud screech resembling a woman's screams assaulted their ears.

"Peacocks," Mark identified the sound. "Downright scary when you hear it in the middle of the night. You'd think someone was being murdered." He turned at a mailbox designed to look like a touring car from the 1930s with the name Walker written on the sides in elegant script. "Dad found a Duesenberg that needs some of his tender loving care," he explained. "Hence, the new mailbox."

"Hence?" Nora arched an eyebrow. "I didn't know they used that word in comic books."

"I've been known to read something meatier than the latest Marvel classic."

Nora looked out the window again. Her stomach gave a little lurch. She lowered the window and took several deep breaths.

"Are you okay?" Mark asked.

"I'm fine," she said quickly. "It just got close in here for a moment."

Mark drove up a winding driveway that ended in front of a sprawling house painted a pale dove gray with colonial blue trim. Cars, trucks and SUVs took up enough space to qualify for a small parking lot.

As Mark helped Nora down then rescued Brumby from the back seat, a woman walked out the front door. Anyone looking at her easy smile would know she was the mother of the Walker clan. Her brown hair was a few shades lighter than Mark's coffee-colored hair and held gold and silver highlights due to Ginna's skill with color. Her blue eyes danced with laughter as she bent down to greet Brumby who'd waddled up to her, his stubby tail beating back and forth with doggie glee.

"We were wondering when you two would show up!" She straightened up and threw her arms around Mark. Not an easy feat since he was several inches taller. She pulled his head down so she could kiss him on the cheek. "Hello, my dearest baby boy."

"Hi, Mom." He kissed her back. "You look gorgeous."

"Now that you've given me the praise I am due, you may

join the others. Go on with you. I want to talk to Nora.'' She patted his cheek then moved on to Nora. Cathy grasped Nora's arms, holding her at arm's length. The older woman studied her with the intensity of a scientist viewing something important under a microscope.

Nora resisted the urge to squirm under the woman's scrutiny. It was hard enough for her to keep down the panic that was threatening to well upward. She was positive Cathy saw way too much.

Cathy stepped forward and hugged her tightly.

''Have you told my knucklehead of a son yet?'' she whispered in Nora's ear.

Her panic level shot up another hundred degrees. She had the presence of mind to play dumb. ''Told him what?''

Cathy shot her a look that said Nora wasn't fooling her one bit. ''That you're having his baby.''

Nora's gaze frantically shot both ways to make sure Cathy wasn't overheard.

The older woman's face softened with her smile.

''There are some things that just can't be hidden,'' Cathy murmured. ''I've always had the gift of knowing when a woman is pregnant. Now, have you told Mark?''

Nora shook her head. ''I'm still trying to make sense of it all.''

''How long have you known?'' Cathy asked.

Nora hesitated. That was all the answer Cathy needed.

''Obviously, you've known longer than the past few hours. I suggest you find a way to tell him before you go into labor.''

''Mark isn't…'' She paused, not wanting to offend her baby's grandmother. ''He doesn't…''

''So you haven't told him yet. You don't think he can handle the idea of being a father,'' Cathy said softly.

Relieved the woman understood without Nora saying anything that might insult Mark in the end, Nora nodded.

Cathy smiled. ''Mark might act the age of his nieces and nephews, but I know he has qualities that haven't even been tapped yet. I can assure you that once he learns, he won't run to some far-off island. I think he'll make a wonderful father. So, tell me when the two of you started dating again.''

''Oh no, we're not seeing each other again,'' she said, dismayed again how her stumbling explanation sounded. ''What I mean is, this was…'' How was she supposed to tell Mark's mother that it was a night when she'd desired comfort and he had been there to provide it? ''It's not like I'm some sex-crazed woman who dragged the first available man into her bed. I guess I can't say I dragged this unwilling man to my bed. I mean he was definitely willing.'' She uttered a squeaky sound then clapped her hands over her mouth. Horror washed over her like a cold shower. She wished she'd thought to keep her mouth shut a lot sooner.

Cathy chuckled. ''I had an idea something happened between you two.''

''How could you think that?''

''Mark.''

Nora's feelings of horror returned. ''He said something to you?'' She didn't want to even imagine what Mark might have said. Not that she hadn't said much more than she'd intended.

Cathy shook her head. ''No, he's a gentleman. But sometimes it's what someone doesn't say that's more telling than what someone says.'' She slid her arm around Nora's waist and guided her into the house. ''Are you feeling all right?''

''I felt a little nauseous coming over,'' she confessed. ''Morning sickness has become my new non–best friend.''

''Mark's driving can make anyone feel a little nauseous,'' Cathy said. ''Let's find some crackers for you. Promise me if you feel tired, you'll go inside and lie down in one of the guest rooms.''

''Won't that look a little odd?''

''With this crowd, it's easy to get lost. If anyone asks, I'll hint you're off somewhere.''

When the two women entered the kitchen, Ginna, Gail, Brian's wife, Abby, Jeff's wife, and two other women were busy mixing dips, adding spices to salads and forming hamburger patties.

''About time you got here,'' Ginna greeted her friend. Her

eyes lit up when she saw the pan in Nora's hands. She took the pan and set it on the counter. "Perfect! You made your brownies!"

"They're staying in here," Gail said, lifting a corner of the cling wrap. "No way we're allowing those animals out there to enjoy something this good."

"As if there would be any left once we take our share," Abby chimed in, swiping a small square. She popped it in her mouth and closed her eyes as she slowly chewed. "I swear, there are days these are better than sex."

"Don't forget to share!" One of the other fireman's wives, said, coming up for a square. Sherie's face lightened with bliss as she nibbled the fudgey treat. "Oh my God, Abby's right! These are fantastic. What is your secret?"

Firemen's and paramedics' wives and girlfriends alike grabbed a brownie.

Nora laughed. "It's no secret. I use buttermilk and French vanilla coffee in my recipe. It gives the brownies more flavor."

"Nora makes the absolute best brownies," Ginna declared. "I have her recipe and do everything it says, including the coffee, but they're still never as good as hers." She picked up a second square. "I'll be running an extra mile for each piece I eat." She heaved a sigh before biting in. "It's worth it."

"Mommy?" Five-year-old Trey Stone walked in and snagged the hem of Ginna's shorts. "I'm hungry."

"And to think breakfast was only a couple of hours ago," she told him, dropping a kiss on top of his head. "Here." She handed him a slice of cheese. "Just don't tell anyone where you got it. We don't want all you kids tramping in here demanding food."

He stuffed the cheese in his mouth while energetically nodding his agreement. He then noticed what Ginna held in her other hand. His eyes lit up.

"Can I have some?" His gaze remained fixed on the piece of brownie.

"Oh, honey, we're sorry, but they're for mommies only," Abby spoke up with a sweet apologetic smile.

His face fell. "Daddy can't have any either?" he asked.

''No, he can't,'' Ginna lied without a qualm.

Trey stood there for a moment. His small face was solemn with his concentration. ''So if only mommies can have it, Emma can't have any, right?'' He referred to his twin sister.

''That's right,'' Ginna said.

He brightened. ''Okay.''

''Don't tell Emma,'' she warned him.

''A secret from Emma.'' His face lit up even more. There was nothing he enjoyed more than knowing something his sister didn't. ''Yeah!'' He ran out the patio door.

''God love him. She'll worm it out of him in three seconds,'' Cathy pronounced. ''And be in here one second after that.''

Ginna shook her head. ''Trey's discovered it's too much fun to know something Emma doesn't. But tonight he'll probably tell his dad we were eating food that was for mommies only.'' She polished off her brownie in two bites.

''Will Mark mention you brought brownies?'' Abby asked Nora.

Nora looked out the window and noticed Mark was with several men. He was laughing and talking, with his hands punctuating his part of the conversation.

''I think he's forgotten all about them.'' She looked farther off and saw that Brumby was being alternately petted and cuddled by Abby and Jeff's twin daughters who sat on either side of the bulldog.

''They think Brumby is one of their stuffed animals.'' Abby glanced out the window. ''It's a good thing he's so patient with them.''

''When he feels he's had enough, he'll wander off and find a nice shady spot for a nap,'' Nora said. She noticed Cathy had unobtrusively left a packet of crackers on a corner of the counter. She telegraphed her thanks with a smile. She turned back to the other women. ''What can I do to help?''

''WHEN DID YOU and Nora get back together again?'' Brian asked when Mark approached the group of men that included his two brothers and new brother-in-law. Brian tossed him a can of beer.

"We're not exactly back together," he replied. "I just saved her the drive over."

"You mean you saved her listening to Dad expounding on why she would buy a foreign car when he got a look at her Beetle." Jeff grinned.

"He's going to have to come up with a new speech now that he bought that Duesenberg, which if I remember correctly was manufactured in Germany," Mark pointed out.

"That was back when cars were built by master craftsmen, not put together on an assembly line," Jeff said, familiar with their father's arguments. "When windows would have etched designs on them, small vases for roses set in the back, seats of buttery-soft leather, sometimes even a hand-carved dashboard."

"When cars were works of art," Brian continued the well-known discussion with which all the Walker children had grown up. With their father well known as an antique car restorer, it was natural they'd be familiar with every automobile known to man.

Brian had driven a classic Corvette Sting Ray until Gail's pregnancy. Without hesitation or a qualm, he'd traded it in for an SUV. Ginna kept her 1966 classic Mustang convertible, but now it carried two child safety seats in the back seat. Even Jeff had once owned a 1967 RoadRunner muscle car, which was put aside for an SUV for his rapidly growing family.

Mark thought about his siblings' choice of vehicles and wondered if that wasn't the beginning of their downfalls. He had always stuck by his beloved Ford pickup. He mourned the day Brian sold his 'Vette, because Mark had secretly lusted after the sports car, but now he viewed it rationally. Once a Walker traded in their much-loved vehicle for something more practical, their life was over.

"Uncle Mark!" Luckily, he had the presence of mind to hand his beer to his brother and hold up his arms when a tiny blond hurricane jumped up, confident her uncle would catch her.

"Carrie!" he shouted as loud as she did. He kept his arms

around her waist as she wrapped her legs around his. She leaned back so she could study his face.

"How do you know I'm not Casey?" she demanded.

"Because Casey would have jumped on my back like the little monkey she is," he informed his niece, adjusting his grip before she slid down to the ground.

Carrie leaned back far enough that she could bend backward, with her head hanging down so that her blond ponytail brushed the ground. She squealed with delight as she was swung from side to side.

"Da-darn, take out my ears, will you?" Mark grumbled, wincing as the strident sounds assaulted his eardrums. "What is it with girls and ear-splitting screams?"

"You think that's bad, try it at 2:00 a.m. when one of them wakes up and thinks there's a monster under her bed," Jeff told him. "Or when they've been out to the movies with their uncle Mark who has loaded them up with candy."

"And brought them home hyper and ready for meganightmares." Abby walked up and tickled the back of her daughter's neck. As if on cue, Carrie squealed again. All the men winced. Abby smiled. "Next time I'll just let them spend the night with you, Uncle Mark," she cooed, patting Mark's cheek with a little more force than necessary.

"Ow!" He reared back. "What was that for?"

"Call it payment in advance, handsome," she said. "I'm sure something will come up before the day is over."

Mark glared at his sister-in-law. "You used to be this shy sweet person who didn't speak above a whisper. What happened?"

Jeff made choking sounds. "That was Lauren who was so quiet," he said.

Abby tapped Mark's cheek again. This time a little harder.

"It's amazing Nora's willing to spend more than five minutes with you," Abby scolded. "You do remember that you brought Nora, don't you? If not, I'll be only too happy to remind you what she looks like. If you men want to be useful, you'll help Lou and Theo with the barbecue." She walked off.

"The woman is the devil incarnate," Mark pronounced,

looking at his oldest brother. "Are you sure she didn't cast some spell that turned you into her sex slave?"

"What can I say? She thinks I'm incredible."

At Jeff's deadpan announcement, the rest of the men broke into laughter. They were all familiar with Abby's take-no-prisoners methods. None of them were sure if they pitied Jeff or envied him his wife.

"Good, the women are finally bringing out some food," Eric, one of the firemen, announced.

Mark turned around. His gaze instantly zeroed in on Nora, who emerged from the house carrying a large platter. She was laughing and talking with some of the other women who were also carrying food.

Brian noticed the direction of Mark's gaze. He nudged Jeff and jerked his head toward the house then toward Mark. Jeff easily noticed what Brian had. The two brothers broke into broad grins.

He's toast, Brian mouthed, recognizing a look that had once been on his own face.

"So what have you been doing?" Mark asked, walking up to Nora and taking the tray out of her hands.

"Secret girl stuff," she replied. "The kind that could cost you your manhood if you found out."

"You women are downright bloodthirsty." He shook his head in wonder. He set the tray down where she indicated it needed to go.

"It's our nature," she said airily. "Just as you men like to stand together and discuss guy stuff, we women discuss girl stuff."

"Mom didn't drag out the baby pictures again, did she?" He discovered by standing just behind her, he could inhale the fresh subtle scent of her hair, which reminded him of a waterfall. He was tempted to loosen her hair and watch the coppery tresses tumble down.

She looked up with a smile. "Don't worry, your dignity is safe. Although I see she added more pictures to the collages in the hallway."

"Emma and Trey," he said. "They were pretty excited when she asked for pictures of them so they'd be up here too. She said they're her grandchildren too."

"Nora! Do you still drive that Martian car?" Lou Walker's voice rang out over the various conversations.

Nora looked to her left and smiled at the man walking up to her. He none too subtly edged his son to the side and threw his arms around her for a bear hug.

"Admit it, you're jealous of my sweet little baby," she laughed, used to the older man's teasing. From the first time he saw her lime-green Beetle, he had called it a Martian car.

"Jealous of something I could kill with my flyswatter?" He stepped back and surveyed her from head to toe. "Gorgeous as ever. If I wasn't married…" His voice fell off.

"Hey, stop flirting with my date or I'll tell Mom," Mark grumbled good-naturedly.

Lou waved him off. "Aren't you supposed to be doing something useful?"

"I am. I'm helping Nora."

Lou gave a snort. "More like making yourself look good."

Nora studied Lou and knew this was what Mark would look like in later years. The Walker men were all tall, imbued with a masculinity that seemed to bring out a woman's femininity. She had no doubt Cathy couldn't resist Lou any more than Nora had been able to resist Mark.

"Next time, don't wait so long before you come out to see us," Lou told her. "It's been too long since we last saw your beautiful face, Nora, me girl," he said in an Irish brogue he liked to use when she was around.

Nora smiled. "I guess saying I've been busy won't work with you."

He nodded. "I'd know better." He glanced at his son. "Is he behaving himself?"

"Has he ever?"

"Once. When he was about six minutes old." He dropped a kiss on top of Nora's head. "Make sure you eat all your steak and everything that goes with it. You need some meat on your bones."

"I'll do what I can," she promised.

He shot her a mock glare. "See that you do." He hugged her again and headed for the other side of the large patio. "Tell the kids they'll need to dry off soon if they want to eat!" he shouted to the group seated by the swimming pool before he moved on to oversee the barbecue grill. Within minutes, Lou and Theo, Lou's father, were good-naturedly arguing over the best way to grill a steak.

"Some things never change." Nora shook her head, amused by the scenes unfolding all around her.

Even with the large group, the chaos was carefully orchestrated with some bringing out salads, condiments and anything food, others helping with the barbecue, and the remaining reining in the kids and steering them toward the barbecue where they'd receive their choice of hamburgers or hot dogs. Those with larger appetites chose both.

Nora helped carry out another bowl of potato salad before Mark kidnapped her and seated her at one of the tables.

"I'll get your steak for you," he offered.

"A small one," she told him.

"All right, tell me all." Ginna slid onto the seat beside her the moment Mark was out of earshot.

"All? Well, millions of years ago…" she began.

"Idiot," she said affectionately. "You know very well I'm talking about Mark and the fact that you arrived with him."

Nora shrugged. "He offered to drive and I accepted. Gas conservation and all that." She reached across the table and snagged a potato chip out of a large bowl. She swiped it across the top of some dip and brought it to her mouth.

Ginna rolled her eyes. She looked around and lowered her voice. "The last time you ever mentioned anything about Mark, you pretty much said he could eat dirt and die."

Nora affected a nonchalant smile. "Dirt just isn't what it used to be, is it? Fine. You want the story. He picked me up at the airport when I came back home. I decided it was time I put the past where it belonged. We talked things out and everything is fine. That doesn't make us an item or anything. Just one person doing a favor for another." *And somewhere along the line, we made love and I'm pregnant. The thing is, I don't know how to tell you.*

Ginna's eyes narrowed. "What are you hiding from me?"

"Nothing," Nora said too quickly. "Where're Lucie and Nick?"

"They're having a mother-son weekend in San Diego. Lucie wanted bonding time. Nick wanted to attend a computer show. Lucie won the coin toss."

"Hey, sis, why don't you go hunt down your husband," Mark suggested, climbing over the bench in between the two women and none too gracefully pushing Ginna farther down.

"No need to," she said sweetly, smiling at Zach who seated himself across from her. He handed her one of the plates he held. "Where are Emma and Trey?"

"They're happy as clams at the kids' table."

"Look at this." Abby stood next to Zach. She looked over her shoulder. "Honey, there's room over here."

"Oh God!" Mark moaned as Abby sat down across from him. Jeff came up behind her and set a plate in front of her. Mark looked at Abby's steak. "What, they didn't have raw meat for her? Ouch!" He jerked his legs back under the bench but not fast enough to avoid Abby's kick. "Why do you always have to go after me?"

"Because you're the perfect target." She picked up her knife and began cutting her meat into bite-size pieces.

"Room for two more?" Brian and Gail took the last spots at the table.

"Only if you'll trade places with me," Mark told his brother while directing his glare at Abby, who merely smiled.

"You are so much fun to torment," she cooed with a wicked smile.

"Don't let her know she's getting to you," Jeff advised.

"Easy for you to say," Mark grumbled.

Nora had forgotten how much energy the Walker siblings exuded when they were together. Not physical but mental energy where talk flew fast and furious around the table. They didn't need to catch up on gossip since they kept in constant touch with each other.

She wondered if Mark felt the shift in energy that she did. The three married couples each shared a bond that excluded everyone around them. They weren't intentionally rude, just connected in a way few would understand. Nora envied them sharing what she knew she would never have the chance to achieve.

"Next time, I'll find us a table about a hundred miles away," Mark murmured near her ear. "Or maybe in another country. On second thought, let's find another galaxy. One that's far, far away." His breath was warm against her ear.

She ducked her head and concentrated on her food.

"You get me Han Solo and I'll be on the next spaceship."

Chapter Eight

"Teams ready?" Theo's voice boomed over the group.

They shouted "Yes!" and one threw the football up into the air.

"Hey, where are the pom-poms, short skirt and cute little crop top?" Jeff asked Abby as he slid his arm around her waist.

"I thought this time you could wear the cute little skirt and top and man the pom-poms," she suggested with a broad laugh.

"I'd pay money to see that," Ginna chuckled, straightening out a lawn chair and sitting down.

"As you can see, he's got the legs for it," Abby told her, putting her chair next to Nora's. "A little hairy maybe, but a good leg waxing could take care of that. Go team go!" She threw her arms up. "Show them who's boss, honey!"

Ginna twisted at the waist and shot her sister-in-law a "you have got to be kidding!" look. "I think the one who will wipe up the field will be Zach."

"Yay, Daddy!" Emma hopped from one foot to the other.

"Yay, *our* daddy!" Carrie and Casey shouted, jumping up and down. "Clean the grass!"

"Their version of wiping up the field," Abby explained.

"Eric, honey, be careful!" Janice, his date, called out.

Ginna leaned toward Nora. "Janice is a flower artist," she confided.

"Meaning?"

"Meaning she works in a flower shop, but she feels it makes her sound more intelligent if she calls herself a flower artist," she murmured.

"Don't tell me. He met her when he was in the flower shop buying flowers for someone else."

Ginna nodded. "The flowers were for Katie, the day-care worker who he met when he went with Jeff and Abby to Casey and Carrie's open house."

Nora looked across the grassy expanse toward Eric and Mark, whose heads were together as they discussed strategy. She knew the men were good friends. She felt an unsettling sensation in the pit of her stomach. Good friends because they're so much alike? She recalled the times she and Mark had met with friends, Eric always had a different woman with him. She reached down and picked up a glass of ginger ale in hopes it would help settle her stomach. As she tipped the glass to her lips, she glanced up and found Gail's eyes on her. There was something too knowing in her gaze.

Nora reminded herself that Gail was a pediatrician not an obstetrician and looked back toward the playing field. Her pulse tripped a few beats as she watched Mark pull his shirt off over his head. His chest was hard-muscled and tanned a rich bronze color. She took another sip of her drink in hopes of quenching her sudden thirst.

"Think they'll overdo it like last time?" Gail asked the women.

"Of course they will, dear," Cathy assured her. "They're showing off for us. Lou pulled a thigh muscle the last time he played with the boys. And strained his back."

Abby nodded. "Jeff could barely the move the next day."

"Brian couldn't lift his arms over his head." Gail chuckled. "I think the men are forgetting they're no longer eighteen."

"Maybe they're forgetting, but that doesn't mean we'll let them forget," Ginna said. She suddenly jumped up clapping. "Woo-hoo, Zach! You go, baby! Oh no!" She groaned when Jeff got the ball from Zach and went running in a zigzag pattern with Mark fast on his heels.

Nora had no warning. Her eyes widened in horror as she

realized a freight train known as Jeff Walker was heading straight at her. Their eyes met in shared panic as she jumped up out of her chair in hopes of getting out of the way. Too late since he slammed into her at the same time and they fell to the ground with Jeff on top of her.

"Jeffrey, get off her this minute! She's pregnant!" Cathy cried out then clapped her hands over her mouth. By then it was too late.

Nora was wheezing as Jeff jumped off her and reached down to pull her to her feet.

"Are you all right?" he asked as the rest of the group circled them.

She pressed her hand against her chest as she tried to pull air into her lungs. The scene before her was unreal. Everyone looked as if they were playing the game Statues. Ginna stared at her friend as if she couldn't believe what she'd just heard. Cathy looked apologetic as she stood there with her hands still covering her mouth. But it was the expression on Mark's face that was the hardest to look at. Shock mingled with a dawning comprehension as his mother's announcement sunk in.

"Oh my God." Ginna was the first one to break the charged silence that encompassed everyone. "Nora!" she screamed, throwing her arms around her friend. "Why didn't you tell me? How long have you known? When did this happen?" she demanded, then noticed the optical line of tension between Nora and Mark. "Oh…my…God," she whispered, looking from one to the other. "*Mark?* Mark is the father?" She released her friend and advanced on her brother with murder in her eyes.

"Gin," Zach's quiet voice carried easily to his wife's ears. "I don't think this is a good time."

Ginna stopped short and turned to her husband. She took a deep breath, then another, and slowly nodded. "You're right," she said quietly.

Cathy moved through the group until she reached Nora. She put her arms around her in a protective gesture.

"That's enough from all of you. Right now, I'm taking Nora up to the house," she said calmly. With the deft touch she was known for, she skillfully maneuvered Nora up to the house.

Ginna was hot on their heels, but Mark edged her out by physically picking her up and moving her to one side.

"This has nothing to do with you, Gin," he said quietly.

"Yes, it does! She's my best friend and like a sister to me."

"Come on, honey." Zach intervened and pulled her gently away.

Mark looked back at the house where the two women had disappeared. He felt as if he'd taken a hard punch to his gut.

Nora was pregnant with his baby. He was going to be a father!

For a moment, he felt the world whirl around him. He wouldn't have been surprised if he'd passed out cold. Instead, the world righted itself, but he still didn't feel too steady on his feet.

Shouldn't there have been some kind of warning to ease him into the situation?

Then he remembered the source of the news. He walked quickly up to the house and slipped into the kitchen. When he reached the hall, he heard the soft sound of Nora's tears and Cathy consoling her. He stopped just outside the guest room.

"He hates me," Nora cried out. "I know he does."

Mark swallowed the giant lump in his throat. *No, he doesn't, but he's sure scared as hell.*

"I don't believe that, dear," Cathy replied. "Mark was just surprised, that's all. I am so sorry I blurted the news out that way. I was so afraid you were hurt when Jeff slammed into you like that."

She should have told me. Mark leaned his shoulder against the wall. *Why didn't she tell me?*

"Do you feel all right? You're not having any pain, are you?" Cathy asked solicitously. "Jeff hit you pretty hard."

Mark straightened up. Dammit, he was the one with the medical training! And he was the father, to boot. Didn't that count for anything? He should be in there looking after her.

He threw his shoulders back and walked into the room. His heart twisted into a painful knot when he saw Nora's tear-stained face. She sat on the edge of the bed with Cathy sitting next to her. His mother's arms were around the younger woman's shoulders. She looked up at the intruder.

"Not now, Mark." Cathy spoke quietly but firmly.

He knew that tone of voice only too well. The five Walker siblings knew better than to argue with their mother when she used that voice.

"This concerns me." He was ready to make his argument. He noticed Nora refused to look at him. He hated to think she was trying to hide from him. Did she think he was going to come in here and say hurtful things to her? Or, even worse, insist the baby couldn't be his? All he wanted to know was why she'd kept the news from him. He didn't need to be a scientist to count back and figure out how long she probably had known. "Nora and I need to talk, Mom."

Cathy Walker's eyes sparked blue fire. "Yes, the two of you do need to talk, but *not now.*"

Mark watched her tighten her hold on Nora. Did she think Nora needed protection? Protection from what? From him?

His mother stared back at him. She wasn't about to leave them alone.

"Go on back outside," Cathy said quietly.

"Nora? Is that what you want me to do?" he appealed to her.

She kept her face turned from him.

He clenched his jaw. "Nora? Do you really want me to go?"

"Mark, go outside." Cathy's tone told him she wouldn't say it again.

He nodded jerkily and walked out of the room.

Mark's head was whirling so much he had to stop for a moment to collect his bearings. When he went outside, he found most of their friends gone.

Ginna walked up to him. Her cheeks were still bright with emotion, but she looked calmer. Mark still kept his distance.

"I'm sorry I yelled at you," she said in a low voice.

Mark grinned. "No, you're not."

Her return smile was pure guilt. "You're right, but I didn't give you a chance to defend yourself." She threw her arms around his neck and hugged him. Her lips tickled his ear. "I swear to you, if you do anything to make her cry or feel the least bit miserable, I will hurt you." She stepped back.

"If I did anything like that, I'd expect a hell of a lot more than that," he said honestly. "I didn't know, Gin. I swear to God if I had—" He stopped. What would he have done if he knew? What was he going to do now that he did know? He suddenly felt dizzy. The world momentarily turned black.

"Hey, little brother, don't pass out on us," Brian advised, grabbing hold of his arm.

"If you're lucky, the feeling might even go away by the time the kid turns twenty-one," Jeff said from the other side.

"How did this happen?" Mark said more to himself than the others.

"I knew we should have told him the truth when he was five and asked us where babies came from," Jeff told Brian. "But no, you wanted him to believe circus elephants brought babies."

"No jokes!" Mark shook them both off. "Not one damn joke." He stalked off.

Ginna turned around to watch him leave then looked back at the house. She started off then paused. "He's right, no jokes," she warned before she ran across the patio.

Brian and Jeff looked at each other.

"Remember how you felt when Abby told you she was pregnant?" Brian asked.

Jeff nodded. "I thought an atom bomb had gone off inside my head. I'd barely recovered from the news when we found out we were having twins."

"I literally lost the ability to breathe," Brian recalled. "Gail was trying to find an easy way to tell me over dinner. She said she got nervous, so she just sort of blurted it out." He chuckled, shaking his head in wonder as he recalled that night. "The trouble was, I had just popped a radish in my mouth. She thought she'd have to use the Heimlich so I wouldn't choke. I think my biggest hurdle was convincing Gail I was already in love with her."

"Yeah, you were pretty tense during that time," Jeff recalled.

The two brothers turned to watch their younger brother walk away. His stride was long and rushed, his body taut. They knew exactly how he was feeling. But they also knew that their understanding of what was going through his mind wouldn't make it any easier for him.

"Something tells me this is going to be harder on him than it was on us combined," Jeff said.

"Yeah, but he'll make it okay. Still, my money's on Nora. She's got enough smarts for both of them. Did you see the way he's kept one eye on her since they got here? I'd say the guy is hooked and just doesn't know it yet." Brian looked around. "Guess we'd better get over there and help the wives clean up. I'll get some trash bags out of the garage."

"Good." Jeff headed for the patio area.

"I DON'T NORMALLY CRY," Nora confessed, dabbing her eyes with a tissue.

"Hormones," Cathy pronounced. "You'll cry, you'll laugh, you'll want to kill someone. Namely, whoever is within range. And by that, I mean your favorite victim will be male because they don't understand what we women go through."

"I didn't plan to tell him that way."

"When were you going to tell *me?*"

Nora looked up to find Ginna standing in the doorway. Ginna's lovely features were a picture of misery. Nora held out her hand and Ginna came in. She crawled onto the bed and sat cross-legged next to Nora, who was seated against the headboard with Cathy seated on the other side of the bed.

Nora sniffed. "Oh, I don't know. Maybe I'd wear one of those T-shirts to work that says Baby on Board or Pregnant, Please Don't Pat My Belly."

"That would get your point across," Cathy said dryly. She stood up. "I'm going to get you something to drink. You're spending the night here and no arguments." She wagged her finger at Nora.

"I know better."

Ginna looked over her shoulder as her mother left the room. She turned back to Nora and mouthed counting to ten.

"When did you and Mark get back together?" she asked once she was sure her mother was out of earshot.

Nora shifted so she could curl her legs under her body. "It was one of those things. I was depressed when I came back from Seattle and he was there," she said lamely.

"I always thought the reason you didn't come over here as often was because of Mark. That deep down you still felt something for him." Ginna's eyes were expressive as she gazed at her friend.

"I was so over Mark," Nora insisted then blushed as Ginna shot her a telling look.

"Oh honey, you're over Mark and yet you're pregnant by him? Try again," she drawled.

Nora could feel the weariness steal over her. "Please, no more questions," she pleaded, sliding down until she was lying prone.

Ginna unfolded her legs and climbed off the bed. "You look like you're ready for a nap."

"Ready and more than willing," she admitted.

"I'll tell Mom you're resting." Ginna headed for the door. "I'll be back in the morning to pick you and Brumby up. Unless you'd rather Mark…?"

Nora looked undecided.

"I'll call first," Ginna started for the door.

"Ginna." She stopped and turned around. "Don't hurt Mark."

Ginna grinned. "You know me so well. All right, I promise not to leave any marks." She held her hand up with the two fingers upright in the Boy Scout salute.

"You were never a Boy Scout," Nora reminded her.

"Oh, I had a few in my time." Ginna twitched her hips as she left the room.

Nora pulled the comforter down to reveal the pillow and lay back down. Within seconds, she was asleep.

"WAS HE NUTS?" Ginna asked, pacing back and forth the length of the kitchen.

Cathy sat at the breakfast bar squeezing a quarter of lime

into her glass of Diet Coke. She picked up her glass and sipped the sparkling liquid.

"Did he have a death wish or something?" Ginna continued ranting and raving without bothering to wait for a reply. She wasn't expecting one. "It had to be the night he picked her up at the airport when she came back from Seattle. My best friend, Mom! My idiot brother had sex with my best friend and got her pregnant! What was he thinking?"

"I realize times have changed, dear, but I don't think the theory has changed that it still takes two to make a baby," Cathy said mildly. She idly picked through the nut dish, found what she was looking for and plucked out a hazelnut. "Are you going to blame Nora too? Did you tell her she was an idiot for not taking precautions with your equally idiot brother?"

"Of course not!" Ginna looked horrified at the idea. "Mom, Nora was vulnerable. Her grandmother just died. She didn't know what she was doing."

Cathy arched an eyebrow. She dug through the nut dish again and brought up a cashew. She handed it to Ginna. "I remember the first time Mark and Nora came out here as a couple. You could see the connection. The problem was, they chose not to recognize it and they parted. Mark licked his wounds by reaffirming his masculinity with too many women and Nora walled off a part of herself. That wall is coming down. Not easily, but it's coming down. I think her grandmother would be very happy to know that. So, what I want you to do, is leave your brother alone and be careful what you say to Nora. Let them figure this out for themselves."

Ginna leaned over, bracing her forearms on the counter. She picked up her mother's glass and took a sip. "You act as if this was something fate decreed."

"Who says it wasn't? After all, Jeff ended up with the woman he'd battled with all through college. Brian went out on a blind date with a woman who was his total opposite. Now they're married and have a daughter. You went on a trip and found someone in the seat next to you. Why shouldn't it be Mark's turn now?"

"Come on, Mom. Mark's ideal age group is four," Ginna pointed out. "His kid will grow up before he does."

Cathy shook her head. "There are depths to your brother that even I don't know, but I have an idea we'll be seeing them in the coming months."

Ginna heaved a sigh. She raked her fingers through her rich brown hair that she'd left in loose waves that day.

"I promised Nora I wouldn't hurt him," she said with a little regret.

"Don't try to figure it all out in one day, dear," Cathy advised, patting Ginna's hand as she took back her drink. "Why don't you pack up your husband and children, go home and have the perfect family evening where you'll chase them around the house because they won't want to take their baths. And once they're in bed and asleep like the little angels they are, you can give your husband an opportunity to chase you around the house." She slid off her stool and walked around the bar to hug her daughter. "Go, my child. Enjoy your evening."

"I told Nora I'd call in the morning and come back to take her home," Ginna said.

"We'll see how it goes in the morning," was all Cathy would say.

Cathy walked with her outside. They found the brothers and Zach hauling trash bags to the garage with Casey, Carrie, Emma and Trey helping by carrying lawn chairs to the end of the patio. Brian was the first to see them.

"Notice how she shows up when all the work is done," he grumbled good-naturedly. "Nice of you to appear, princess."

"Nice to see you did such a good job of cleaning up," she retorted with a saucy smile. "Hey, handsome, wanna go home and put the kids to b-e-d." She spelled out the last word.

"You spelled *bed* and we're not going!" Emma declared with a familiar mutinous expression on her face.

"Of course you're not going to bed," Ginna said, swinging her up into her arms. "We need baths first."

"Baths, aghhhhh!" Trey made a face.

"Enjoy your evening, dear." Cathy patted her shoulder as

she leaned over to plant a kiss on Emma's cheek. "And don't give your parents too hard a time," she teased.

"I won't, Grammy, but sometimes Trey does."

"And I'm sure he has help." Cathy wasn't fooled by the little girl's angelic face.

She stood in the driveway ten minutes later, waving off the last of her family.

"You can come out now," she called after the last vehicle was out of sight.

Mark emerged from the stand of nearby trees. "How'd you know I was there?"

"Mother's intuition." She took his arm to stay his motion when he started to head for the house. "She's asleep."

"Then I'll wait until she wakes up."

Cathy shook her head. "Let her have tonight to sort things out."

Mark spun in a tight circle. His face was a tight mask of frustration.

"Why didn't she tell me? Was she planning to…?"

"No," she said firmly, easily guessing the direction of his thoughts. "She would never consider that. Nora's still feeling fragile. Give her a little time."

For a moment, he looked as if he was going to argue with her then he apparently changed his mind. "Can I come over for breakfast?"

"Only if you first stop at Ed's Bakery for their Danish."

Mark nodded jerkily. He started to move off then halted. He turned back.

"Mom—" He stopped as if unsure what to say next or just couldn't bring himself to say the words because then he'd air his fears.

Cathy patted his cheek. "The best thing about pregnancy is the months you have to prepare for it. You'll have plenty of time to get used to the idea, dear."

"What if Nora won't let me get used to it? What if she doesn't want me to have anything to do with the baby?" He hesitated before saying the last word.

"That's not Nora's way," she said firmly. "Now, go home

and get a good night's sleep. The two of you can discuss this after you've thought things through.''

Mark put his arms around his mother. The faint scent of Chanel No. 5 tickled his nostrils. For as long as he could remember his mother had worn that fragrance. Even now, he considered it a comforting scent because it always brought him good memories.

"I love you, Mom," he murmured against her hair.

"You better," she teased lightly. "Go home, Mark. Try to relax."

He released her and dug into his shorts pocket for his keys. "Will you tell Nora—" He shook his head.

"You can tell her once you've found the words."

Cathy watched Mark head for his truck and drive away.

"My baby boy has finally grown up," she murmured to herself. "Now if he'll just take the time to find it out for himself."

She turned back toward the house, mentally figuring where she would display future pictures of her next grandchild.

I'M GOING TO BE A FATHER.

Mark couldn't breathe.

Nora is having my kid.

Black spots danced in front of his eyes.

We made a baby.

Oh yeah, he was definitely going to pass out.

He blindly made his way to the couch and dropped to the cushions before he fell down.

During the drive home he kept seeing how Jeff had accidentally run into Nora. Mark's first thought was she might have been hurt, then he had been almost brought to his knees when his mother had shouted that Nora was pregnant.

Since then, the questions flooded his mind, and so far he hadn't been able to get one answer.

How long had she known she was pregnant? Why had she told his mother before she told him? Dammit, he was the father! She had to have known that morning as they drove out to his parents'. Did she know the last time they talked on the phone? She hadn't even dropped any hints!

He racked his brain for the slightest clue. It wasn't easy but he forced every stunned brain cell to perform at optimum level. There had to have been something, a word she'd said, something. The times he'd seen her could be counted on one hand. Nights he'd spent with her even less.

Come on, Walker. Basic biology says it only takes once.

He flopped back against the couch and rubbed his face with his hands. He suddenly held them out and stared at the palms. They were damp.

"I'm not father material," he said out loud. "That's my brothers' jobs. They're the dads. I'm the fun uncle that takes the kids out for wild days of adventure and brings them back hyper and filled with junk food."

Mark felt his breathing constrict again.

He recalled the look of pleasure in his mom's eyes. There was nothing that his mother loved more than the idea of prospective grandchildren. Each grandchild was given a quilt she made that was created from their father's own baby clothes. She was presently working on quilts for Emma and Trey using Ginna's baby clothes because she didn't want them to feel left out. He'd told her she was more than welcome to sneak in any of his clothes she'd kept. She'd just smiled. That smile scared Mark because it meant she knew something he didn't. Today she had definitely known something he didn't.

"Hey, Mark, pick up!" Brian's voice seemed to echo throughout the room.

Mark's head snapped up. He had been so lost in his thoughts he hadn't even heard the phone ring. He leaned over and snagged the cordless phone's handset.

"Did you ever stop to think that I didn't pick up because I might not be home or I just didn't want to talk to anyone?"

"I knew you were home, and if you hadn't picked up, I would have said I'd be over there in twenty minutes. You would have picked up then."

Mark called him a less than brotherly name that would have

once earned him a trip to the bathroom and a mouthful of soap if his mother had heard him.

To make matters worse, Brian just laughed.

"You okay?" he asked, his voice now quieter.

This time Mark laughed, but there was no humor in the sound.

"Oh yeah, I'm just fine. After all, I found out today I'm going to be a father. Doesn't that make any guy's day?" He wished he smoked so he'd have something to do with his hands. He needed something to settle the earthquake rolling around inside him.

"Which means you're still in shock. You're so overloaded you can't even take it all in. You have that wild thought that maybe it's a mistake. You can't imagine how it happened, although you know very well *how* it happened. So, which do you feel?"

"All of the above and even more than you've mentioned," he admitted.

"Have you talked to Nora?"

"She's spending the night at Mom and Dad's." He pressed his palm against his stomach. The last time he had felt like this, he'd indulged in a burrito-eating contest with Eric at a fair. He'd had major heartburn for a week.

"Don't bite my head off for asking this, but do you know for sure that—"

"Do *not* even go there, Brian. If you want to keep your head where it belongs, you will not finish that sentence." He let his brother know there was no doubt in his mind and there shouldn't be any in Brian's.

"Okay. Look, you want to talk, just give a call or come on over. You know I'm here for you, little brother."

"I know," Mark murmured. For all the competition between brothers, they were always there for each other when it counted. Mark appreciated Brian's support, but he wasn't ready to talk to anyone. "I think for now I'm going to crash early. I'm hoping things will look clearer in the morning."

"I guess it's a good thing we don't go back on duty until

day after tomorrow. I guess you'll be going back to Mom and Dad's tomorrow,'' Brian said.

There was no doubt in his mind what he'd be doing tomorrow. The decision was made, and in his mind, there was no going back. He feared this was only the first of many scary decisions.

Mark took a deep breath. Once he said the words out loud, he knew there would be no going back.

Chapter Nine

"Good morning, dear, did you sleep well?" Cathy greeted Nora when she walked into the kitchen. The older woman wore a bright pink velour robe and looked entirely too wide-awake for Nora, who didn't consider herself a morning person.

"Yes, I did, thank you," she replied as if she hadn't expected to. "Thank you for leaving some crackers for me." When she woke up, she found a small plate of crackers on the nightstand. After a few, she discovered her stomach wasn't so touchy when she got up.

"I used to nibble on a few before I tried getting out of bed. I didn't seem to feel as sick that way." She handed Nora a mug. "Ginger tea. I know it's not the same as coffee or even a decent second, but believe me, your stomach wouldn't appreciate coffee right now anyway."

She accepted the mug and sipped it cautiously. It tasted better than she thought it would since she'd always been a hard-core coffee drinker.

"Thank you." She slid onto one of the stools at the breakfast bar.

"Think you can handle some food now?"

Nora mentally cataloged her stomach. "I would love something."

Cathy was soon whisking eggs in a bowl and pouring them into an omelette pan.

Nora cupped her hands around the mug, feeling the warmth steal through her palms.

"You'll feel even better after you eat." Cathy slid a golden omelette onto a plate. She set it on the breakfast bar along with a plate piled high with toast and another with bacon. "Let's see. I have orange honey, raspberry jam and blackberry preserves for your toast."

Nora's eyes widened with horror. "Oh, Cathy, I can't eat all that food without exploding!"

"That's what I'm for." Lou walked into the kitchen. He looped his arm around Nora's shoulders for a one-armed hug as he dropped a kiss on top of her head. "Sleep well?"

"Yes, I did," she said with some surprise.

"Whereby you wouldn't have if you'd gone home. You would have lain awake worrying all night. Sometimes, sleeping in a strange bed can be a good thing." Cathy looked at her husband. "I suppose you want an omelette too."

"A real one," Lou stressed.

She opened the refrigerator door. "Egg whites are better for your cholesterol."

"But not as tasty." He poured himself a cup of coffee and brought over the pot as if to top off Nora's mug.

"No caffeine for me," she said regretfully.

He winced. "Sorry." He handed the second cup to his wife. "One whole egg and two egg whites?" he bargained.

Cathy heaved a sigh. "Don't blame me if the doctor puts you back on that strict diet."

Nora spread raspberry jam on her toast and bit into it while cutting her omelette into bite-size pieces. Golden cheese oozed out of it.

"Is there anything you can't cook?" she asked.

"Custard," Cathy said promptly. "I can't bake custard to save my life. It's the same when I try to bake a custard pie. It always comes out watery."

"There was that sausage casserole you once tried making," Lou said, straddling the tall stool next to Nora.

"We don't mention that." Cathy placed a glass of orange

juice in front of Nora along with a glass of milk. "Drink both of them," she ordered.

Nora settled for sipping the juice in between bites of omelette and toast.

"I've always loved this kitchen," she mused. "It's so large yet it's warm and comfortable."

"It cost me a small fortune to get it this warm and comfortable," Lou grumbled good-naturedly. "I rebuilt that Model A to pay for the kitchen."

"We needed the size what with all the kids and their friends," Cathy explained, handing Lou his plate. He blew her a kiss and dug into his breakfast.

Nora looked around again. She saw the white curtains with an ivy pattern trailing along the bottoms that was echoed in tiles along the counter. Along one side of the room were polished oak glass-fronted cabinets holding everyday dishes and fine china and glassware. Another corner held a large round oak table and eight chairs but room for probably four more without crowding anyone. The tablecloth was the same pattern as the curtains. A green dish towel hung on a rack over the sink.

She could smell the cooking scents in the air, the rich aroma of coffee mingling with toasted bread and jam.

"When I was growing up, Grammy Fran would fix me oatmeal on cold days," she recalled. "I hated cold days because I hated oatmeal. She told me it would stick to my bones. I told her that it would also glue my papers together. She'd always laugh and pop a piece of toast in my mouth." She absently mimicked the movement.

A shave-and-a-haircut knock on the back door announced their visitor before he walked inside.

"Hey, Ma." Mark kissed her on the cheek. He gazed hungrily at the food. "Am I in time for breakfast?"

"One day, I'd like to have someone cook *me* breakfast." Cathy returned to the stove.

"I made you toast this past Mother's Day," Lou reminded her.

Cathy looked over her shoulder at Nora and mouthed "burned black" at her. Nora giggled.

"Are you going to eat that piece of bacon?" Mark asked, taking the stool on the other side.

She shook her head. Mark wasted no time stealing the piece and popping it into his mouth.

Nora blinked her eyes.

"What is with that shirt? Some kind of test pattern? Because all I see are spots and red splotches," Lou said.

Mark looked down. "Dalmatians and fire trucks. I think it's kind of cool since I couldn't find a shirt for paramedics so I got the next best thing."

Lou sighed. "I guess it's better than some of the disasters you've worn."

"I'm making a statement," Mark defended his choice.

"Good thing you wear a uniform. That way you don't scare your patients with some of your choices."

"Says the man who thinks he can wear three different shades of green and it's all right," Cathy pointed out.

"Comes from the woman who has twelve pair of black shoes yet like the rest of us only has two feet." Lou toasted her with his coffee cup.

"I have ten pairs of black shoes and they all serve a different purpose," Cathy said self-righteously. She turned to Nora and Mark. "Why don't you two go out onto the patio? It's a lovely morning, not too chilly." She handed Mark a filled plate.

Mark looked around. "Where's the Brumb?"

"He's out in the backyard with Jasmine." Cathy mentioned their German shepherd also known as the family's oversize lapdog. "I gave them each a steak bone, so they'll be occupied for hours."

Mark picked up Nora's plate along with his own. "Does that sound good to you?"

She picked up her juice glass and the plate with the toast. "All right."

Nora set out the plates and silverware while Mark adjusted the table's umbrella so the morning sun wouldn't hit them directly.

"You better eat your food before it gets cold," she advised, sitting down in one of the chairs.

"Mom makes great omelettes," he said, forking up a mouthful. "She used to make them on Saturday mornings before our Little League games."

Nora pushed around her food until she chose a small piece and brought it to her lips.

"She'd also make these great orange-iced rolls," he continued. He heaved a sigh and dropped his fork on his plate. "Oh hell, I can't do this small talk."

"Thank God," she breathed in relief. "I'm sorry. I am so sorry. You don't have to think I'm going to make things bad for you because I'm not."

Mark held up his hands. "Wait a minute, what are you sorry for?"

"For getting pregnant! I wasn't thinking that night and…"

"And I was there too," he pointed out. He set down his fork, carefully aligning it with his plate. He looked up. "Nora, I'm sorry this happened. I don't think this was in your life plan, but I will be there for the baby. From now on, you can know that you can count on me. I want to be there. I intend to help out financially and every other way I can help."

"Thank you," Nora said numbly. She hadn't expected him to act so gracious. "But I'm doing fine."

"You're not going to be able to work your entire pregnancy," he said. "And with you being self-employed, you don't have maternity leave. I know how it works, Nora. You won't see any income when you're not working. Please don't be proud. Let me help where I can whether it's with your own expenses, medical expenses, whatever you need to set up a nursery. And when the baby's born, I'm more than willing to help in any way. I'll take the baby for you whenever I can."

She slumped back in her seat. "It sounds as if you've done a lot of thinking about this," she said, surprised.

"Only for about the last fifteen hours." He picked up his coffee mug and sipped the hot liquid. "I'm equally to blame."

"No, not blame," she said quickly. "Let's not use that word in regards to the baby."

He nodded. "Fine by me. So tell me, when did you find out you were pregnant?"

Nora winced. "Remember the night we went to Syd's Place? I saw my doctor that morning."

"A month?" He did some mental calculations. "No, six weeks ago! Why didn't you tell me that night? How could you keep it a secret for so long?"

"I didn't know how to say it!" she retorted, feeling her temper rise.

"Didn't know how to say it?" he snapped. "How about, 'Remember that night we spent together, Mark? Guess what? We made a baby!' Did you think about saying that?" His voice rose.

"Yes, I thought about saying that! But I didn't think the moment was right," she argued.

"Didn't think the moment was right," Mark repeated. "So when would you have considered a perfect moment? When you were in labor? When the kid was graduating from high school?"

Nora shot to her feet. "There is no reason to be sarcastic. Fine, I didn't tell you the minute I found out, but I was still getting used to the news. Then I come home and there you are. Before I knew it, you've kidnapped me and my dog."

He also stood up. "You went willingly!"

"It was still more like a shanghai," she argued, tossing her napkin onto the table. "You know what? You are an impossible man to talk to. You don't listen! You never listen! You do what you want and the hell with everyone else. Well, guess what, Mark Walker, the hell with you!" She spun on her heel and stalked back to the house.

"This isn't over!" he yelled after her.

Her reply was the door slamming shut behind her.

Mark dropped back into his chair muttering curses on stubborn women. A soft whine sounded near his knee. He looked down and found Brumby gently pawing at his leg.

"Your mistress is a stubborn woman," he told the dog as he fed him a piece of egg.

"Son, one thing you need to remember for the coming

months is that no matter what you say to a pregnant woman you will be wrong. Just smile, admit you're wrong and take i from there.'' Lou stopped by the table. He held his coffee mug in one hand.

"She's known for weeks. And she's talked to me since then She could have said something.''

"Like I said, apologize, and if you're lucky she won't murder you. Well, I've got a carburetor to rebuild.'' He ambled off toward the large garage where he housed his automobile-restoration business. "Welcome to the club, Mark.''

"What club?'' Mark called after him.

Lou looked over his shoulder and grinned. "The Daddy's Club.''

Mark slumped back in his chair. There was that word again. He didn't have enough time to learn to be a dad. He wondered if Nora would mind having a longer pregnancy than the usual nine months. Maybe it could last a few years or so. By then, he might be ready for fatherhood. He dropped one hand and absently scratched Brumby's ears. "You're getting a younger brother or sister, Brumb. I bet you'll be a great big brother, but don't worry, you won't be ignored. I'll take you for walks and play ball with you. Whatever you want to do.'' He felt a slight pressure against his leg. He looked down and groaned. "Okay, I can see exactly what you want to do.''

Nora walked outside and stopped short at the sight before her.

"Making friends with my dog will not help your case,'' she said coolly.

"He was the one who came on to me.'' Mark gently pushed Brumby to one side.

He could have sworn her lips twitched, but the movement was quickly masked so he wasn't sure if he'd just imagined it. He hoped that meant she wasn't still angry with him. Then he saw the spark in her eyes.

Oh yeah, she still wasn't too happy with him.

She stood in front of him with her hands folded in front of her.

"I will not deny you access to the baby,'' she said primly.

"If you're willing to help out with the larger expenses, I'm not too proud to accept any help. I can add the baby to my medical plan if you don't want to add him or her to yours. Or we can see which one has the better benefits." She looked as serene as a woodland stream.

"I'll check on mine as soon as possible and let you know," he replied, treading lightly. He remembered his dad warning him about hormones. Memories surfaced of Jeff and Brian moaning about Abby's and Gail's erratic moods during their pregnancies. And wasn't there something about prospective mothers getting some kind of nesting instinct? Nora might want to put everything in order right away. His imagination took over. Or was there another reason she wanted to have things in order?

"Are you feeling all right?" he asked.

She looked surprised by his question. "Other than morning sickness, I've been all right, why?"

"With all you've been talking about, I felt as if something might be wrong,"

Nora's eyes flared emerald fire. "There is *nothing* wrong with me or the baby. Obviously, you haven't been listening to me. I merely wanted you to feel a part of the pregnancy. Maybe we need to talk when you feel ready to listen." She turned on her heel and walked away. "Brumby, come!"

The bulldog looked up at Mark as if to say, "Sorry, guy, but she's the one who feeds me." He got to his feet and trotted after his mistress.

"Damn that woman!" Mark closed his eyes and leaned back in his chair. "I stayed up half the night trying to figure out what to say to her, left my apartment early this morning without even a cup of coffee to get my internal engine running and came out here only to have her insult me when I'm trying to do the right thing."

"Mark."

He opened one eye. His mother stood at the edge of the patio. He noticed she'd taken the time to dress in jeans and a long-sleeved plaid cotton shirt in varied shades of blues and greens with a blue sweater.

"I'm taking Nora home," she told him.

"I told her I'd take her home," he protested.

"I don't think that would be a good idea, dear."

"What would be a good idea, Mom?" He was feeling beyond frustration by then. "What in the hell does Nora think is a good idea? Has she figured out that she needs a guy with the daddy gene? Is that the problem here? If that's the case, I could have told her that right off."

The last thing he expected to see on his mother's face was pity.

"I think that's something you'll need to figure out for yourself, dear." She walked back to the house.

Mark heard Nora's voice mingled with his mother's and soon the sounds of Cathy's car moving down the driveway. A cold nose nuzzled his hand. A tan and black German shepherd whined and pushed at his hand again.

"Hey, Jasmine," he greeted his parents' dog. "You're probably the only sane female I've been around for the past two days."

The dog planted her front feet in his lap and licked at his face then gave another woof and pushed off with her feet as she jumped back and ran off.

"Augh!" Mark gulped for air. "Great. One female unmans me with words. Another tries doing it with her paws." He slowly rose to his feet. He started to walk gingerly away then recalled long-honored rules. He turned back, picked up the dishes and carried them into the house. After rinsing them off and putting them in the dishwasher, he wrote out a note and put it on the counter before he left the house.

ALL THE WAY BACK to his apartment, Mark replayed each word Nora had said to him and what he'd said in return. Try as he might, he couldn't understand what he'd said that she'd found so objectionable. He'd been tempted to go out to the garage and talk to his dad, but if his dad was rebuilding a carburetor, he'd expect Mark to help and Mark didn't visualize spending his day off working on a car.

The minute he got back to his apartment, he threw off his

jeans and shirt and pulled on running shorts and a tank top. He walked down to a park near his house and took off on his favorite trail.

Long ago, Mark discovered he could solve his problems easier when he was running. All he needed was a decent trail and he could convince himself he could solve the problems of the world. He wasn't surprised that Jeff and Brian were closer to each other than he was with them. It had nothing to do with the age difference, but because Mark tended to keep his problems to himself.

When he reached the fork in the path where the left side would take him up an incline for the more experienced runner and the right for the novice, he didn't hesitate in turning left. Ten minutes later, he was running in place at the top of the incline. Below him were one of the two baseball fields. One field was empty while on the other one was a man and a small boy. Mark was too far away to get much of an idea of the boy except that he couldn't have been more than six or seven. The man, obviously his father, was hunkered down, showing the little boy how to properly hold the small bat and how to hit a home run.

Mark knew he should have kept on running, but he couldn't stop watching the duo. The man stood a short distance from the boy and threw the ball underhanded in an easy pitch. The boy swung too soon and completely missed the ball. His shoulders drooped and he looked frustrated. The man straightened up and went over, again showing him what to do. Mark couldn't miss the patience in the man's manner as he worked with the little boy.

How many hours had his dad spent with him showing him how to pitch a curveball? How to bat? How to properly throw a football? No matter how busy Lou was restoring a car, he always found time to play with his sons.

Mark could see that same attitude in his brothers. He remembered last Christmas when Jeff put together two tricycles for his girls. It hadn't been a pretty sight. Luckily, the twins never saw, or heard, their dad's frustration putting the bikes together. The next day, Jeff was out there watching them hap-

122 *Pregnancy Countdown*

pily pedal on their tricycles and making sure they didn't fall off. He recalled Brian sitting cross-legged on the ground with a sleeping Jennifer draped across his shoulder.

His two brothers had turned into their father.

Mark had no aspirations to be Father of the Year. He had no biological clock ticking away, no sudden need to procreate a mini Mark just because he was over thirty.

He had joked that the daddy gene stopped at Brian and that was fine with him because it gave him more time to play. It wasn't entirely true.

How was he going to tell his father and brothers that he didn't think he could live up to their standards of fatherhood? That he didn't think he could be the great dad figure they'd been from the beginning?

Mark considered himself the fun-loving brother. He was the guy always ready at a moment's notice to head down to Mexico for fishing. Or take off for a weekend of nightlife in Las Vegas. Jeff and Brian couldn't do that. Instead, their time off was spent with their kids, even looking after them to give Abby and Gail a break.

Mark figured he wasn't meant to have that kind of responsibility.

Then fate had played a crazy joke on him. It took Nora and him, mixed them up together in a situation where they couldn't stop themselves, and the result was a baby.

He had trouble visualizing a little person who would call him Daddy. This was a new chapter in his life and he wondered how he would handle it. Could he be a real dad to his child and not just a father, a sperm donor?

So much for his run clearing his mind. All it did was give him a lot more questions to figure out.

NORA DROPPED another damp tissue into the wastebasket with one hand while pulling another out of the box by her hip. She sniffed and blew her nose in a less than ladylike manner.

Brumby whined and pawed her leg, which was covered by a taupe, rust and cream–colored afghan her grandmother had knitted for her.

After a dinner of her favorite Chinese chicken salad, Nora changed into her favorite flannel nightgown and settled down to a movie marathon.

"I'm okay, boy," she sniffed, reaching down to give Brumby a reassuring pat. "I never realized a car commercial could make me cry. But the little girl was so cute." She wiped her eyes.

Earlier in the day, after Cathy dropped her off at home, Nora left the house to do some grocery shopping and pick up some books on pregnancy at the library. Cathy had mentioned there were some excellent Web sites on the Internet, but Nora was one of the very few who were still computer illiterate. She had a computer, but she only used it to keep records on her clients and type an occasional letter.

Nora spent the afternoon reading books on pregnancy. She wasn't surprised to learn morning sickness can happen any time of the day or night and roller-coaster emotions due to her changing hormones were normal. Been there. Done that.

After she ate her dinner, she sorted through her collection of DVDs and pulled out every romantic movie she owned. She lit several candles and set them around the room to add to the mood even if it was just her as audience. Between the movie marathon and a brand-new package of chocolate-covered graham crackers, she felt content.

All it took was a scene in one movie showing an automobile commercial and she was crying as if she was watching a sad film.

Nora blew her nose again. She reached down and scratched Brumby behind the ears. He uttered soft growling sounds.

She smiled at her dog's sounds of pure joy. "Typical male. It doesn't take much to satisfy you as long as I find the right spot."

In a way, it didn't take much to satisfy Mark either, did it, Nora? Just that flick of the finger or even a flick of the tongue in just the right place.

"Out damn thought," she paraphrased Shakespeare in a desperate attempt to halt the flood of memories.

Easier said than done once the door had been opened.

Nora recalled the incredible care Mark took with her, as if she were some fragile piece of china. He acted as if they had all the time in the world. His ignoring her entreaties when she was positive she would go insane if he didn't take the final step she needed for fulfillment. The cool touch of his fingertips stroking her inner thigh may have lit the flame, but she experienced flash point when he replaced his fingers with the heat of his mouth. It was as if he knew exactly where her most sensitive areas were. That he could easily arouse her with a mere word. And in the end, how he made her feel as if she was the most beautiful woman in the world.

No wonder she had woken up that morning with a smile on her lips. The man was definitely a gifted lover.

Not that everything that happened that night had been one-sided. That night, Nora had gotten the chance to discover what drove Mark wild. His unbridled response had made it easy for her to throw herself into her explorations.

She shifted uneasily on the couch as a low simmering heat developed deep within her belly. For a moment she considered dousing herself with her glass of lime-flavored water. Instead, she settled for stuffing another chocolate-covered graham cracker in her mouth and chewed furiously.

Of course, he knew how to make her body sing. How many women had he dated—if you wanted to call it that—since they had broken up? How many women had he made love to since then?

She jammed another cracker in her mouth.

"I wish I had some marshmallows and candy bars," she mused with an unladylike sniff. "I could fix some killer S'mores with these graham crackers."

She drifted off in thought, thinking of heading for the grocery store to pick up the needed supplies. Then she realized acquiring the necessary ingredients would require her getting dressed and going out.

Nora looked down at Brumby who was shamelessly begging for his share. "Too bad Vons doesn't deliver." She named the grocery store that was a few blocks away.

'I WANT TO GO to your doctor's appointment with you.''

Nora frowned. She hadn't slept well the night before, so she didn't feel at her sharpest. She had no one to blame but herself and two packages of chocolate-covered graham crackers. Her first appointment wasn't until late morning, so she took her time getting up, which her stomach greatly appreciated.

"Who is this?" she asked sweetly.

"Very funny, Nor."

"Ah yes, the infamous Walker growl. Why do you feel the need to go to my doctor's appointment with me?"

"Because this baby is mine too. I want to be with you every step of the way." He lowered his voice. "If I give you my schedule, are you willing to work around it?"

She had told him she wanted him to be a part of the baby's life.

"Of course I will." She shifted onto her side. "My next appointment is scheduled in two weeks on Monday."

"I'll be off duty on that day. Just tell me what time and where and I'll be there. Or I can pick you up," he offered.

Nora strained her ears in an attempt to identify the background noise. "Are you at the station?"

"Unfortunately," he grumbled. "Do you know what they do to prospective fathers here?"

"No, I've never been privy to that form of male bonding." Her lips curved in a smile. She wasn't sure what was going on, but she had a pretty good idea that he was the butt of everyone's joke.

"They get a cake that looks like something from a baby shower. Then they make up a condom tree as a reminder why you're going to be a father."

"Meaning if you'd used one and so on," she said.

"Exactly. Then they bring in a baby safety seat, which is a pretty nice one, by the way. I'll drop it off to you after I'm off duty. The guys bought quality," Mark said. "But they added something to the car seat. They put in a doll that cries. And wets," he muttered. "I have no desire to see what else the doll does."

Nora couldn't hold back her giggle. "I think that's sweet."

"These guys aren't sweet. They're diabolical. They also gave me six books on bringing up baby. I've been told I will be tested on their contents." He didn't sound eager about the prospects. "I think they meant it."

"Who originally thought up the idea to give male baby showers?" she asked, certain she already knew the answer. All she heard was a mumble. "What was that? I couldn't understand you."

He heaved a deep sigh. "I said it was my idea. We gave one for Brian and it sorta took off from there."

"Which meant Brian and the others decided they had the chance to come up with major payback," she guessed correctly.

"In spades," he admitted.

Nora smiled. She knew Mark's penchant for practical jokes. "But they didn't have your style, did they?" she said. "They dared enter your arena for the wild and wacky, but I bet they didn't come up to your standards."

"True." He sounded mollified by her verbal soothing of his ruffled feathers. "I, at least, would have come up with a better limerick on the cake."

"Then it sounds as if they hadn't truly studied the master," she cooed. She wiggled her toes under the covers. "Give them credit for trying."

"I'll give them an A for effort."

"Next time you'll be in charge and you can show them how it's done," she reminded him.

Silence hung heavy from the other end of the phone line.

"You just patted me on the head, and if you could have you would have given me a cookie, wouldn't you?"

Nora ignored the suspicion in his tone. "Of course not. But you feel better, don't you?"

"You've spent way too much time with my sister," he groused.

Nora glanced at the clock and gasped. "I have to go or I'll be late! Thank them for the safety seat and bring me a slice of the cake too." She disconnected the call and almost flew off the bed. Luckily, by then, her stomach had settled down.

She quickly showered and applied makeup. As she dressed, she stood sideways to gaze at her profile in the mirror. She pouched out her tummy to get a better idea what she'd look like in a few more months.

"So will I look as if I swallowed a Ping-Pong ball or a beach ball?" she mused, turning this way and that, entranced with everything that was going on inside her.

She reached for her favorite heather-green pants and discovered she couldn't fasten them.

"I guess this is goodbye until next year," she murmured, hanging them back up. She settled on a smoky-blue dress that wasn't fitted around the waist and paired it with midheeled slides that were nothing more than a few strips of leather in two shades of gray.

After making sure the doggie door was unlocked for Brumby, she ran out of the house.

Nora reached the Steppin' Out Salon and Day Spa in record time. She parked next to Ginna's classic black Mustang convertible and hurried through the back door. The moment she crossed the threshold she felt herself instantly relax thanks to the hint of fragrance in the air that CeCe, the owner, felt was calming to the soul. Nora swore the aroma was never the same from day to day, but it always seemed to be just what she needed.

As if thinking her boss's name was a magic spell, CeCe seemed to materialize from the end of the hall. As always, the dark-haired woman personified elegance. With her classic cheekbones, full-lipped mouth and a figure any woman would admire she could have been thirty or sixty. To date, no one had been able to figure out the mystery that was their boss.

"How are you feeling, *chérie*?" the older woman asked in her lightly accented voice. "Your stomach is not upset this morning?"

Nora felt her jaw drop. "How did you know?"

CeCe smiled. "Some things a woman just knows." She laid her hand on Nora's arm. "If you start feeling unwell, you must go lie down. Or see if Phoebe can give you one of her aro-

matherapy facials. I always found sniffing a sprig of mint
helped. We also have some ginger tea that should help you.''

"I'll remember that. Thank you.'' Nora walked out to her
station. Ginna was standing behind her chair talking to Cheryl,
one of the nail techs who worked in the salon, as she deftly
threaded the golden-brown strands into an intricate braid that
hung down Cheryl's back.

"Braids always make me think of Heidi,'' Cheryl said, staring in the mirror as Ginna worked.

Ginna laughed. "I dare Gary to call you Heidi.'' Her fingers
were a blur of motion as she mentioned Cheryl's boyfriend.

"We're still in that bliss part where we think neither can do
any wrong.'' She sighed. "And he's so darn cute.''

"Is there anyone here who isn't in the first throes of love?''
Nora asked, stashing her purse in a bottom drawer at her station.

"Me,'' Phoebe confessed. She picked up a tube of hand
cream on the counter and squeezed a dime-size dollop into the
palm of one hand. "Blind Date Central let me down again.''

"Welcome to the club,'' Nora told her. "I gave up because
it seemed all I dated were duds.''

"The only good man who was up there was my brother and
you all missed out,'' Ginna announced.

"No offense, Gin, but Brian's too nice,'' Phoebe explained.
"I like someone a little dangerous.''

"This last one wasn't dangerous?'' Nora asked.

"This last one's idea of living dangerously was to leave his
credit cards at home,'' she said glumly.

The other three women immediately offered their sympathy.

"What about you, Nora?'' Ginna asked, a sly look in her
eyes. "What do you consider the perfect man?''

*Irreverent. Fun-loving. The kind of man your grandmother
adores.*

Not that she'd dare admit that to her friend.

Nora settled for a bland smile and a stock answer. "Someone
who's breathing.''

Chapter Ten

"Are you sure you don't want me to go with you to your doctor's appointment?" Ginna asked. "I can cancel my lunch with Zach."

"As crazy as it sounds, I can still drive myself," Nora replied.

Ginna dropped into Nora's chair. "Nora, you are one of the most together people I know. Well, except for that insane dating period you went through, and we won't even discuss that philosophy professor you dated."

"As if I would know he believed I was his queen four thousand years ago," Nora argued.

"On another planet!"

"Actually, in another galaxy. And let's not forget that Mrs. Crockett has otherworldly visitors all the time."

"At least they give her some incredible things to write about. Did you read her latest yet?" Ginna picked up a brush and ran it through her hair. "Zach wants to send her roses." Her eyes took on a sultry cast as she recalled that night.

"I'm still waiting for you to give me back the last stories she brought in," Nora reminded her.

Ginna twisted her hair up on top of her head and secured it with a couple of pins. "I'll make a copy. So, you're sure you don't want company at the doctor's?"

Nora looked in the mirror and watched the front door open. Mark stepped inside.

"Very sure." She watched him smile and speak to the receptionist, point in her direction and head her way.

"Ladies. Actually, one lady, one pain in the butt." Mark grinned at Nora. "Are you ready?"

Ginna looked at her brother then at Nora. "He's going with you?"

"He *is* the father," Nora reminded her.

Ginna swiveled in her chair so she could face Mark.

"I still haven't forgiven you," she stated in an imperious tone.

"I still haven't forgiven you for telling Lynne Michaels I had a nasty rash in an unspeakable place," he countered.

"She didn't have to believe me."

Mark shook his head. "You have no idea how evil this creature is," he told Nora.

Nora looked at Ginna. "It would have been funnier if you'd have faked some photographs of some kind of icky rash to give her."

"Rats!" Ginna snapped her fingers in frustration. "I could have used you back then." She smirked at her brother. "Never underestimate the power of friendship, little brother." Her gaze slid over him. "Don't you own any normal shirts that are acceptable for when you go out in public?"

Mark looked down at his shirt. The blinding profusion of turquoise and red macaws perched on green branches that boasted bright yellow blossoms made him an easy target. "It's a gloomy day. I thought the shirt would cheer it up," he said simply.

"Or blind it," she muttered.

Nora slipped on her jacket. She picked up her purse, settling the strap over her shoulder. "We have to go."

"I'll want details," Ginna called after them.

"She's not just sneaky, she's also very bloodthirsty," Mark said as he guided Nora out of the salon.

"I think you greatly exaggerate your sister's talents." Nora slipped on her sunglasses to shield her eyes from the afternoon sun.

Mark grinned again as he put on his sunglasses also. Nora

momentarily regretted his covering up those brilliantly colored eyes.

"Do people ever ask you if you wear colored contact lenses?" she asked.

"All the time. They can't believe somebody would naturally have this color eyes. I bet you get asked a lot if your hair color is natural." He disarmed the alarm and helped her up into his truck. He stood by the seat as she reached for the seat belt. He covered her hand with his, stopping her action. He used his other hand to tuck a strand of hair behind her ear, then flicked the gold stars and crescent moon that dangled from her ear. "Pretty." He looked into her eyes as he spoke the word.

She felt the warm brush of his fingers against her ear. A tingle started at her ear and moved into a part of her brain that was guided by her emotions.

"Thank you," she whispered, unable to take her eyes off him. "They're my favorite earrings."

He took the seat belt from her and stretched across her to secure it. She discovered he smelled like fresh lime.

She knew there a good reason she liked the smell of lime.

Mark turned his head to one side and smiled at her. Not the cocky all-male smile he usually flashed. This was something softer, almost intimate. And a heck of a lot more dangerous to her peace of mind.

"I wasn't just talking about the earrings," he murmured.

She couldn't stop her lips from curving in an answering smile. "I know."

His face was so close to her that their lips almost touched. For a moment, she would have sworn he was going to kiss her.

"If you're a good girl at the doctor's I'll take you to lunch afterward," he said.

"That's funny. I'd already assumed you were going to feed me afterward."

Mark shook his head. "Saucy wench."

"I've never heard of that place. But as long as they serve good food, I'll be happy." She settled back in the seat, moving away from his touch.

He shook himself off. "Right." He closed the door and walked around to the driver's side.

Nora glanced out the window and noticed Ginna standing at the salon's front window. She wiggled her fingers at her friend as Mark drove off.

"Dr. Jackson's offices are in the Stafford Medical Center," she told him.

"I know where it is," Mark pulled out into traffic. "How did you choose him?"

"He was on the list of recommended obstetricians my doctor gave me. I narrowed down the names to the ones on my medical plan and visited them. Quite a few of my clients go to him and highly recommend him." She pulled down the visor. She looked at Mark. "You don't have a mirror."

Mark cursed under his breath as another driver cut in front of him. "Why would I have a mirror there?"

"So your dates can check their makeup." She dug into her purse and pulled out a small mirror and a tube of apricot-colored lip gloss. She carefully applied it then dusted some blush on her cheeks. "Didn't anyone tell you that a mirror on the passenger-side visor is a requirement?"

"I didn't realize seeing a doctor required a full makeover," Mark commented.

"More like making one feel better."

Mark frowned at her reply. "Aren't you feeling good? You're not having cramps, are you? Or spotting?"

"My, my, I'm impressed. You read the books they gave you," Nora teased.

"I'm a paramedic, sweetheart. They make sure I already know these things," he reminded her. "Otherwise, they won't let me ride in the paramedic truck. Or drive, for that fact."

"Has it been quiet for you? Last night's news showed a multicar pileup on the freeway," Nora said.

Mark's lighthearted expression dimmed. "It was bad," he said crisply.

Nora immediately sensed the incident wasn't something he wanted to talk about. She realized she wasn't used to seeing him looking somber.

"Brumby has a new hobby," she announced, deciding a change of subject was in hand.

By the relaxed set to his shoulders she saw that she'd succeeded.

"What is he up to now?"

"When he hears the kids playing in the park, he runs outside to the back fence," she explained. "He'll sit there staring at the fence as if he can see right through it and see the kids playing. I've seen him sit there for hours, that stub of a tail wagging." She chuckled. "He doesn't bark or try to jump at the fence. But his tail will start going faster the more excited he gets. Sometimes I think it will fall right off because he wags it so fast."

"You have a very strange dog," he laughed.

"I consider myself lucky he entertains himself so easily," she replied. "He loves to go after tennis balls. We do that for exercise and he loves the dog park where he can socialize."

"Bulldogs aren't exactly known as lapdogs," Mark pointed out.

"No one told Brumby that. Sometimes I think he's convinced he's a poodle." She leaned over and touched his arm. "There's the center."

Mark flipped the turn signal and swung the truck into the parking lot.

"A lot of pregnant women are going in here," he commented, pulling into an empty space. "Is there an epidemic?"

"Stafford's an OB/GYN center for women, although there are also a couple pediatricians who have their offices here," she explained.

"One-stop baby center."

"Pretty much." She accepted his hand as she climbed out of the truck. A gust of wind caught the open ends of her jacket. Mark grabbed the ends and brought them together. He slipped the zipper into the tab and pulled it upward.

"We can't have you catching a chill," he told her with a smile as he brushed hair away from her eyes.

"Thank you." She smiled back.

Did Nora's eyes always look like liquid emeralds?

From the moment Mark woke up that morning he'd felt as if he was gearing up for something. His stomach felt as if someone had dumped a quart of acid into it and every muscle felt as tight as a drum. He wasn't sure why he felt that way. Then he saw the note on the refrigerator door. He'd tacked up a reminder that Nora's doctor's appointment was today.

He told himself going with her was doing the right thing. That he would do what he could for her. His father and brothers would expect it. Brian sure had supported Gail. He'd practically held her hand from the moment he learned she was pregnant. Mark admired him for it. He knew the least he could do for Nora was be there for her as he was today.

When he had secured her seat belt, he caught hints of fragrance in her hair and around her. Something that made him think fresh and clean like mountain springs and waterfalls.

At least it's nothing to do with liquid emeralds again.

Nora's cheeks were flushed from the cold air. She walked briskly, easily keeping up with his longer strides that he shortened for her benefit.

She'd dressed warmly in a knit dress that he'd call orange, but he was sure there was another name for it. He'd tried not to stare, but he'd swear her breasts were fuller and he could see a slight rounding to her belly. She'd clipped her hair at the nape, but the wind stole strands loose so that they flew around her face.

Mark felt as if he'd ventured into unknown territory from the moment he stepped into the building. Music that floated in the air was meant to relax the visitors, colors were soft, muted and all geared for the feminine soul. The walls were even painted pale pink! He hunched his shoulders wondering if he shouldn't tell her he'd wait for her in the truck. He opened his mouth ready to say that but instead asked which floor the doctor's office was on.

"We go to the second floor," Nora explained, heading for the bank of elevators.

Mark looked around at the women walking down the hallway. He felt like the proverbial bull in a china shop. Was he the only man in the entire building? He suddenly found it difficult to breathe.

"Mark, are you all right?"

"Huh?" he looked down at her and noticed concern darkening her eyes. *They are like liquid emeralds.* "No, I'm fine, although it does seem a little warm in here." He resisted the urge to check his collar even though he knew there was no way the shirt's open collar could be too tight.

She swayed slightly in his direction. "Don't worry. All these double-X chromosomes aren't contagious," she said in a mock whisper just as the elevator door slid open. "You'll still be your supremely male self when you leave here."

"I hope so." He hoped he didn't sound as prayerful as he thought he did.

Mark almost panicked again when Nora opened a door. The waiting room was filled with women. Not one to consider hiding behind a woman's skirts, he nevertheless stayed on Nora's heels as she approached the receptionist's desk.

"Hi, Michele," she greeted the young woman as she signed in.

"Hi, Nora," she said beaming. She looked quizzically at Mark. "Can I help you?"

"I'm with her," he explained.

"Don't you work with Rick Gibson?" she asked, mentioning one of the firefighters at Mark's station.

"Yeah, I do. You know Rick?"

"I dated him about a year ago," Michele explained. Her eyes slid over him appraisingly. "Ginna does my hair. That's nice you're helping out Nora."

"That's me, Mr. Nice." He grinned, all the while thinking his friend seemed to be dating them younger all the time. He couldn't imagine Michele had been out of high school all that long. He realized he was standing there alone and Nora had seated herself. He hurried over to take the chair next to her. "Considering the number of people in the area, it's surprising how many you run into that you either know or know of." He lowered his voice. "I didn't say anything, since I wasn't sure if you wanted her to know I'm the father."

She didn't lift her head as she scanned the magazine's table of contents.

"Since it's already known you're the father and you will be listed on the birth certificate as the father, I don't think it matters who all knows."

He could have sworn icicles literally dripped from the words.

Considering she was fine all of two minutes ago, he couldn't imagine what he could have done wrong in that short a space of time, unless it was because he hadn't admitted he was the father.

One other thing was also rearing its head inside his mind. His feelings for Nora. That was something he was going to have to figure out, because what happened one night meant he and Nora were connected for years to come.

He was aware of the fragrance of her perfume and the soft rustle of her clothing as she shifted her body in her chair, shrugging out of her jacket. She laid it over her lap. Out of the corner of his eye he could see her hands as she leafed through her magazine. She wore little jewelry. He noticed the two gold bracelets on her left wrist and a ring on her right hand along with the dangling earrings that entranced him. A dark orange stone set in gold winked at him.

Something Jeff once said suddenly slipped into his mind.

I could be blind, mute and deaf and I would still know when Abby is near me. A part of my soul will always recognize her.

At the time, Mark put down the pronouncement to a man who was crazy in love. He couldn't imagine that would happen to him.

So why did he feel as if a part of Nora had stolen inside him?

Needing a distraction, Mark leaned forward and examined the selection of magazines before him. He was relieved to see the assortment wasn't all meant for prospective mothers. He considered the weekly newsmagazine safe and picked it up. As he flipped through the pages, he was aware of the chilly presence next to him.

He had no idea what he might have done, but it must have been a doozy.

''Nora Summers?'' a nurse appeared at an inner door.

He started to rise, but Nora stayed his movement.

''You don't need to be present for this part of the examination,'' she told him.

''Nora, I'm a paramedic,'' he kept his voice low. ''I've delivered babies and it's not as if I haven't seen—''

''Do not go there.'' She held up her forefinger in the universal sign to be quiet or else. She practically pushed him back into his chair. ''You can come in when he's finished.'' She turned around and walked toward the waiting nurse.

Mark opened his magazine again and tried to concentrate on a story about a small town that had voted the fire station's canine mascot as mayor.

''Who says he couldn't do a good job?'' he muttered.

Ten minutes later, he'd finished the magazine and gone on to another. A half hour after that, he had to keep himself seated instead of pacing the room. He looked around. Why weren't women coming out of the back? Or did the office have a separate exit?

Was there something wrong with Nora or the baby? Why hadn't they called him?

He began drumming his fingers on his knees. He never considered waiting one of his strong suits.

''Is this your first?'' A woman seated a few chairs over asked, noticing his impatience.

''Ah, yes,'' he cleared his throat. ''Yes, it is.''

She smiled. ''My husband wanted to know everything the first time around too. This is our fourth.'' She patted her burgeoning belly. ''It's pretty much old hat to him now.''

Mark looked at her more closely. ''Wait a minute. Didn't you have twins a few years ago?''

She slowly nodded. Then her face lit up. ''I know you! You were the paramedic who responded to my husband's call the night I had the twins. That night was so crazy. My water broke, I was in heavy labor and he couldn't get the car started.''

Mark laughed as the memory of that night kicked in. ''He was convinced something would go wrong, while you were so calm it was almost scary.''

She laughed along with him. "I had to be calm. My husband was creating enough trouble with his constant questions."

"He was better than some. I've had some of them ask if they can take pictures," he explained. "And now you're on your fourth? You're a brave woman."

"We decided this one will be our last," she replied.

"Mark?"

He'd been so engrossed in their conversation he hadn't realized Nora had come out.

"Are you all right?" He half rose out of his seat.

"Just fine. Why don't you come on back?"

"You're lucky with your first one." The woman smiled at Nora. "At least your husband won't lose his cool if you go into early labor too soon like mine did. He'll know what to do."

"Let's hope he won't have that chance," Nora replied. "I like the idea of a hospital, doctors and nurses."

"Don't we all." She chuckled.

Mark stood up and followed her to the rear of the suite of offices.

"I was wondering if you were being kept prisoner back here," he muttered.

"There're three doctors in the office and it's very, very busy," she replied, heading to the end of the hall. "It's your typical doctor's office. Not a mad scientist's laboratory or dungeon."

"I just want to meet him."

She stopped so quickly he almost ran into her.

"Do not ask him about his credentials or how many babies he's delivered or anything else," she said. "Do you hear me?"

Mark blinked at her fierce tone. "Okay."

"You are here because I said you can be here. That's all." She turned back around and walked into the open doorway. "Mark, this is Dr. Jackson. Doctor, Mark Walker, my baby's father."

Her baby's father.

Those two words hit Mark like a sledgehammer to the knees.

He managed a smile as he held his hand out to the doctor. He recalled seeing the man before.

"I've seen Mark in the emergency room a few times." Dr. Jackson stood up and reached across his desk to take Mark's hand. "It's nice to meet you."

Mark nodded. "I just want to hear that Nora's okay."

"More than okay. Everything looks great. Nora is taking excellent care of herself, the baby is right on schedule. I want to do a sonogram next month. We're anticipating a healthy baby in five months."

"Sounds like a plan to me," Mark said, relieved to hear good news.

"Nora said you wanted to hear it for yourself, so I hope that settles your mind?" the doctor asked.

"Definitely. Thank you."

"Fine, then, Nora, I'll see you in a month. If you have any questions or if you ever experience cramping or bleeding, call me immediately."

"I will. Thank you." Her smile was degrees warmer for the doctor than it had been for Mark.

They left the office with Nora leading Mark toward a rear door.

"Don't you need to make your next appointment?" he asked.

"That's already been taken care of," she replied.

Since several people were waiting at the elevator, Mark didn't say anything. He helped Nora on with her jacket before they walked outside.

Salt air from the ocean was strong as they crossed the parking lot. Mark noted the charcoal-colored storm clouds overhead and wondered if they'd have rain by nightfall.

As before, he helped her into the truck and secured her seat belt. And, as before, he turned his head to look at her face.

His mouth was close enough that a kiss would have been inevitable. He took a chance and lightly covered her mouth with his.

"Your lip gloss has an interesting flavor," he murmured.

"It's champagne flavored." She breathed the words, staring

into his eyes. "It's part of CeCe's cosmetics line we carry in the salon."

He stole another kiss before drawing back. "It suits you. Let's get you fed before I take you back to the salon. Wouldn't want sister dearest accusing me of keeping you malnourished."

Nora watched Mark cross in front of the truck and climb in the driver's side. Her lips still tingled from his kiss.

"What are you hungry for?" he asked.

You. "I've been craving Italian food lately," she said. "Spicy antipasto, garlic bread, huge beef stuffed ravioli or fettuccine Alfredo."

They looked at each other and grinned. "Gianni's!"

Mark wasted no time in starting up the truck and switched on the heater to warm up the interior.

"And we're late enough to miss the lunch rush. I haven't been there in months," he said.

"Neither have I." Nora was surprised that they were so clearly on the same wavelength. Then she remembered that they'd eaten at Gianni's Italian restaurant several times when they'd dated. The circular booth in the rear of the restaurant had been theirs. It afforded them just enough privacy where they could trade kisses and sit as close together as humanly possible.

What had she thought back then? Had she imagined she and Mark would have a long-lasting relationship?

The moment she considered that outcome, her fears took over. Every time Mark flirted and joked with a woman, all she could see was the resemblance to her father. And she feared she would turn into a paranoid, bitter woman like her mother.

She felt that unsettling emotion when Mark smiled at the receptionist, and even when he was talking to the woman in the doctor's office.

What if it's just his way and he's not flirting the way Daddy always did? What if he's just one of those men who genuinely likes women but wouldn't dream of cheating on the woman he's with? What if you made a mistake back then, Nora? If so, you need to do the right thing.

Why did her grandmother's voice intrude at the oddest times?

"Nora? Did you fall asleep?" he teased.

She hadn't realized they'd arrived at the restaurant until Mark spoke.

"When I was little, I was convinced my conscience had a voice," she said.

"And he spoke to you anytime you thought about getting into trouble?"

Nora nodded. "Except the he is a she," she said, unaware she used the present tense. "My grandmother."

"Whoa, and I bet Fran made sure you toed the line."

She was grateful he took her seriously. "No matter how many times my friends dared me to take a candy bar from the market on the corner, I wouldn't do it because I was convinced Grammy Fran would know. Sometimes I think she still knows what I do," she whispered.

Mark leaned over and touched her chin, turning her face toward him.

"Then let's give your conscience a great meal so she'll take a nice long nap," he said quietly. "And while she's napping, we'll head down to the beach, take off all our clothes and go body surfing."

Nora arched an eyebrow. "It's, what? Sixty degrees outside and looks as if it's going to rain at any moment? We'll have to wait until the temperature drops to at least fifty."

"Oh yeah, my kind of woman." He got out of the truck and came around to help her out.

They were still laughing as they entered the restaurant. Since the place wasn't busy, they chose the enclosed patio that held warmth and a lot of light even with the gray sky overhead. A waterfall set in one corner lent serenity to the atmosphere, while strategically placed hanging plants added color.

Nora asked for sparkling water with a slice of lime while Mark ordered a Diet Coke.

They didn't need to study their menus as they gave the waitress their selections.

"You take that eating-for-two philosophy seriously, don't you?" Mark teased Nora.

"You'd be amazed at the advice I've gotten from friends and clients," she replied, taking a piece of still-warm Italian bread out of a woven basket. She spread butter on it then nibbled away. "Some people seem to think if you're pregnant, they can tell you what you should and shouldn't do. I've also been told the time will come when people think they can pat my belly."

"You don't have enough yet to pat."

She looked down at her lap. "It's coming."

"Yeah, which is why I want to talk to you about something."

Nora noticed the serious tone. "Such as?"

"I think I should move in with you."

Chapter Eleven

"What?" Nora's voice was almost an ear-splitting screech.

"I said—"

"I know what you said." She put down her piece of bread. It wasn't heavy enough to do much damage to him anyway. "What prompted you to come to this conclusion?"

Mark started to answer but stopped when the waitress appeared with their salads. She set the plates in front of each of them, asked if they needed anything else. When they told her they didn't, she left them alone.

"We can talk about this after we eat," Mark said, picking up his fork.

She didn't pick up hers. "No, I think we'll discuss it now. You are not moving in with me."

"There's a good reason why I should be there with you." Mark said. "What if something happens where you might need immediate assistance?"

"I dial 911."

"What if you can't? Brumby's smart, but he can't use a phone," he argued.

"And what if something happens to me when you're on duty?" she said, triumphant she had the perfect argument. "Not that anything would. You heard the doctor. I'm in excellent health. I don't need a baby-sitter."

"I can do all the heavy work around the house. When you get ready to turn a room into a nursery I can help with that."

Nora studied Mark. "When I'm ready to set up the nursery and you want to help, fine, but you're not moving in."

"Then will you promise that you'll call me if you need anything at all? No matter what time of day or night, and if I'm on duty, you'll call the station?" he persisted.

"All right, just to make you happy, I promise," she said flippantly.

"I mean it, Nora. I want you to promise me."

She was stunned by the intensity in his voice. "All right, Mark, I promise," she murmured. She picked up her fork and began to eat.

Apparently relieved, he also began eating. During their meal, they traded stories about their work. Nora told Mark about Mrs. Crockett and her alien erotica. Mark almost choked on his tortellini.

"You're putting me on," he accused her.

"Ask Ginna. My client looks like the typical sweet little old lady who would serve you lemonade and cookies," she told him. "Except she has a family tree of these incredible people and she is very serious about her alien visitors. When you listen to her, you start believing it too. When she asked me if I'd read some of her writing, I thought I'd be reading these sweet stories. Instead, I'm reading something that should be rated triple X."

"We were once called out to a house because the wife was trapped," Mark said. "What we didn't find out until after we got there was that she was trapped in the bathtub with her big toe stuck in the faucet." He momentarily had a faraway gaze. "That was interesting."

"Don't tell me. She was young and beautiful."

"Not according to the married guys."

"You never find naked men stuck in a tub?" she asked.

"Not lately." He leaned back as the waitress left their meals and took away their salad plates. "Most of the time the calls are for the elderly or someone's having chest pains, or motor vehicle accidents."

"And delivering babies." She cut a ravioli square into fourths.

"That was some night." Mark shook his head. "We got a call from this guy who was totally panicked. His wife's water had broken, he'd gone out and found his car wouldn't start and that their nearest neighbor was on vacation. By the time we got there, he was a wreck and she was trying to get him to do the breathing exercises with her so he'd relax. There was no time to get her to the hospital. She delivered practically then and there. Her husband collapsed and said since they'd had twins, that was it. His nerves couldn't take it. Since she's now expecting their fourth, I guess he's toughened up."

"You really enjoy your work, don't you?" Nora asked, realizing she was seeing a new side to him.

"I can't imagine doing anything else," he said sincerely. "The funny thing was, Brian and I never thought we'd follow the same career path or end up with Jeff at the same station."

"They claim it's so they can keep an eye on you," she said, remembering hearing the two brothers joke about their younger sibling.

"They've always liked to feel important." He stole a ravioli off her plate and chewed on it reflectively. "Very good."

"Concentrate on your own food." She pretended to stab him with her fork.

"What time is your next client?"

Nora glanced at her watch. She was dismayed to see how time was flying. "I've got to be at the salon in an hour."

"I'll have you back in plenty of time," Mark promised.

Later, as they drove to the spa, Nora thought over the past few hours, which led to thoughts about the past couple of years. She'd enjoyed the time she'd spent with Mark. At the doctor's, she'd felt that unease when he'd flirted with the receptionist and even when she came out and found him talking to another woman. If she'd been honest with herself, she would have admitted there was no reason for the feeling. It wasn't as if they were married or even in a long-term relationship. But something was there between them. Just as there had been something before.

Nora had been hurt after their breakup. While she'd been the one to break up with him, it still had hurt to do so because she'd truly cared for Mark, and had even thought she might be falling in love with him. She opted to end the relationship before it was too late.

Except, breaking up with him didn't mean that she could shut her feelings off like a faucet. She'd sat home alone on many a weekend night with only her chocolate-covered graham crackers and chick flicks for company. When the spa's blind date bulletin board appeared, she'd studied it with great care. She'd admitted to herself she wasn't too picky. She wasn't asking for much. Someone who had a great sense of humor, had the same likes and dislikes as she did, had a steady job, didn't have a police record, and if he was mentally stable, so much the better.

It turned out most of her carefully chosen men didn't have the qualities she was looking for and the few who did bored her to tears.

One thing about Mark was that he never bored her.

He irritated her to no end. He made her laugh and he made her angry. And, damn him, he made her feel. But she had to admit he never bored her.

"Here we are with time to spare," Mark announced.

Nora blinked and looked around. She'd been so lost in her own thoughts she hadn't realized he was now parked in front of the salon.

"Thank you for going to the doctor's with me and for lunch," she said huskily, still feeling a little unsettled after her introspection.

She would be so much better off if she didn't think so much!

Mark unbuckled his seat belt and turned to face her. His grin was her first warning. His words were her next.

"I prefer actions to words," he murmured just before his mouth covered hers.

This time, her emotions overrode her sensible side. She rested her hands on top of his shoulders and leaned into him. Feeling her response, he immediately deepened the kiss.

Nora had never considered Mark's taste before, but this time her senses were heightened as his tongue swept through her mouth. She felt as if she was indulging in something forbidden, like the triple-hot-fudge sundaes she lusted after once a month.

Hard to believe, but she'd finally come up against something that was even better than her favorite sundae. And it wasn't a monthly craving either. This one was turning into a pretty near-constant hunger.

"It's that lip gloss," he murmured against her lips as he unzipped her jacket and slipped his hand inside to palm her breast.

She couldn't help smiling. "That isn't where I wear lip gloss," she whispered back.

"Really? Maybe you should try it there and I can let you know if it works." He moved on to nibble on her earlobe.

Nora felt the heat rising from within to bloom outward where his fingers lightly rubbed her nipple. The sensation sent shock waves through her body. She couldn't remember ever seeing fireworks with her eyes closed before.

"We could get arrested!" she gasped, pulling back.

Mark's grin was decidedly lopsided. The same shock she felt was echoed in his eyes.

"Good thing I'm friends with most of the cops in this city."

Nora looked down and found her nipples standing out against the fine knit of her dress. Her fingers trembled as she tried to zip her jacket back up. In the end, Mark brushed her fingers away and zipped it for her.

"Have dinner with me tonight?" he murmured.

"I'm working late," she said, still in a daze from his kiss.

"I'm flexible." He flashed his killer grin. "Wait a minute, I guess you already know that." He took great care in pulling her hair out from under her jacket collar and spreading it over the material.

"I'll get home around eight," she told him.

"I'll be there." Mark climbed out of the truck and loped around the front to open the door for her and help her down.

When Nora turned around to face the salon, she saw a row of curious faces looking outward. The face that stood out the most belonged to her best friend.

"Ginna will demand full details." She gave a sigh.

Mark leaned down to whisper in her ear. "Tell her we blew off the doctor's appointment. That we went to a sleazy motel and did things even she couldn't imagine."

Nora felt her face warm with her blush. "I don't know. She can imagine a lot. And on that note, I'm going in before we do get arrested."

"I'll see you later." Mark's words followed her.

Nora barely crossed the threshold before Ginna pounced on her.

"What was that out there?"

Nora faced her squarely. "Ginna, I'm surprised at you. You're a married woman and you can't recognize a kiss?"

"You two acted pretty cozy." She stayed on Nora's heels as Nora walked to the back of the building.

"He just kissed me goodbye," Nora said, determined to keep it casual.

"Honey, that wasn't a kiss, that was a nuclear meltdown," Ginna pronounced, following her into the private area allocated for employees. She dropped into a chair, crossing her legs. Her fog-gray calf-length wool skirt parted at the knee, revealing a good portion of leg clad in sheer gray tights and darker gray high-heeled boots. Nora had teased her that with her sheer tailored blouse the color of morning mist added to the combination, she only needed a whip to look like a fledgling dominatrix. For winter, Ginna had added warm honey-colored highlights to her hair, which was pulled up and back in a loose knot of curls with a strand artfully curved down one temple. Her only jewelry were her engagement and wedding rings and fat gold hoop earrings. "For a minute, I thought the two of you would be ripping off each other's clothes right then and there."

"I'm sure you would have stepped in to save me," Nora said dryly, hanging up her coat. She was grateful her nipples didn't show as much anymore under the fine knit.

"Nora, I love my brother, but you're my best friend."

"Family comes first," she said.

Ginna shook her head as she stood up. "I have always thought of you as another sister, which makes things very strange right now," she muttered wryly, "but what I want to say is that Mark may be related to me by blood, but if he does anything to hurt you I will kick his butt."

Nora turned around. "Do me a favor and if there's a problem, let me do the butt kicking." She hugged her friend. "But I thank you for the gesture. Don't worry so much. You know, I can't wait until you get pregnant."

"Zach and I are doing our best." Ginna hugged her back. "All right, I promise to back off a little." Nora arched an eyebrow. "All right, a lot!"

Paige appeared in the doorway. "Nora, Mrs. Crockett is here," she announced.

"Thank you, Paige."

Ginna watched the willowy woman walk away. "Rumor has it Paige is engaged to a senator's son."

"I heard it was an ambassador's son."

The two women walked out together.

"Which means she isn't engaged at all," Nora said.

"True." Ginna sighed. "We need more scandals in here."

"My having your brother's baby isn't enough for you?"

"No, I can't pick on you as much as I can the others."

"My dear, you are positively blooming!" The elderly woman sang out when Nora came into view. She reached up and hugged the younger woman. "I'm sure the baby will be as beautiful as you are."

"I guess my secret is out now," Nora laughed.

"I love little babies," Mrs. Crockett declared. "You must tell me when you are due. I always regretted Mr. Crockett and I didn't have children."

After that, Nora didn't worry about saying a word because Mrs. Crockett had much to tell her.

"My stories are going to be published!" she announced happily.

After hearing the disclosure, CeCe came out with a bottle of champagne and a glass of sparkling cider for Nora, so they could celebrate.

"We will have a special celebration for you later on," she

told Nora, putting an arm around her waist. "Just remember to listen to your body. If you need to rest, you must do so."

Nora protested the older woman's suggestion even as she knew it wouldn't do any good. CeCe firmly believed whatever she said was to be followed.

For the rest of the afternoon Nora imagined she could still taste Mark on her lips. She was looking forward to their evening together. Who knows, maybe they'd even re-create that kiss.

She fairly flew out of the salon after her last client and made a quick stop at the grocery store to pick up something for dinner.

As she unlocked the front door, she could hear her phone ringing.

"Damn, damn, damn," she muttered, jiggling her key as she realized it wasn't unlocking easily. She practically jumped over a happy Brumby to grab her phone. "Hello? Hello?" She grimaced then saw the tiny red light blinking on the handset indicating someone had left her a voice mail. She pushed the button for voice mail and tapped out her password.

"Nora, hi, it's Mark. I called the salon but they said you'd already left and I guess you had your cell phone off. Look, babe, I'm sorry, but I'm going to have to beg off dinner tonight. Something's come up, so I'm going to be out of town for a little while. I'll call you when I can."

Nora could hear he sounded rushed. She also heard something else in the background. Men's voices and one faint one yelling at Mark to hurry up.

Her movements were slow and methodical as she pressed the number on her handset that would delete the message.

She'd been raised not to waste food. Otherwise, she would have thrown out the steaks she'd purchased for dinner instead of putting them in the freezer.

"I guess it's just us, sweetie," she told her dog. All animation left her voice and her body.

Mark had found something more enjoyable to do than spend the evening with her. Nora swallowed convulsively and felt the hot sting of tears in her eyes.

She had been right to begin with. She was better off without
Mark in her life. For all she knew, he'd grow bored with their
baby too.

Rash decisions are never the right ones.

"I don't need a conscience," she grumbled. She fixed
Brumby's dinner then a salad for herself. She discovered she'd
lost her appetite and only ate because she knew she needed to.
Not that it stopped her from consuming half a package of chocolate-covered graham crackers that evening.

She was grateful that she had a full schedule the next day
so she wouldn't have much time to think about Mark who she
had dubbed "the rat."

She hoped his evening out with the boys had been a total
bust. She hoped some sweet young thing he tried to pick up
told him he was a nice guy but way too old for her. She hoped,
well, everything she hoped was about as bad as it could get.
And then she hoped for even worse.

By the time she waltzed into the salon the day after, she felt
her armor was well in place.

"Can you believe those guys?" Ginna asked as she poured
herself a cup of coffee.

Nora sniffed appreciatively and sighed. She missed her coffee with sad desperation. Decaf and herb tea just wasn't the
same.

"Which guys?" she asked absently, settling for inhaling the
aromatic fragrance of Ginna's coffee. Her mouth cried for just
one sip.

"My brothers for one."

Nora stiffened. "Not really," she stated in a tone that indicated she didn't want to hear any more.

If Ginna read the signs, she ignored them. "They were
packed up and out of here within an hour," she went on. I
guess it's pretty bad up there, so they wanted to do what they
could to help out."

Now she was confused. "Help out? Help out what?"

"The fire," Ginna explained. "Didn't you see it on the
news?" Nora shook her head. "There's a wildfire up in the
Sierras. I forget exactly where. Jeff, Brian, Mark and some of

the other guys at the station took their vacation time so they could go up and help. Their decision was so quick, they barely had time to pack. Wait a minute, Mark must have told you when he called to cancel your date.''

Nora shook her head.

''He only said something came up,'' she said dully.

Ginna looked at her closely, noted the faint shadows under her eyes and slight droop to her mouth.

''And you thought the worst, which is pretty easy to do with Mark,'' she guessed.

Nora sat down because her legs wouldn't hold her.

''My dad used to call my mom and tell her something came up and he wouldn't be home for dinner,'' she explained in a low voice. She didn't feel Ginna's hand on her shoulder. ''He was usually out with another woman.''

''I can see little brother still needs to work on his communication skills.''

Nora didn't miss a news report after that. She knew catching sight of Mark was impossible, but it didn't stop her from hoping. She worried when she heard about firefighters getting hurt, one even killed in the fire. She told herself paramedics might not be close to the fire, but there was always a chance something could happen, couldn't it?

THREE WEEKS LATER, and Mark was still gone. She had one telephone message from him while she had taken Brumby to the dog park.

Sorry I'll miss the doctor's appointment. I hope you're okay.

''The man definitely needs to work on his communication skills,'' she muttered. This time, she didn't delete his message.

Nora discovered her morning sickness was lessening and she was growing rapidly. She looked at her house and realized she soon would have to shop for furniture for the nursery.

Halloween night, she tied a pumpkin-orange bandanna around Brumby's throat and handed out candy to trick-or-treaters.

''Are you havin' a baby?'' one little boy dressed as Scooby Doo asked.

"Yes, I am." She smiled, dropping candy into his bag.

"I figured. You're fat like my mom and she's havin' a baby too. Thank you!" he shouted as he ran off.

"Just think, Brumby, in four years, we'll be escorting a little charmer like that one," she said wryly, preparing herself for the next onslaught of kids.

NORA HAD GROWN fascinated with the many changes of her body.

Her breasts were definitely fuller. None of her clothes fit her. No surprise there, since most of them were designed to be slim-fitting. Ginna offered to go shopping with Nora one afternoon.

"I look as if I swallowed a soccer ball," Nora grumbled, turning sideways and looking at her profile in the mirror.

"At least maternity clothes aren't ugly the way they used to be," Ginna commented. "We have some pictures of Mom when she was carrying us." She shook her head. "I can't imagine any woman got pregnant back then for the wardrobe."

Nora held up a bronze silk top. "Last year I wore that copper sequined top with the skinny straps and that gorgeous black silk skirt." She sighed. "Now it wouldn't cover even a fourth of me."

"So where is Mark taking you?"

"Mark isn't taking me anywhere."

"But he got—" Ginna clamped her mouth shut.

Nora stilled. "So he's back."

For once, the loquacious Ginna was at a loss for words.

Nora was grateful for her silence. She'd decided her separation from Mark was good for both of them.

One phone call in a little over three weeks wasn't enough.

For the rest of the afternoon she refused to allow Ginna to even say Mark's name.

"I'm sure there's a good reason why he hasn't called yet," Ginna said desperately. "They only got home a couple of days ago."

"A couple of days ago," Nora repeated. "Ginna, you're not making it better. My hormones are out of control, I already feel like a human beach ball and last night I discovered that eating chocolate gives me heartburn. Need I say more?"

"No, you've pretty well covered it all."

Nora knew her friend better and feared what would happen next. But Ginna remained silent on the subject of Mark after they got back to her house and she helped Nora put away her new purchases.

"Everything will be fine," Ginna assured her, giving her a hug. "See you tomorrow."

"We don't work tomorrow," Nora reminded her.

"Oh, right, we don't." She smiled brightly.

Nora told herself she didn't spend the evening waiting for the phone to ring. She didn't hope someone would show up at her front door.

"Artificial insemination," she said just before she fell asleep. "I was impregnated by artificial insemination."

THE ALARM CLOCK wouldn't stop ringing.

Nora fumbled for the clock and realized that wasn't the source of the strident sound. Nor was the phone. It took a couple of minutes for her to realize it was the doorbell interrupting her sleep.

"Go 'way," she mumbled, pushing her face farther into her pillow in hopes it would deafen the sound. All she accomplished was almost suffocating herself. "Whoever you are, I hate you." She slowly pushed herself out of bed and pulled on a robe and blindly searched for her slippers.

Alternately trying to shush an excited Brumby and cursing her uninvited visitor, she made her way to the front door. "What?" she snarled, flinging open the door. Her mood wasn't improved when she found a perky-looking Ginna standing on the doorstep.

"You look terrible!" Ginna exclaimed, brushing past her. "Didn't you sleep good last night? You should have after we walked the entire mall yesterday. I can see we've got some work ahead of us and not much time to do it in."

"What are you talking about?" Nora followed her back to her bedroom. "Time for what? We didn't have plans for today." She paused, searching her memory. She was afraid she'd missed something when Ginna left the night before. "Did we?"

"Not exactly." Ginna opened Nora's closet door and rummaged through the contents. "This is last-minute. We decided you have to come with us."

"Who is we and where do I have to come with you?" Nora dropped back onto the bed then flopped backward. "I'm really tired, Gin. You go on. I'll catch up."

"No excuses. You're already up. All we have to do is get you dressed. We have to hurry though. Abby's outside waiting for us and we still have to pick up Gail. Here we are." She pulled out a sweater the color of cinnamon. She tossed it onto the bed. She looked back at her friend. "Come on, Nora!"

"For what?" she shouted back, ready to snarl. All she wanted was to crawl back into her nice warm bed. She looked at the clock and groaned. "It's not even seven o'clock!"

Ginna found a pair of deep navy leggings and put them down next to the sweater. She studied her friend.

"You look like you've gotten bigger just since last night."

"Thank you so much for that glowing compliment in regards to your future niece or nephew. Now go away." She started to curl back up on the bed.

Ginna grunted as she pulled Nora to her feet. "Abby has a decaf latte waiting for you. Afterward, we're all going out to breakfast. But first—" she made a *ta da!* gesture— "the park and our rah-rah session."

"Our what?" Nora asked.

"Rah-rah session," Ginna replied. "We head to the park, watch the guys do their jogging in their cute little T-shirts and shorts, and we cheer them on."

Nora gave her a look that pretty much said, *you've got to be kidding.* Except she knew Ginna wasn't joking.

"No," she said firmly.

"Yes." Ginna explored Nora's drawers until she found what she was looking for. She tossed underwear on the bed.

Nora grumbled the entire time Ginna pushed and prodded her into getting dressed, brushing her hair and adding a light touch of makeup.

"About time," Abby grumbled as Nora carefully climbed into the front seat of the SUV. Abby nodded toward the steam-

ing cup in one of the cup holders. "It's not as good as caffeine
but you'll find it's a close second. Ginna, you want to let Ga
know we're on our way?"

Ginna pulled out her cell phone and spoke Gail's name. "
love these voice-activated phones. Zach gave it to me." Sh
grinned, brandishing her new toy. "Gail! It's Gin. We're o
our way and should be by your house in about ten minutes
Don't worry, we've got coffee."

"Says you." Nora stifled a yawn. "We don't have to hav
this rah-rah session, do we?"

"It's good for you. It's female bonding," Abby replied
"We haven't been able to have one for the past month. W
decided it was time to get out and do what we do best. Nov
that you're part of the team, so to speak, you have to com
with us."

"If this is bonding, why can't we do it over breakfast?"
Nora said hopefully as she sipped her hot brew. Her appetit
had significantly increased in the past few weeks.

"This is so much better." Ginna leaned forward. She hel
her insulated cup in one hand.

Nora closed her eyes and inhaled the rich coffee aroma em
anating from the back seat. She hoped it would allow her t
believe she was drinking the real thing.

"You've really blossomed since the last time I saw you,"
Abby commented.

"I'm hungry all the time," Nora admitted. "There're time:
I think Brumby's afraid he'll end up on the dinner menu."

"What has your doctor said?"

"That I need to watch my weight."

"And when was the last time Mark saw you?"

"About thirty pounds ago."

Abby chuckled. "It just feels like thirty pounds."

Nora tried curling up in the deep bucket seat. While the
leather seat was as comfortable as an easy chair, her temporary
bulk wouldn't allow her to perform too many contortions.

"Feels more like a hundred and thirty," she muttered.

"Wait until the ninth month," Abby advised. "You won'
be able to see your feet, you'll waddle like a duck, spend three-

quarters of the day going to the bathroom and you'll convince yourself the baby is never coming out of there.''

"Gee, thanks for that glorious look into my future." Nora heaved a sigh. "You do know that if men carried the babies, pregnancy would probably last a month, tops.''

"I'd give them an hour," Abby said.

"The two of you are not helping my decision to get pregnant!" Ginna sang out.

Nora looked at Abby, who grinned back at her.

Twenty minutes later, after picking up Gail, Abby pulled into the parking lot at one of the city's largest parks. She opened the back of her vehicle and hauled lawn chairs out, handing one to each woman. They set off to a spot everyone but Nora was aware of. When they reached the edge of the park, they found several other women there.

"Hey there!" Marge, one of the firemen's wives, called out. "We were afraid you'd be late." The women exchanged hugs.

"Sleepyhead didn't want to get up," Ginna explained then made introductions to any of the women Nora hadn't already met.

"There's nothing like an early-morning rah-rah session to start a day right," Patti, another wife, declared with a smile.

Nora tugged at Ginna's sweatshirt. "You do know that I will punish you for dragging me out to this," she said in a low voice.

Ginna ignored her as she looked down at her watch. Realizing verbal battering wasn't getting her anywhere, Nora settled in her chair to sulk.

She told herself this was not the way she wanted to see Mark again.

"Hormones," Abby pronounced, looking at her face. She dropped into the chair on her other side.

"My hormones are perfectly fine, thank you," Nora stated with great dignity.

"They're coming," Gail announced with a hint of excitement.

Curious, Nora leaned forward to see what was going on then quickly leaned back hoping she looked disinterested.

A moment later, about fifteen men wearing gray T-shirts and navy shorts were running in staggered lines on the path created along the park's edge for serious joggers. Nora easily recognized Jeff, Brian, Eric and Rick. One man wearing a bright red shirt stood out among the others. Mark.

As the men approached, the women jumped out of their chairs, leaping up and down and cheering loudly. Several of them clapped. A few seconds before Mark ran past her, Nora stood up. Jeff rolled his eyes at his wife while Brian raised his arms in victory. Mark turned his head at the same moment Nora stood up. He appeared startled at seeing her then his gaze settled on her burgeoning belly. He stumbled so badly his arms mimicked a windmill to keep himself upright.

"Been running long, baby brother?" Ginna hooted.

Mark spared a quick glare for his sister before turning back to Nora. He slowed his pace.

"No rest stops here, Walker," one of the men called out. Mark immediately picked up his pace and continued running.

Nora resisted the urge to look after him.

Damn him, he looked good. That only made her feel cranky.

"And our reason for coming here was because...?" she asked Ginna.

"There's nothing like a little eye candy to start the morning," Abby said. "And how thoughtful of them to come out here today so we'd have a nice place to watch and ogle. Did you all see Mark's face when he saw Nora? I thought he was going fall on his face," she chuckled.

"Please tell me we're going to breakfast now," Nora pleaded. "I'm starving!"

"We'll see them on the next lap then we'll go," Ginna told her.

Gail put her hand on Nora's arm. "Are you all right?"

Nora smiled weakly. "Physically, I'm fine. Just hungry, but that seems to be constant with me."

"Along with what's been going on," Gail said knowingly. "I know the feeling. Brian and I had our ups and downs during my pregnancy. I guess I didn't make it very easy for him."

"Do you regret it? Oh, not Jennifer, just the way it happened?"

Gail smiled. "At first I couldn't believe that I'd had sex with a virtual stranger. Believe me, it wasn't my plan at all. And Brian is the total opposite of any other man I'd dated before. It still isn't easy for me to relax, but he's showing me it can be fun. Maybe our courtship wasn't traditional and Jennifer's conception was unusual. But it all turned out great and now when I look back, I know I wouldn't have it any other way. Don't be mad at Ginna for her bulldozer ways. She worries about you."

Nora rested her hands on top of her belly. "I'll just wait until she's pregnant. Then I can torture her even more than she's trying to torture me."

"Abby would heartily approve." Gail laughed.

"Gail?" Nora hesitated. "Would you be able to take on a new patient in about four months?"

"Your baby? Of course I will!" She hugged her. "As for everything else, don't worry. It will all work out."

Nora didn't tell her that just because it did for her didn't mean it would for her.

She was having enough trouble. Once she'd seen Mark, her memories went on overload. Not just the memory of his hand sliding across her breast, but also the taste of him.

She feared it would be easier to go without coffee than to go without Mark.

Chapter Twelve

Could Nora be having triplets? She was healthy, wasn't she. She didn't look as if she could safely carry that much weight. He was afraid that morning if she leaned over any farther she'd fall over.

Questions raced through Mark's mind as he kept replaying those few seconds in his mind.

The crew had gone out for a morning run. Mark was grateful for the physical release after the last weeks of nonstop work and little rest. He was convinced he'd never get the smell of wood smoke out of his clothing. He'd volunteered to help out at fires before. As fully trained paramedics, Mark and Brian treated firefighters and volunteers for smoke inhalation, burns, a few broken bones and even treated one volunteer who suffered a heart attack. Time to think wasn't an option. He only ate if someone pushed him toward the food tent and slept when steered toward a cot. He only saw Jeff and the others when they returned to the camp for much-needed rest and food.

Mark knew he should have tried to call Nora more when he was up north. Except free time hadn't been an option. It seemed whenever he had an extra five minutes, he spent it sleeping, as did everyone else there. When he'd mentioned his worries to Brian, his brother had assured him Nora knew the score.

"You don't think I don't worry about Gail?" he'd said late one night when they were seated near one of the patio heaters that had been set up around the camp area. "You've volunteered before, Mark. When we're in situations like this, we have more things to worry about than those we left behind. We know they're safe. That's what counts.''

Except the day after they returned home, they went on duty to relieve those who'd doubled up to cover those who were gone. The men were relieved the shift was slow. If nothing else, they were able to catch up on their sleep in between their station duties.

Now that Mark was feeling more human, he had time to think about Nora.

"Hey, Walker number three, your turn for kitchen cleanup tonight," Eric reminded him.

"Yeah, yeah." He continued staring off into space, then turned to Brian. "Did Nora look all right to you? I mean, she looked so—so—"

"Big?" Jeff was the one to finish his sentence for him. "Remember when Abby was pregnant with the twins? She gained sixty pounds. Her mother told her she'd never get the weight off and tried to get her to diet all through her pregnancy. Abby told her as long as the doctor said she was healthy, she wasn't going to worry. Once she stopped nursing the girls, she was out running and pushing the stroller. I think Abby's the perfect mother. Keeps the home running smoothly. The woman is amazing."

"The man can be as romantic as a tree stump," Brian muttered, shaking his head.

"Hey, Mark, your mama-to-be looks as if she's having sextuplets," Eric joked. "What does the sonogram say?"

"And here we thought you'd be the last guy to get caught in the fatherhood trap," Rick inserted. He looked at his buddies. "There must be something about the Walker men that drives women crazy and gets them pregnant." His grin turned to mock terror as Mark advanced on him. His pleas for help were ignored by the others. They told Rick he was on his own.

There was nothing they enjoyed more than watching one of their own get soaked with a bucket of dirty wash water.

MARK STOOD on the sidewalk looking inside the salon. Lat afternoon had turned dark, so the lights were on.

He could see Nora energetically brushing a woman's hai and wielding her magic with a curling iron. Had her smile always lit up her face like that? Did looking at her always give him such a jolt to the solar plexus?

Nora was having his baby.

How could he have let her get away from him?

He stood there not feeling the cold night air as he watched her.

He wanted her. He wanted the whole package. Nora, the baby, even her crazy dog. Now all he had to do was convince her. He took a deep breath.

"It's a public place, she can't throw me out," he muttered heading for the door and pulling it open.

In another life, Mark would have flashed the lovely recep tionist one of his charm-filled smiles. Tonight, his attention was centered on someone else in the middle of the salon. He quick ened his step when he saw her reach for the set of drawers by her station. "What are you doing?" he growled, grabbing the cabinet a millisecond before she did. "You shouldn't be mov ing furniture." The cabinet almost slid from his hands.

Surprise at his appearance lit up her eyes then amusemen took over. "As you can see, it can be moved with the touch of one finger." She demonstrated by gently pushing the cabine with her forefinger.

"You're pregnant, you have to be careful," he insisted, un able to take his eyes off her protruding tummy.

"I am careful." Nora lowered her voice. "What are you doing here? Mark!" Her voice sharpened when he didn't re spond.

His head snapped upward. "Are you sure you still have about four months to go?"

Her jaw worked furiously. "What exactly are you asking?" she asked, tapping one foot.

He didn't need a knock upside the head to realize his error. "Oh no!" He held up his hands. "It's just that you're so—so—"

Nora crossed her arms in front of her chest.

"Well proportioned," Mark settled for the safest set of words.

"Hi, Mark," Cheryl greeted him as she walked past. She glanced past him toward Nora.

"Good night, Cheryl," Nora said pointedly.

Tell me everything tomorrow, Cheryl mouthed at her.

"Was that your last client?" Mark asked.

Nora nodded.

"Do you want to go get some dinner?"

"It has to be a quick one. It's been a long day and I'm tired," she told him.

"If you'd rather, I can pick up something and bring it to the house," Mark suggested. "Is there anything in particular you might like?"

Nora thought for a moment. "Coconut shrimp and jasmine rice from Syd's Place," she replied.

"I'll call in the order while I'm driving there," he promised.

"And their garlic cheese bread," she called after him.

Mark walked back and grabbed a pen and a sheet of paper from her station and began writing. "Garlic bread," he muttered.

"And see if you can get a couple bottles of their key lime sparkling water," she suggested. "None of the stores carry the stuff and I love it."

"Water." He kept on writing.

"And see if they have any peanut-butter-cup cheesecake left." Nora smiled brightly.

Mark wrote furiously then looked up. "Anything else?"

She thought for a moment. "Just a green salad with their dressing."

"That's it?" He sounded unsure.

"Of course it is. I'm supposed to watch my weight. I'll see you at the house then."

Mark tucked the paper in his jacket pocket. "I hope the truck can hold all this," he muttered as he left the salon.

Nora smiled at Mark's departing figure. She had missed him. She'd been angry and upset when he'd canceled their dinner

at the last minute without any explanation. She'd understoo
when Ginna told her the reason for his abrupt leave-taking. Sh
just wished he'd told her himself.

"Not that I won't let him suffer a little," she murmured
herself as she gathered up her coat and bag.

Brumby greeted Nora with doggie growls and ecstatic how
when she walked in the door.

"As if you don't use your door when I'm gone," she tol
the bulldog, bending over awkwardly to scratch the top of h
head.

She figured she had enough time to change her clothing an
replaced her knit dress and flat-soled half boots for sag
colored soft knit pants and a roll-necked tunic.

She rubbed the aching small of her back as she set o
glasses, plates and silverware then fed Brumby. She hadn
been home more than twenty minutes when Brumby's excite
barks as he scrambled for the front door alerted her to Mark
arrival.

"Just in time," she greeted Mark as she opened the doo
She sniffed the appetizing aromas coming from the bags an
boxes he carried.

"I thought I'd need a forklift to get all this out to the truck,
he grumbled, walking into the kitchen. After he set the bag
on the counter, he shed his jacket.

Nora noticed his shirt was a little more sedate today. Pine
apples scattered across a dark green background.

Nora rummaged through the bags and set the contents ou
on the table.

"I have been craving their shrimp for the past few days,
she said. Easily guessing the steak sandwich was Mark's, sh
set it on the second plate.

Mark tossed Brumby a French fry, which the dog nearl
inhaled.

"I got some onion rings too," he told Nora.

"They're one of the things I had to give up along with coffe
for the obvious reason, along with chocolate and anything bar
becued. They give me heartburn," she replied, looking at th
crispy-fried rings wistfully.

"Then why the cheesecake? You know, the chocolate one," he reminded her.

"Some things are worth the gallons of antacid I'll have to drink tonight." She stole a slice of garlic cheese bread and bit into it. "Mmm."

Nora concentrated on her food while Mark shared small bites of his sandwich with Brumby.

"Didn't you eat any lunch?" He watched her eat with ladylike precision.

"Once the morning sickness left, my appetite seemed to have doubled," she replied.

"I can tell. So you're feeling fine?" Something occurred to him. "You had your sonogram, didn't you?"

She shook her head. "I had to reschedule my appointment."

"Then I can still be there?"

"Of course." She picked up another shrimp. "Why couldn't you tell me where you were going?"

Mark hesitated. "I didn't want you to think I was trying to impress you."

"Why would you think that?"

"Because some guys like to show off. They'll do the 'Gee, babe, I'm leaving tomorrow to fight a big fire. Anything could happen to me'," he said wryly, tossing the last piece of steak to Brumby, who caught it in midair. "We went up there because they were shorthanded."

Nora noticed Mark hadn't looked at her during his recitation. She knew most people would assume his lack of eye contact meant he wasn't telling the entire truth. She sensed that wasn't the case with him. She could see the hint of color along his cheekbones.

Mark was embarrassed!

"Mark, I know you, Jeff and Brian have volunteered at the big wildfires before," she said softly.

He picked up one of the bags they hadn't emptied. "I bought two pieces of cheesecake," he told her. "I almost asked for three pieces so I'd be assured of getting one." He slanted her a grin.

Nora studied Mark. When had he changed from the kid at

heart he'd always been? She had seen him as her father's clone
but her father wouldn't have bothered helping out strangers in
need. But she was still wary. Sometimes people who were too
good to be true were just that: too good to be true.

"I can make coffee to go with the cheesecake if you'd like,"
she offered.

"You can't have coffee," he pointed out.

"Don't remind me," she groaned. "At least I can smell it."

"Does it help?"

She shook her head. "But I take what I can get." She got
up and moved around the kitchen. Pretty soon, the rich aroma
of coffee filled the air and the cheesecake slices were on plates.

Nora used the side of her fork to slice a bite off. She closed
her eyes in bliss as the rich flavors of chocolate and peanut
butter exploded in her mouth.

"I can't believe you ate everything." Mark hunched over
his arms protectively guarding his plate. "You didn't even
leave a grain of rice behind."

"Eating for two has its advantages."

"And you're feeling all right?"

"Feeling perfect. Brumby and I take walks every day down
to the dog park or just to the park here if we don't feel like
going too far."

Mark didn't even say anything when Nora swiped the last
bite of his cheesecake. He helped her clean up the kitchen after
they had finished.

Nora leaned against the counter as he put away the glassware.

"My sonogram is day after tomorrow," she said. "If you'd
still like to go."

Mark's eyes lit up. "Yeah, I would."

"It's at 8:00 a.m."

"I'll pick you up," he offered. "Maybe we could get a late
breakfast afterward if you don't have any appointments."

"I kept my morning free since I didn't know how long the
procedure would last. Breakfast sounds good."

He held the ends of the dish towel between his hands.

Nora knew it wasn't due to his not knowing what to do with

it. Cathy Walker had trained all of her children to be self-sufficient in the home. Mark grew up doing more than his share of kitchen duty along with his tasks at the fire station.

"I'm sorry it happened this way," he said slowly. He grinned crookedly. "I mean, here we'd been split up for the past couple of years and then…" He gestured awkwardly toward her swollen stomach. "I feel like I should apologize. I should have taken precautions that night."

"Maybe it's one of those things that's meant to be." She rested her hand on her stomach. "I consider the baby a gift," she murmured. Then she laughed. "This little one is very active."

"Kicking?" He kept his eyes directed on her stomach.

"And punching and rolling." She took his hand and laid it against her then slowly moved it around. "Ah, right there." She looked up. "Do you feel it?"

Mark kept his hand against her belly. "Do you think he'll go for football or soccer? Maybe volleyball or hockey."

"Whatever *she* wants to play is fine with me."

Mark grinned. "Fifty-fifty chance we'll have a boy."

"And fifty-fifty it will be a girl."

"Are we going to let them tell us what the sex is?"

"For a while I thought I wanted to wait and be surprised, then I decided I'd rather know," Nora said. "Is that all right with you?"

"Sure. Then I'll know whether to pick up a pitcher's mitt or ballet slippers." He kept her hand on her belly, but now his touch was warmer, more caressing as his palm traveled along the womanly curve.

Nora heard that a woman's sex drive could be heightened during pregnancy. All those extra hormones had something to do with it. She'd felt it that day Mark had taken her to the obstetrician's office. First when he'd zipped up her jacket and lightly kissed her. She'd felt it even more when he kissed her again.

Tonight, she felt the heat moving through her like a river of white-hot lava and all he'd done was touch her stomach. How would she feel if he touched her bare skin?

Fingers light as a butterfly's wing sliding across her collar bone. Palm, lightly callused, cupping her breast, moving slowly down her stomach. Feathery touches everywhere as if knowing exactly what would make her sigh with pleasure. She would want to reciprocate in kind, but her muscles would feel so relaxed she wouldn't be able to move.

That's how she would feel.

She raised her head. She could see the same look mirrored on Mark's face.

Ask him to stay the night.

Oh sure, ask him to see you looking like a walking and talking beach ball. That would ruin the mood!

She moved away, allowing his hand to fall away.

"I'm pretty tired," she murmured. "It's been a long day for me."

If he was disappointed by her rejection, he didn't show it.

"Then I'll see you day after tomorrow." He picked up his jacket off the chair he'd draped it around.

Nora followed him to the front door.

"Thank you for dinner." She smiled, but it felt like an effort.

Mark reached for the doorknob then stopped the motion. He spun around and had her in his arms before she could react and his mouth was on hers before she knew his intent.

She didn't think of pushing him away. Not when she wanted him so badly. She parted her lips and allowed him entrance as she slid her arms around his waist. Her belly wouldn't allow them to get as close to each other as they'd like, but it didn't stop their mouths from feasting on each other.

Ask him to stay!

Not a good idea!

Sure, it is.

Mark leaned back slightly and smiled at her. "I have told you how beautiful you are, haven't I?" He then stepped back. "No matter how hard it is." He grinned wryly at his own joke. "I'm going to be a gentleman and leave now." He stole another kiss then walked out the door. "Don't forget to secure the dead bolt," he said over his shoulder.

Nora's fingers trembled as she shot the dead bolt. She knew she was in for a sleepless night.

MARK COULDN'T BELIEVE a woman could be so pregnant and not burst open like an overripe melon. Thoughts of every science-fiction mōvie that had an alien bursting out of a human being came to mind.

"Now, this will feel a little cold," the technician warned Nora just before she smoothed a colorless gel across her bare stomach.

Mark noticed that even though she was prepared, Nora still sucked in her stomach as the gel touched her skin. She turned her head and looked at him. He walked over and took her hand, lacing his fingers through hers.

"Now let's see if the little one will pose for us." The technician moved the scanner slowly over her belly. "Just keep your eyes on the monitor and you should be able to get a good look at your baby."

Mark stared at the monitor. He stared entranced by the wavy lines that soon took shape.

He was looking at his baby!

"He's one active little guy," he said hoarsely.

The technician chuckled. "Judging by the lack of certain equipment, I'd say *she's* one active little girl," she told him. "Congratulations, you're having a daughter." She pushed a button for photographic copies.

"A little girl," Nora whispered. Her laughter was shaky.

Mark's fingers tightened its grip on her hand. "Oh my God, a daughter," he muttered. "I'm the guy mothers warn their daughters about and I'm having a daughter. What's wrong with this picture?" He was in shock and didn't see the look of amusement pass between Nora and the technician.

"It's common among men," the technician said. "They realize they'll be watching those horny kids sniffing after their daughters. They're afraid they can't handle the pressure."

"I can handle the pressure!" Mark said indignantly. "I'll just tell the boys what my dad told my sisters' dates. 'There's a lot of empty land out there and I've got a big shovel.'" He looked at the photograph the technician gave him. "A little girl," he whispered. His knees suddenly buckled. He blindly groped for a chair.

Nora started to rise then realized there was no way she could. "Mark, are you all right?"

"It just hit him," the technician explained. She peered at him closely. "No, he's not going to pass out."

"Says you," he whispered, staring at the picture. "There's spots before my eyes."

"He's a paramedic," Nora told her.

"Doesn't matter. I've had doctors pass out. Wait until the delivery," she said knowledgeably. "He's the kind who will crash fast."

Mark was still staring at the picture when they walked out of the doctor's office.

"What do I know about having a daughter? Except for protecting her from jerks like me," he said. Dismay was written on his face as he looked at Nora.

Nora reached his truck before he did and stood by the passenger door. "If it will make you feel better, I'll let you give her *the talk.*" She started laughing. "You should see your face!"

"Don't scare me like that." He had to press the button for his alarm system twice before it deactivated.

"Breakfast?" Nora prompted as he helped her into the truck. "I'm starving."

"Hmm? Oh, yeah."

Mark didn't want to admit his head was still spinning at the news.

"Now I can fix up the nursery for a little girl," Nora said. "I wanted to know the sex so I could decorate accordingly."

"I'll do the heavy work," Mark volunteered.

"You know how to hang wallpaper? Stencil walls?"

"Sure I do," he bluffed. He made a mental note to get his brothers to help. He figured they'd know how to hang wallpaper and stencil walls, whatever that was.

"Um." Nora didn't look convinced.

By mutual agreement, they stopped at a local restaurant known for its home-style cooking and large portions.

"I'm having a daughter," Mark announced to the waitress the moment they were seated in a rear booth.

"Congratulations." She smiled brightly. "Too bad you don't have the fun of going through labor, too." She winked at Nora as she went off to get coffee for Mark and orange juice for Nora.

Mark looked at Nora. Since the day promised cold and rain, she'd dressed in an olive polo-style sweater and matching leggings. Even her flats were the dull green color. He wondered if she'd hit him if he teased her that she could be in a martini. Then he remembered his brothers talking about how women had no sense of humor when they were pregnant, so he decided it might not be a good idea to tease her. This morning, she'd swept her hair up into a ponytail and only wore her dangling stars earrings. He noticed her nails were polished a bronze color. She looked so beautiful his heart ached.

"We can do this," he said.

She looked startled then laughed. "I think we already have."

"No, what I mean is *we* can do this. Raise the baby together. Be together."

She leaned back against the seat. "I told you we would share custody."

"Why not more?"

"Because there's too many differences," she told him.

"You didn't think so six months ago." He winced the moment the words left his mouth. "I'm sorry, that's not what I meant."

Nora's eyes flared bright green. "Yes, it is." She was silent as the waitress left their drinks. They gave their orders and watched her leave. Nora held up her hand when Mark opened his mouth. "Could we hold off on this discussion until after we eat?"

Mark nodded. He was positive the meal lasted forever. Nora kept conversation casual and he spoke by rote. But he knew something was bothering her. He feared what bothered her was him.

All through breakfast, Nora wondered if she shouldn't just explain why she felt the way she did. Tell him about her fears.

"You don't work until this afternoon?" Mark asked when they drove back to her house.

"I'm not going in until one." She unlocked the door and led the way inside. They walked back to the family room. Mark collapsed on the couch then picked up Brumby and set him on the cushion next to him. Nora took the chair across from them. She linked her hands in front of her.

"I've never said much about my father," she began. "Mainly because he left us when I was young."

"You only said your parents were divorced," he replied.

Nora sighed. "It was really more than that. My mother was very insecure. Anytime my father even talked to a woman, my mother was convinced he was hitting on her. He liked to flirt and she used to think it was going beyond that. They'd go out a lot at night and they were always fighting when they came home. My mother would accuse him of taking a woman's phone number and my dad would call her a nagging bitch. Pretty soon he got fed up with all her accusations and he left. What I couldn't understand was that he left without me," she said in a voice that left her disconnected from the subject. "He never even said goodbye to me. I remember hearing my mother on the phone demanding he give up all his girlfriends and come back to her. Of course, he didn't." She took a shuddering breath. Mark started to say something but she shook her head. "Please, let me finish this first."

Mark nodded.

Nora pressed her fingertips against her temples.

"My father paid alimony and child support with the stipulation he never see me or my mother again," she continued. "We moved in with Grammy Fran. Later on, I came to realize that Grammy Fran had practically ordered my mother and me to stay with her. My mother continued thinking my father would come to his senses and come back to us. Grammy Fran took over all the mom duties. She enrolled me in school, made sure I got there on time, joined after-school activities and had a normal life, even if my mother was lost in her own little world.''

''So you think I'm like your dad,'' Mark guessed.

''No!'' she shouted at him. ''He was not my dad, he was just a sperm donor. He was nothing more than a signature on a check every month. A dad is like your dad and your brothers. A dad is someone who cares about his kids. Who believes in the word *family*.''

''But you think I'm like him.'' Hurt crossed his face when her silence was his answer. He thought for a moment. ''Is this why you broke up with me? You thought I was like him? I never cheated on you. In fact, I never cheated on any woman I dated on a regular basis.''

''You never dated a woman on a regular basis. Three dates was usually your limit. Everyone calls you the three-strike date!'' She curled up in a tight ball.

''Not until after you dumped me. I was hurt, dammit! All I could think about was you. What could make you think I'd cheat on you when you were the only woman I wanted to be with?'' Mark jumped to his feet and paced the length of the room. ''Why didn't you tell me any of this back then? We could have worked things out.''

''I didn't see working things out when you had firefighter groupies hanging all over you.'' She glared at him.

''Great, just great,'' Mark muttered, turning in a tight circle before facing her. ''Then you remember a hell of a lot more about that night than I do. You know what I remember?'' He pointed his finger at her. ''I remember picking you up because we were going out for dinner. I remember you wearing a cute little turquoise sundress that had crisscross straps across the back. You had one of those temporary tattoos on your shoulder. A small red rose. Your hair was shorter then, curlier. We went down to Corona Del Mar for dinner then stopped at that club the guys hang out at. A new band was playing and we wanted to dance. After we'd been there for about an hour, you suddenly turned cold. You acted as if you were spoiling for a fight. I'd barely gotten you home before you told me we were through. I asked you why and you said you didn't need to give me a reason. Just don't call you again. Then you slammed the door in my face. That's what I remember.''

Nora stared at him openmouthed. ''You remember what I wore?'' she whispered. ''Even the tattoo?''

He nodded. ''I remember everything, Nora. The only woman I would have cared hanging over me was you. If someone else was flirting with me, I was polite and that was it.''

She shook her head. She was hearing a different side to the story and having trouble comprehending it.

''Maybe it looked like I was flirting that night,'' his voice softened. ''I don't know. But I do know the only woman who had my attention back then was you.'' He picked up his jacket. Before slipping it on, he picked up Brumby and set him on the floor. ''But I guess it's easier to remember what you want to, isn't it?''

Nora remained curled up in the chair. The sound of the door softly closing was like a death knell.

She felt guilt dump acid into her stomach. Then the baby kicked as if offering her own opinion. Nora placed her hand on her abdomen. ''You're going to tell me I was wrong, aren't you?'' Another kick was her answer. She heaved a deep sigh. ''That's what I was afraid of.''

Chapter Thirteen

Mark wasn't his usual enthusiastic self during his next shift at the station. Sensing his need, the others left him alone.

He'd come to more than one decision during this time.

He wanted Nora to realize he wasn't like her father.

He wished he'd known two years ago what he knew now. Maybe times he'd been polite to a woman looked like flirting. Especially to someone as sensitive to it as Nora was. He would have been more understanding about her feelings.

Since today was a sunny day, Mark had taken a chair outside so he could be alone with his thoughts.

"So, Jeff, what all are you and Abby doing for your anniversary?" Brian asked as the two brothers walked outside. Jeff had a basketball in one hand and was bouncing it up and down.

"Oh man!" he groaned. "That's why she's been hinting about a getaway weekend at the Del Coronado." He mentioned the popular hotel in San Diego.

"And you didn't pick up on hints that I'm sure were less than subtle?"

"The girls were down with the flu then Seth caught it," Jeff replied. "I'll get her something she's wanted for a long time."

"We'll watch the kids if you want to take Abby out for a nice romantic dinner," Brian offered.

"She's so tired lately she'd probably prefer staying in," Jeff said.

Mark caught Brian's attention and grimaced at him. Brian nodded. Both brothers knew Abby would not prefer staying in.

"Either of you know how to wallpaper and stencil?" Mark asked.

Jeff and Brian exchanged looks.

"She's getting ready to set up the nursery," Jeff said.

"And she'll want everything just right," Brian added. "You can't make any suggestions because she'll tell you you don't know what you're talking about. If you ask her if she's feeling all right, she'll think you're telling her she's fat."

"If you offer to rub her back she'll accuse you of just about everything known to man," Jeff said. "Then there's labor." Both brothers groaned.

"Gail turned into a raving maniac during her labor," Brian recalled. "She was downright scary."

"You want scary, be with Abby when she's in labor," Jeff said. "If she could have gotten her hands on something sharp, I probably would have lost something important." The other two men winced in sympathy.

"Thanks a lot, guys." Mark stood up and picked up his chair. "Now that you've shared your expertise in these matters, I am now going to go inside and cut my throat."

"We're always here to help, little brother," Jeff called after him.

"Call on us anytime," Brian added. He stared at Mark's departing figure. "He didn't mean that, did he?" he asked Jeff. "He really meant that to be a wave, right?"

"He could have been pointing at the sky," Jeff suggested. "Of course, he wouldn't have used that particular finger, would he?" He bounced the basketball a couple times. "I tell you, good advice just isn't appreciated the way it should be."

NORA WAS TIRED when she got home from work. She was used to working even longer days and had never felt her energy level lag. Now she learned she couldn't stand on her feet all day. She took advantage of CeCe's advice and rested whenever she could.

At the moment she just wanted to collapse on the couch and put her feet up.

She realized she wasn't going to have that peace and quiet when she saw a familiar pickup truck parked in her driveway with the front end facing outward. She also felt her heart get a little kick start when she saw a bare-chested Mark in her front yard pushing a lawn mower over the front lawn. He'd left the garage door open and Brumby was secured by a long lead that was wrapped around Mark's truck's rear bumper. The bulldog barked and strained forward to greet her as she carefully climbed out of her little Bug.

"Hey there!" Mark grinned at her. He shut off the mower and walked over to the front steps where a large water bottle resided. He twisted off the top and drank deeply. He poured the rest of the water over his chest. "Hi, honey, how was your day?"

Nora stopped long enough to pet Brumby and scratch him behind his ears.

"Long. What are you doing?"

"I'd say I was mowing your lawn for you," he said. "Ginna mentioned you'd fired your gardener because he was doing a lousy job. You're right. He wasn't doing much more than the basics. Your plants needed feeding and your grass definitely needed to be aerated. I got the back lawn done too. I see what you mean about the Brumb. He sat facing the back fence the whole time a bunch of kids were playing in the park. I think he enjoyed himself as much as the kids did." He picked up a hand towel and wiped the sweat off his chest.

Nora's mouth went dry as she watched his hand move across his chest.

Had it always been this muscular? His tan had faded some because of the winter weather, but his skin still retained a hint of dark gold color.

"Nora?" He looked at her inquiringly. "You okay?"

"Fine," her voice came out squeaky. "Fine. This was very nice of you."

He stepped forward. "I like your hair." He brushed his fingers against the wispy curls feathering her cheeks.

Nora touched the short curls that lay against her neck. "I asked Ginna for something easy to take care of and she sort of went crazy with the scissors."

"Cute. Like you." He stepped even closer.

She inhaled the heated scent of his body. Thoughts of dragging him into the shower and soaping him all over ran through her mind.

"Ah." She found it difficult to get past the picture of a naked Mark in her shower. "I feel like I should fix you dinner as a thank-you."

Mark shook his head. "Actually, I'm kidnapping you to my place. I figured I'd soften you up first with my landscaping skills." He wiggled his eyebrows in a comical manner. "Come on, Nora," he urged softly. "I promise I won't give you food poisoning. Mesquite-grilled chicken kabobs, potatoes baking on the grill. S'mores," he added as further inducement.

Nora swallowed a soft moan.

"You fight dirty," she whispered.

He grinned when her stomach growled loudly.

"Your eyes may say no but your stomach says yes. Come on, it will be fun," he invited. "Brumby can come too."

"Let me change first."

"I still have to edge the lawn and put the tools away," he told her. "Why don't you change into something comfortable, we'll go eat at my place and I'll have you back home in bed before you yawn once. If you'll give me your keys, I'll put your Bug away when I'm finished."

Nora's mind went traveling again. Now they were out of the shower and into bed. She noticed she didn't resemble a baby whale in her private fantasy. In fact, she looked pretty darn good.

"I'll be out as soon as I change."

In Nora's mind she might have been moving swiftly, but she was actually waddling more than running as she searched through her wardrobe for something that wouldn't make her look, well, pregnant.

"Your daddy's doing things your grandfather would never have done," she told the tiny kicker inside her belly. "Lawn work was beneath him.'' She tossed items of clothing out of the closet. She'd kept her pregnant wardrobe limited to some knit pants and skirts with elastic waistbands and loose tops. She couldn't find one thing that could be considered remotely sexy. At least nothing that she could wear at this time. She sighed with regret when she looked at one of her favorite tops. It was a black sequined halter top she usually wore with a skinny black silk skirt that had a slit up to the thigh. When she wore that outfit with her favorite black satin high-heeled slides, she felt invincible.

Tonight, she settled for a V-necked teal knit top with black leggings and black flats. She fluffed up her hair and exchanged her gold studs for the dangling stars and moons Mark liked so much. With a touch of golden coral blush, coral lipstick and mascara, she felt ready for pretty much anything. When she walked outside, she found Mark sitting on the top step with a contented Brumby leaning against his hip. Mark looked up and smiled.

"You looked cute before, but now you look downright beautiful." He dropped a light kiss on her lips. "I'd like a hell of a lot more, but I'm pretty grubby right now."

"I wouldn't mind," she murmured, leaning toward him.

Mark's eyes flared blue. "Ah, honey, now that's the kind of thing I like to hear. But not when your neighbors are watching us." He took her arm and escorted her to his truck.

Nora had been to Mark's apartment when they were dating before. She noticed the lack of dirty laundry and commented on it.

"I wanted to impress you." He grinned.

She grinned back. "You have."

"You want something to drink?" Mark asked her as they walked into the apartment. He headed for the small kitchen.

"Yes, thank you. Whatever you have." She walked around, noting only a few changes. His television set was now a bigscreen, the furniture seeming to be centered around the TV and his stereo system. She wouldn't be surprised if his mother hadn't helped him choose the couch and chairs since they were a durable fabric in an oatmeal shade with navy throw pillows for accent. She saw a family photo on a side table. "Do you mind if I put on some music?"

"Choose whatever you like." He returned carrying two glasses. He handed one to her.

Nora lifted the glass to her lips and sipped. "How did you get this?" she asked, pleased to discover it was her favorite lime-flavored sparkling water.

"There are some stores that carry it." He unlocked and opened the patio door. "Want to sit out here while I grill the food? Luckily, it's not too cold. Oh, one more thing." He disappeared into the kitchen and returned with a large beef bone that he presented to Brumby. The bulldog accepted the bone with his usual dignity and headed for the patio with his prize.

"Mind if I take a shower?" Mark asked once he'd turned on the patio light and started up the barbecue.

"Not at all. I'll sit here and relax." She smiled up at him.

It wasn't long before Nora heard the sound of water running. The picture of Mark in the shower ran through her mind again. She shifted uneasily in her chair.

"Hormones," she muttered. "All hormones."

Needing to do something other than sit there and imagine him in the shower, she got up and went back into the kitchen. Her exploration yielded plates and silverware that she set out on the small table on the patio.

When Mark returned, he was dressed in a pair of jeans shorts and a dark red T-shirt. His hair was still damp from his shower.

"I thought you were going to relax," he teased her when he saw the table already set up.

Nora blinked. "I can't believe it. You actually own a shirt in a solid color?"

He looked down at his chest. "Sometimes I surprise even myself." He checked the fire then put the potatoes on the grill.

"This is nice," she commented, looking out over the landscaped area complete with a small running stream. "Very restful." She watched a man in shorts and tank top running along a path. "Do you use the trails for your runs?"

"I like another area where there're some hills to make my

run more interesting.'' He settled in the chair next to her and stretched out his legs.

Nora looked down and noticed Mark's feet were bare. She never thought of a man's feet as sexy, but there was something about his that inspired fantasies.

She started.

"The baby?'' Mark asked, noticing her movement.

She nodded. She took his hand and placed it on top of her belly.

Mark's eyes widened as he felt a thump under his palm then another. ''Damn!'' He laughed. ''With a kick like that, she's definitely going to grow up to be a soccer player.''

"Try sleeping with someone doing somersaults inside you,'' Nora groaned. ''She's definitely a night owl. It always seems the minute I get comfortable in bed, she starts her gymnastics. It's like sleeping with a Mexican jumping bean.'' She smiled, letting him know it didn't bother her as much as she claimed.

"It must be one wild sensation.'' He got up to turn the potatoes and put the kabobs on the grill. ''That's why women have the babies.''

"True, you guys wouldn't be able to handle monthly cramps.'' She shifted in her chair.

"Hey, we're tough guys,'' Mark argued.

"When a member of your sex gets a simple cold you think you're dying,'' she teased.

"You're spending way too much time with Ginna,'' he grumbled. ''So, what did you think of the last Ducks game?'' He mentioned an ice hockey team.

"Changing the subject?''

"There is no way I can win the battle of the sexes, so I'm not even going to try,'' Mark said, getting up to check the chicken. ''Let me know when you're ready to set up the nursery and I'll help.''

"I was thinking about looking for furniture next week.''

"My truck can hold pretty much anything you'd want to take with you,'' he offered.

Mark noticed Nora's smile. ''What?''

"I'm seeing this new side to you and I don't know what to think," she replied.

Mark leaned over and planted his hands on her chair arms. "Then don't think. Just feel," he whispered just before brushing the lightest of kisses across her lips. "Nice. You're wearing that champagne-flavored lip gloss again."

"All my lip glosses have that flavor. It's my favorite," she murmured.

"And rapidly becoming mine," he said against her lips as he stole another kiss.

Nora didn't have to order her arms to move upward and curl themselves around his neck. They did that all on their own. She could smell the familiar hint of lime warmed by his body heat.

She could have told herself her response was all hormones, but she knew better. The sensation was too elemental. She felt her breast swell under his touch, her nipple harden as he rubbed his thumb over the aching peak.

It would have been so easy. All she would have had to do was stand up and suggest they continue this in his bedroom. Except a part of her wanted this part to go on. The man was romancing her and she was determined to enjoy every second of it.

"Mark," she said his name in a breathy sigh.

"Hmm?" He transferred his attention to the curve of her neck.

"I think it's starting to burn."

"Oh, honey, I was burning the second I saw you." He nibbled her earlobe.

"I mean the chicken."

It still took a second for her words to form a coherent statement in his mind. Mark slowly raised his head.

"You did promise to feed me," she murmured.

"Right." His smile showed some regret but understanding. He straightened up and walked over to the barbecue. "Just in time." He used tongs to pick up the potatoes then piled the kabobs on a serving plate to set in the middle of the table. "Madam." He grasped her hands and pulled her to her feet.

"That's the fastest I've gotten out of a chair in months," she laughed as he seated her at the table.

"I have my uses." Mark offered her the serving plate.

"It all smells so good." Nora chose two kabobs and put them on her plate then chose one of the potatoes. She nibbled on the chicken and grilled vegetables. "The man knows how to barbecue."

"Cleanup consists of tossing everything in the trash. I usually use paper plates so there's nothing to wash. I'll even barbecue in the rain so I don't have to clean the kitchen afterward." Mark tossed Brumby a piece of chicken. "Think he's going to be able to handle not being an only child anymore?"

"Knowing Brumby, he'll watch the baby the way he watches that fence when the kids are playing in the park," she replied.

Mark kept the conversation light and easy throughout dinner as he asked Nora what she wanted for the nursery and they compared schedules for nursery-furniture shopping. He leaned back in his chair with one arm draped along the back and watched her with a small smile tipping the corners of his lips.

"What?" Nora asked. "Do I have food on my face?" She looked down at her chest as if she thought she might have spilled something on herself.

Mark slowly rose to his feet and walked around the table to crouch down by her side.

"I enjoy just looking at you," he said quietly. He reached up and cupped her cheek with his palm. "And touching you. My idea of a perfect day is spending it with you."

Her lips trembled. "You don't need to lay on the charm, Mark Walker."

He shook his head. "I mean every word." He glanced past her at her plate. "I think it's getting too chilly out here for you. Maybe we should go inside." He stood up and held out his hand.

She didn't take her eyes off him as she accepted his helping hand. "Yes, I guess it is."

Once they were back inside, Mark closed the drapes. Sensing his presence wouldn't be required, Brumby made his way into the bedroom. Mark pulled Nora into his arms and dropped featherlight kisses along her forehead. In response, she slipped her hands under his shirt and placed her palms against his bare skin.

"I don't think there's anything that feels as good as your hands on me," he murmured. His mouth slid down to the corner of her lips.

"Oh, I can think of something that I'm sure feels even better," she breathed, sliding one hand downward.

Mark sucked in a sharp breath as he felt Nora's hand rest warmly over his zipper.

"Woman, you are dangerous. I don't think I'm going to let you leave tonight," he gasped as he reached for the hem of her top and started pulling it upward. When she started to speak, he touched her lips with his fingertips. "No excuses, Nora. You don't have to worry about the dog because he's here. I'll even set the alarm so I can get you home in plenty of time to get ready for work. Stay with me," he whispered, kissing the side of her neck.

Nora closed her eyes and just luxuriated in the touch of his mouth. She grasped his hands so he couldn't pull her top up any farther. "I don't look the way I did six months ago."

His gaze was solemn with sincerity, but there was no mistaking his desire. "Nora Summers, you are so beautiful you make my teeth ache. That will never change."

She blinked rapidly because the tears were forming so fast. "Oh, Mark, you're making me cry!" she wailed. She felt weak at the knees from the warm expression in his eyes.

Mark laughed softly as he resumed his attack on her top. He pulled it up another inch. "Then let's hear it for your crazy hormones."

"I don't have any appointments tomorrow," she softly admitted.

"Even better." He nibbled on her ear.

Nora heard the intrusion before Mark did.

"Mark!" She grabbed his hands again, staying the motion.

"Nora," he teased as he tugged her top upward.

She shook her head. "No, someone's at your door. Your doorbell just rang."

He leaned in and nuzzled her neck. "What doorbell?"

The melodic chimes echoed again.

Nora snatched her top out of his hands and hurriedly pulled it down. She cast frantic looks at the door as if whoever was on the other side could see her.

"*That* doorbell!"

"If we remain quiet, whoever it is will go away," he whispered against the curve of her ear while his fingers traced her bare skin under her bra.

"No one is going to think you're not home when the lights and stereo are on," she argued, but whispering all the same. She shivered under his touch.

He nibbled on her earlobe. "Best way to make burglars think you're home is to keep the lights and stereo on when you're not home," he murmured.

"Mark, open up!"

Mark slumped. He dropped his head onto his chest and cursed roundly.

Nora smacked him hard on the arm. "Don't you ever say those words around the baby!" she ordered fiercely.

He flexed his jaw. "Go away! I'm not home!" he yelled.

Pounding on the door followed the constant ring of the doorbell. "Dammit, Mark, let me in!"

Nora pushed Mark toward the door. He glared as he reached for the doorknob and threw open the door. He was ready to kill the intruder who dared ruin the evening he'd worked so hard to plan.

"Do not expect to be named the baby's godfather," he snarled at his older brother.

"She threw me out." Jeff rushed past him. He was the picture of distraction when he faced Nora. "Hi, Nora." He showed no surprise she was not only there but looking disheveled. Not that he was looking much better. Jeff's short dark brown hair stuck up in wild-looking spikes and his eyes were bright blue orbs wide with shock. He looked as if a truck had run over him. "She told me to get the hell out of the house and not come back." He dropped onto the couch and buried his face in his hands.

"Abby threw you out?" Mark asked, just to make sure he understood his brother. "Why?"

Jeff shook his head. "I don't know," his words were muffled. "We were having a great evening and then the next thing I knew she opened the front door and threw my keys outside. Told me to go find them and not come back until I'd learned some sense."

"Oh, Jeff." Nora sat down beside him. She touched his arm. "There has to be a reason for her to do this."

He looked up. His blue eyes were now wild with panic. "There was nothing! It's a special night. There we were, celebrating our anniversary and everything was great. Next thing I know, Abby said I have no clue and kicked me out. What am I going to do?" he pleaded with her.

"Mark, why don't you get Jeff something to drink," she suggested.

Mark curled his lip. This was *not* how he'd planned his evening. He made a "he has to go!" gesture to Nora while she glared at him and mouthed, *Do it!*

"I wonder if I have any hemlock in the fridge," he muttered, going into the small kitchen. He kept his attention centered on the conversation going on in the living room as he pulled a can of beer out of the refrigerator. He walked back into the living room with purpose in his stride. "Drink it fast because once you've finished it, you're going back to your own home and working things out with Abby," he told Jeff, handing him the can.

"I can't. She told me not to come back," Jeff moaned, accepting the can. "You know Abby. She never says anything she doesn't mean. I can sleep on your couch, can't I?"

Mark opened his mouth ready to say no way in hell are you staying here but Nora pinched his thigh. He flinched.

"Of course you can stay here," she soothed Jeff as if he were a small boy. She moved to stand up.

"No, he can't," Mark muttered, earning himself another pinch. His glare at Nora couldn't stand up to the one she was

returning. He quickly moved in to take her arm and help her
to her feet. "I drove you here, remember?"

"And you'll drive me home then come back here and talk
to your brother," Nora informed him in a low voice.

"Jeff can go stay at Brian's," Mark argued sotto voce.

"No, he can't. He came to *you*." She picked up her purse
from the table. "Brumby, come."

Mark now understood what it meant to whine. At that moment, he wanted nothing more than to sit there and howl at the
injustice of it all.

The overnight guest he'd planned for wasn't his oldest
brother.

"Jeff, Mark's going to take me home then he'll be back."
Nora spoke gently to the man. She looked sternly at Mark as
he muttered, "Or not."

"Okay," Jeff said. He appeared lost and forlorn as he looked
around the room. "I can't believe she did that," he said sadly.
"It's our anniversary."

"Mark will be back in about ten minutes," she assured him,
patting him on the shoulder.

"This is not how I'd planned our evening to end," Mark
muttered as they walked out to the parking lot.

"He's your brother," she reminded him unnecessarily.
"And he came to you for comfort."

"Jeff has Brian, he has Mom and Dad. Hell, he can even go
to Ginna or Nikki. Why me?" He helped her into the truck
then picked up Brumby and set him in the back seat.

"That doesn't matter, you are the one he came to and the
two of you need to talk."

Mark settled behind the wheel and quickly started the engine.
He switched on the heater. He adjusted the vents so the warm
air would flow directly at Nora.

"I shouldn't have answered the door," he grumbled.

Nora leaned over and kissed his cheek. "Think of all the
good karma you're racking up," she teased.

"Yeah, yeah, yeah." He put the truck in gear.

Mark took his time driving back to Nora's house. He pulled

into her driveway and stopped the truck. He half turned in the seat.

"I bet he won't even miss me."

"Go back and talk to your brother," Nora advised. "Do the male-bonding thing."

Mark helped her out of the truck and walked her to the door with Brumby trotting at their heels after he made a quick pit stop at one of the bushes.

"This isn't how I'd planned our evening to end," he said again as she unlocked the door.

She looked up and smiled. "I know. But maybe there was a reason for my not staying."

"Yeah, a great reason. My idiot brother with the world's worst timing," he grumbled.

Nora stood up on her toes and kissed him lightly. When he tried to deepen the kiss she stepped back.

"Thank you for a lovely dinner," she murmured.

Mark's chest rose and fell with a heartfelt sigh.

"This is one of those times when I wish I were an only child."

She smiled. She reached up and cupped his cheek with her hand. "No, you don't."

"Oh, yes, I do," he said fervently.

"There will be other evenings," Nora murmured.

"I'm holding you to that." He kissed her swiftly and walked away before he did whatever was necessary to talk her into allowing him to stay.

During the drive back to his apartment, Mark called Brian on his cell phone but only got the answering machine. He disconnected without leaving a message. He next toyed with the idea of calling his parents then decided against it. No matter how badly he wanted his parents' advice on how to handle Jeff, it was up to Jeff to call them, not Mark.

When Mark later walked into his apartment he found Jeff still slumped on the couch, his beer can cradled between his palms. Mark couldn't remember ever seeing his oldest brother looking so dejected.

"You look like you lost your best friend," Mark said, detouring to the kitchen long enough to get a can for himself. He didn't want a beer, but he thought he'd make the appearance of keeping his brother company. He dropped into the chair across from Jeff. "What happened, Jeff?"

Jeff shook his head. He stared into the can as if he hoped it held all the answers.

"Hell if I know. I took Abby out to dinner for our anniversary." His voice was as wooden as his expression. "Everything was great. I waited until we got home before giving her her gift. Next thing I know, she's yelling at me. She said I don't understand her. That I have no clue. She told me to get out and not come back until I do get a clue." He lifted his head and looked at Mark. He lifted the can and drank. "Why is she doing this to me?" he moaned.

Mark was stunned as he listened to his brother. He couldn't imagine anything happening where Abby would throw Jeff out of the house. He'd always viewed them as the ideal couple with the ideal marriage. He saw them having the kind of standard he didn't imagine he could ever live up to. He racked his brain to come up with a logical reason but nothing was coming to mind.

He wished Nora had stayed. She might have been able to come up with questions that wouldn't occur to him.

"She was fine before dinner?" Mark asked.

Jeff nodded.

"And everything was okay during dinner?"

He nodded again. "Mom and Dad took the kids for the weekend," he said. "We had the house to ourselves for the first time since Seth was born. I thought we'd continue celebrating. Instead, she kicks me out. Just kicks me out." He kept repeating the words as if he couldn't believe it happened. "She threatened to tear me into little pieces. She would have done it too," Jeff said sadly. "God, I love that woman."

Mark hunched down in his chair and stretched his legs out in front of him. Silence hung heavy between the two brothers.

"Jeff, how did you know you'd be such a great dad?"

Jeff looked up, surprised by the question. "How did I know?" he repeated. "I didn't know. I was scared to death I'd be a failure from the minute I found out I'd be a father to the minute the girls were put into my arms. When I looked into their tiny faces, I knew I would move heaven and earth to do whatever it took to keep them safe and feeling loved. Dad said it was ten percent work and ninety percent just plain not worrying, because it would all fall into place. I thought he was just putting me on. I saw it as his way of soothing new-father jitters, but it turned out he was right." He smiled faintly. "You just sense what needs doing and you do it."

Mark shook his head as if he had trouble believing him. "You make it sound so easy."

"Not easy. You panic the first time they sneeze or get a fever. Late at night, you get up and go in to check on them and then you just stand there watching them sleep and think to yourself this child came from me. It's an incredible feeling. And now..." He shrugged.

Mark looked at Jeff's morose expression and easily guessed what he was thinking about.

Mark felt just as unhappy for pretty much the same reason. He leaned forward to get out of the chair.

"I'll get some sheets for the couch."

Chapter Fourteen

It took all of Nora's willpower not to call Ginna the moment Mark drove away from her house. It took just as much self-control for her not to call her friend the moment she got up in the morning.

Luckily, she only had to wait until she started fixing breakfast. She snatched up the handset before her telephone finished its first ring.

"Hello?"

"If you were still over here I would have served you breakfast in bed."

Her smile came readily. "And what would breakfast in bed have been?" She nestled the handset between her ear and shoulder.

"Well—" Mark drew the word out "—it would have started out with me."

"My, my, the pictures you bring to mind," Nora drawled.

"I hope your pictures are as interesting as mine." He heaved a sigh. "Time for another cold shower."

Nora's smile grew. "Otherwise, how was your night?"

Mark lowered his voice. "My brother is about as pathetic as you can get."

"Did you find out exactly why he and Abby had a fight?"

"We stayed up until about two while he moaned and groaned his life was over. According to him, there wasn't any fight. He could only say that he couldn't understand why she threw him out. He tried calling her this morning, but she hung up on him. He barely said hello before she hung up," he explained. "He's in the shower now. I think the best thing to do is just shoot him and put him out of his misery. Please tell me you slept as lousy as I did."

Before Nora could speak, a soft beep sounded in her ear. "Just a minute, that's my call waiting." She depressed the flash button on her handset. "Hello?"

"Nora, do you have plans for lunch?" Ginna asked.

"Nothing, why?" She sensed Ginna knew of her oldest brother's fate.

"Call it a major estrogen caucus," she said cryptically. "I'll pick you up."

"No, just tell me where to meet you."

"Meet me at Starrs at one." She named one of their favorite restaurants.

"I'll be there." Nora waited as Ginna disconnected. She heard a click. "Mark?"

"Still here. Although I could be over there in about the time it would take you to get back in your bed."

She laughed at his hopeful tone. "Down, boy."

"That's not an easy task," he groaned. "I wish we were going on duty today. Then Jeff would have something to do other than look about as sad as a hound dog."

"Why don't the two of you go for a run or go lift weights or something?" she suggested as she poured herself a glass of orange juice. "Isn't that what guys do when they're depressed?"

"What do women do?"

"Go shopping. Eat chocolate." She turned at the sound of her toast popping up. "Mark, I want to eat my breakfast before it gets cold. I'll talk to you later."

"Next time I'm not letting even the president of the United States interrupt us," he warned her.

"Don't worry, handsome, next time I'll shoot the doorbell myself." Nora chuckled softly at Mark's softly muttered curse as she disconnected the call.

She glanced at the clock. She'd have just enough time to run couple of errands before meeting Ginna at the restaurant.

A few minutes before one o'clock, Nora parked her Bug in ne restaurant parking lot. She carefully extricated herself from ehind the steering wheel and climbed out of the small car.

She grimaced as raindrops started falling on her before she eached the door. She quickly pulled up the hood to her coat nd quickened her steps.

"You made it just in time," Ginna greeted her as she entered he restaurant. "We've got a corner table."

Nora looked down at her tummy. She swore it had grown ust since breakfast. "Good. The last thing I want is to find nyself stuck in a booth." She slipped off her coat as they valked to a table where Abby, Gail and Cathy were already eated.

Nora always enjoyed eating here. She liked the serene atmo-phere with its hanging plants everywhere and a rock waterfall hat covered one wall, with a small pool below populated with olorful koi. She wondered if the peaceful surroundings was he reason for their choice.

As she approached the table, she noticed Abby didn't look s energetic as she usually did and her eyes were shadowed vith weariness. The other two women looked serious. Cathy tood up at their approach and hugged Nora.

"You look beautiful, dear." She kissed her on the cheek.

Nora laughed. "I feel like I should be named Shamu." She nentioned Sea World's whale mascot.

"Yes, but can you jump through a hoop?" Abby hugged er next, then Gail.

Conversation was superficial as the women placed their or-lers with the waitress.

Nora knew these women well enough that plain talk was est. She turned to Abby.

"Jeff's staying with Mark," she said without preamble.

Abby arched an eyebrow. "And you know this because…?"

"I was at Mark's when Jeff showed up. He looked about as hell-shocked as a man can look." She looked at Abby. "All e could say was that you told him he had no clue and to stay gone until he figured it out. What does he need to figure ou for himself?''

Abby didn't look away. ''Did he tell you it was our ann versary yesterday?''

She nodded. ''And the two of you went out to dinner.''

Abby picked up her glass of iced tea and took a sip befor speaking. ''Did he tell you what he gave me?''

''Obviously not something wildly extravagant and roma tic.''

''Something definitely not romantic,'' Cathy agreed.

Abby looked around. She blinked rapidly as if she was tryin not to cry. ''I wanted to give Jeff something extra special fo our tenth anniversary,'' she explained. ''You know what mean. Something he wouldn't do for himself. I was able to ge him season tickets for his favorite hockey team for next seaso It wasn't easy, because I kept hearing they were already gon But I didn't stop. I made calls and I tracked some down. He' got four season tickets for next season. And I—'' she stoppe swallowed and pulled out a tissue to blow her nose, ''—and am the proud owner of a central vacuum system.''

Now Nora understood why Jeff had ended up on Mark' doorstep the previous night.

''Last year he gave me a beautiful pair of earrings that hel the twins' birthstone.'' Abby carefully dabbed her eyes. ''Thi year all he talks about is what a good wife and mother I am He tells people how well I keep the house and raise the kid All of a sudden, I've turned into some drudge.''

''My son's brains have suddenly turned to mush,'' Cath pronounced, patting Abby's hand.

''He has no clue,'' Abby declared. ''That stupid man has n clue!''

''I guess if Brian gives me something much too practical o our tenth wedding anniversary we'll know it's genetic,'' Ga said.

Cathy grimaced. ''It could be. Lou gave me a new engin for our tenth anniversary.''

Ginna shook her head in disbelief. ''And to think Dad is sti alive. Okay, that's it. Zach is no longer allowed to play wit

em,'' she announced. "I don't want him picking up any bad
bits." She looked at Nora. "Now that you've had fair warn-
g, you know you've got ten years to train Mark."

"Mark's on his own," Nora insisted.

"You were at his apartment last night," Ginna pointed out.

"He invited me to dinner and that was all," she said firmly.
e concentrated as hard as she could not to betray herself with
blush. The bane of all redheads was blushing at the wrong
ne. She must have succeeded since Ginna didn't say any-
ing. "Mark drove me home not long after Jeff arrived."

Ginna looked at her closely. "Your suggestion or Mark's?"

Nora tipped her head slightly downward so she could look
wn her nose at her friend. "Mark needed to be with his
other."

"He didn't help him figure things out," Abby muttered.

"How would you know? You hung up on him every time
e called you." Nora held up her hands in defense. "I saw
m when he showed up at Mark's, Abby. He's devastated."

"Good," she said coldly, although her lips wobbled a little.
Maybe I overreacted last night, but it was the last straw. The
an used to be so romantic. For no reason at all he'd bring
e flowers or arrange for Cathy and Lou to take the kids, and
ke me out for dinner and a few hours stolen away in an
egant hotel," she said. Her eyes took on a faraway look as
e recalled those times. She suddenly recovered herself and
ished. Then sorrow took over. "Now he's taking me for
anted like I'm a piece of furniture." She picked at her crab
lad. "He can't come home until he realizes he's been an
considerate idiot."

"Abby, I hate to say this, but I grew up with these guys.
ff's as stubborn as any mule and if you're honest with your-
lf, you have to admit you can be just as obstinate as he is,"
inna said cautiously. "It sounds as if you were pretty harsh
h him last night. What if he gets some bug up his butt and
cides he can do without you?"

"That would never happen," Cathy said firmly.

Abby looked at her sister-in-law with a stricken expression,
if she'd just been struck.

"I'm just trying to play devil's advocate here," Gin pointed out. "That sometimes things don't come out the w we hope. Or maybe Dad will put Jeff out of his misery a reveal the secret," she said in a mock hushed whisper.

"Trust me, your father won't tell Jeff a thing," Cathy sa "He and Theo would say the boy has to figure it out for hi self."

"Way to go, Dad and Grampa." Ginna grinned.

"If you'd seen Jeff's face last night you'd know he'll whatever he can to get back home again," Nora said. "T man is a walking wreck."

"Are you going to give him any hints?" Gail asked.

Abby thought for a moment. "I'm betting on Jeff. Let's pi on Nora now. What exactly were the two of you doing la night?"

Nora hadn't expected the abrupt change of subject.

"He cooked me dinner."

Four pair of eyes swiveled in her direction.

"Mark can't cook," Ginna stated.

"We had chicken kabobs and baked potatoes on the barb cue."

"That explains it," Cathy chuckled. "That's the only me Mark can safely fix without burning anything."

"He told me he mastered the packaged meals," Gail adde "The man is almost domestic."

Once again, four pair of eyes settled on Nora. This time s couldn't blame her burning cheeks on the spicy tortilla so she'd ordered.

"Do not see things that do not exist," she ordered them.

"He's a cutie," Abby pointed out.

"We're sharing the baby and that's all we're sharing." No picked up a tortilla chip and bit into it almost defiantly.

"That's not going to stop us from hoping, dear," Cat inserted. "A mother always wants the best for her children."

"I'm flattered you think I'm the best for Mark, but..." S found herself fumbling for the right words. "It's just not mea to be." She finally settled for what sounded clichéd in her ea but the best she could do.

"Of course, dear," Cathy murmured.

Nora didn't know why Cathy's smile made her nervous, but t definitely left her feeling uneasy.

"Is anyone up for shopping after lunch?" Cathy asked rightly. "It seems everyone is having a sale. Besides, I want o go shopping for my prospective granddaughter!"

Under her deft urging each woman admitted there was that ne special item she was looking for.

'ABBY, it's Mark." He shifted the phone to his other ear as e walked out to the patio where the barbecue grill was waiting. Ie'd tried calling his sister-in-law all day and hung up each ime he heard the answering machine. *Where was she?*

"If he asked you to call on his behalf, you can just forget t," she said coolly.

"I guess you'd have to say I'm calling on my behalf," he oked, waiting for her answering laugh. The frigid silence told im his joke wasn't appreciated. "Ab, the guy's hangdog mis-rable. We're talking he's as pathetic as you can get." He noved the barbecue tools to one side so he could set the platter f hamburgers down.

"Good. Once he figures things out, he can come home."
Click!

Mark reared back. "The woman wastes no words."

"What woman?" Jeff stepped out onto the patio. He carried a plastic bag of hamburger buns in one hand and a plate of cheese and onion slices in the other.

"Your wife. Has she always been this stubborn?" Mark set he burgers on the hot grill. The meat immediately started siz-ling on the hot surface. "You know what you need to do? ust call her up and tell her you're sorry. I bet you could be nome by dinnertime." *And I'd be over at Nora's five minutes 'ater.*

Jeff frowned. "Why should I apologize? I didn't do anything wrong."

Mark mouthed a curse. "Maybe because you'd rather be with Abby than eat my char-grilled hamburgers every night?

Come on, Jeff, it's been a week!'' Longest damn week o
my life.

"It's the principle of the thing. I haven't forgotten our an
niversary once, I don't forget her birthday or the kids' birth
days. We celebrate the anniversary of our first date and eve
the date we think the twins were conceived.'' He circled th
small patio. "I never leave the top off the toothpaste. I tak
the trash out without being asked. I'll take the kids out fo
walks when I'm off duty. I don't leave my dirty clothes on th
floor. I even remember to put the toilet seat down! Dammi
I'm a prize and Abby needs to realize that!''

"Honey, if she doesn't take you, I will!'' A woman calle
out from the pool area.

Jeff clasped his hands over his head in a victory gesture.

Mark closed his eyes. "Now I know why he came here. Pur
torture.''

WHAT WAS MARK doing at her house?

Nora didn't miss his truck parked in front of her house no
the lights blazing inside. Since Ginna was the only person wh
had a key, she guessed how he got in. She drove up the drive
way, activated the garage-door opener and drove inside.

Nora groaned as she tried to slide out from under the steerin
wheel. Right about then, she was looking forward to goin
inside her house and putting her feet up.

She finally pushed the car seat back and slid out of the smal
car.

"At this rate, I'll need a can opener to get myself out,'' sh
muttered, walking in the back door. The moment she steppe
inside the kitchen, appetizing aromas surrounded her. Sh
paused long enough to scratch an excited Brumby behind th
ears. She was amused to see that Mark's dark pink shirt wa
covered with yellow and green surfboards.

"Hey.'' Mark helped her off with her coat and tossed it t
one side at the same time he pulled her into his arms and kisse
her.

Nora felt a flash fire go off inside her. She was ready to jus wallow in his kiss, when the baby kicked. Mark jumped backward.

"It's okay, I'm your father," he told her tummy. He looked up at Nora. "Are you hungry? I brought Chinese."

Nora's mouth was already watering.

"I went to Ming's for our dinner. We have shrimp in lobster sauce," Mark murmured in a low sexy voice. "Orange chicken, egg flower soup, egg rolls, some broccoli beef." He set out the distinctive take-out containers with Chinese writing on the sides. "And, of course, almond and fortune cookies. I also made a stop for a gourmet dog dinner for Brumby. I'm beginning to think dogs eat better than us," he confided.

Nora took the chair he offered. "And here I was trying to remember what I had in the refrigerator. What brought this on?"

"One, I wanted to see you. Two, I wanted to see you. Three, I wanted to get away from Jeff." He took the seat to her right. He used chopsticks to pluck a snow pea out of a container and rubbed it gently against her lower lip until she opened her mouth.

She chewed slowly, savoring the tastes exploding in her mouth.

"Ready for more?" His voice was seductive.

"Oh yes," she breathed.

"Just keep your eyes closed," Mark told her, still keeping his voice low.

She nodded. This time, she bit into a piece of orange chicken.

"Aren't you eating?"

Mark leaned over and brushed his lips across hers. "It tastes better on you," he murmured.

Nora enjoyed her meal bite by bite courtesy of Mark. She had no idea what he would feed her next and loved each surprise he gave her. In between she was given sips of hot tea.

"This is incredible," she said, still keeping her eyes closed.

"And just the beginning," he told her. "Now you can open your eyes for the finale."

She opened them to find him holding a fortune cookie.

"Ready to take a chance?" He arched an eyebrow.

Nora took the cookie out of his hand and broke it open. She unfolded the tiny piece of paper. She scanned the printed word and laughed.

"Well?" Mark prompted.

"'New beginnings are around the corner'," she said. "You rigged the cookie."

"I did not!" He laughed, holding up his hands. "I swear had nothing to do with it. But it's fitting." He stood up, crosse his arms at the wrist and held out his hands. "Come on, littl mama." He pulled her to her feet. "Part two of your surprise."

"Part two? Mark, what are you doing?" Nora asked, now suspicious when he led her toward the rear of the house.

"Don't worry, you're still safe," he assured her, guiding he into her bathroom. He sat her down on the commode.

Nora watched him turn on the tub faucets, keeping a han under the water flow as he adjusted the temperature. He studie her collection of bath products and chose a bottle of bath oi Pretty soon the exotic fragrance of tangerine and vanilla fille the air. He pulled out a box of matches and lit the candles sh kept lined up around the tub.

Nora shifted uneasily. "Uh, Mark."

He turned to her and laid his fingers across her lips. "I'r pampering you, gorgeous."

"I'm not so gorgeous right now," she wanted him to know

"You'll always be gorgeous to me." He turned off the fau cets. "Wait here a minute." He disappeared but returned a few minutes later. He carried what looked like a wine bottle and wineglass. "Nonalcoholic," he announced, showing her the la bel. "It was a very good year."

A laugh escaped her lips.

"Into the tub," he told her briskly.

Nora hesitated. "Mark, the last time…" She paused. "Th last time I was, well, thinner."

"And now you're carrying my baby," he reminded her un necessarily. He fiddled with the top button to her dress.

She decided it was time to just go for it. She stood up an

et him reach for the hem. The dress was loose enough to easily
pull up over her head.

"They're easier than anything else," she explained.

"As if I'd complain about a piece of clothing that's easy to
take off," he teased, setting the dress on the hamper. When
he started to cross her arms in front of her chest, he stepped
closer to stop her gesture. "You are gorgeous," he told her,
looking her straight in the eye. "Do not ever think anything
different. Understand?"

"It's just that I've ballooned everywhere. I can barely see
my feet."

"That's why you need me around." He kneeled down and
helped her slip off her flats. "Sexy," he commented, touching
a toe polished a bright coral decorated with a flower painted
in the middle.

Nora had wondered how she'd feel with Mark seeing her
look, well, pregnant. What she didn't expect was to feel downright sexy and it had to do with the way he looked at her as if
she was the most beautiful woman in the world.

He helped her into the tub where she slid down into the
warm water with a sigh of bliss.

"Good thing you have a big tub." Mark's statement was her
first warning.

She looked up to find him shedding his clothes.

"What are you doing?" she squeaked.

"Easiest way to pamper you is to just dive right in." She
stared at his boxers that boasted dancing poodles as he pushed
them down to the floor.

Mark climbed into the bathtub, seating himself at the other
end. He grinned. "Now, this is fun." He picked up one of her
feet and started rubbing the sole.

"Mark!" Nora grabbed hold of the sides of the tub so she
wouldn't slide under the water.

"I'm just rubbing your feet." He wrapped a hand around
her foot and rubbed the arch.

She started howling.

Then it hit him. "You're ticklish!"

"Yesssss!" Nora choked, trying to pull her foot back, but

her balance wasn't the same as it used to be. "Do you kno
how hard it is for me to have a pedicure without practica
screaming?"

Mark grinned. He gentled his touch on her foot and beg
kneading the sole instead of rubbing it. When he finished,
picked up her other foot.

Nora groaned with appreciation as he kneaded the sorene
out of her feet.

"Keep making sounds like that and I'll be rubbing more tha
your feet," he warned her.

"Promises, promises." She was lost in the sheer sensatio

Mark carefully put her foot down and leaned forward.
quickly realized Nora's stomach wasn't going to let him g
too close. With a minimum of splashing he had her turne
around and leaning back against his chest.

"This is much better," he murmured in her ear.

She started to shift around in the water until she realize
what her movements were doing to him.

"Don't worry about me," Mark said softly, unconcerned
was aroused. "This is all for you." He picked up her mes
sponge and dunked it in the water. He began rubbing it ov
her back.

Nora closed her eyes, leaning back again when Mark strok
the sponge across her shoulders. She felt boneless under
touch. She could easily get used to all this pampering.

"I should have put on some music," he said.

"Just keep on doing what you're doing." She waved h
hand in the air with all the aplomb of the Queen Mother.

"Yes, ma'am," he chuckled as he moved the sponge acro
the top of her breasts. He squeezed the sponge, sending rivule
of water down her skin.

Nora realized that she wasn't feeling so boneless anymor
If anything, she was feeling quite the opposite. For a prospe
tive mother, she was feeling some very un-mom-like sens
tions. Considering what she felt against her hip, she knew Ma
was on the same wavelength.

Just a little lower. She shifted in the water so that his har
slid down to the full globe of her breast. Her breath caught

er throat. She could hear his breathing growing a little labored
hen his fingers grazed her nipple. She moaned as her now
xtremely aroused nipple sent shock waves all through her
ody.

Nora started to turn around, but Mark's hands tightened on
er shoulders.

"Stay the way you are." His whisper had a ragged edge.
lis fingers found her nipple again.

"Mark." She didn't sound much better. "Things could hap-
en just from you touching me there." She wasn't sure if she
as issuing a warning or a promise. Judging from the exha-
tion of air behind her, it could go either way.

His hand froze for a bare second then flirted with her nipple
gain. He rolled it between his thumb and forefinger. She
quirmed under his touch. She felt the tension beginning deep
ithin her belly, and this time it had nothing to do with the
aby.

"Mark!" She grabbed hold of the sides of the tub just as
e implosion seemed to go off inside her. Nora was powerless
gainst the shock waves moving through her. A part of her
ensed Mark's whispered words in her ear as he reminded her
he wasn't alone. By the time she returned to earth, she felt as
she'd been turned inside out. She could also tell that he was
ill very much aroused. She licked her lips. "Wow."

"Wow is right. You were incredible." He kissed the side of
er neck.

"Oh no, I want you with me this time." Nora pushed herself
way from him and would have gotten up but she realized there
as no way she was getting out of the tub without help.

Mark stood up behind her and stepped out of the tub. He
nagged a towel and carefully wrapped it around her.

"I'll mop up the water later," he promised, easily picking
er up in his arms and walking out of the bathroom. "For now,
's just us."

Nora's body was still humming as Mark settled her onto the
ed. He followed her downward.

"Did the doctor say it's all right?" Mark asked, resting his
and on the swell of her belly.

She kept her eyes on his face. "Yes."

"Then I'm all yours." He grinned just as he gathered h
into his arms and kissed her.

Nora felt a pang in her heart at his words. She opened h
eyes and looked at his handsome face. She wondered if the
was a chance he was speaking the truth.

No matter. Tonight, she was going to pretend Mark was
hers.

Chapter Fifteen

Nora's eyelids were at half mast as she blindly made her way down the hall toward the kitchen. She would have preferred being back in bed with Mark's warm body curved around her. They hadn't gotten much sleep. She also would have killed for a cup of coffee but knew she'd have to settle for a cup of decaf. She consoled herself that she could smell the coffee she'd set up in the coffeemaker for Mark before they finally fell asleep.

Her first hint something wasn't quite right was the strange sound coming from the counter by the stove. She forced her eyes open and tried to focus on the dark image that she knew was her coffeemaker. She sniffed. She couldn't detect the rich scent of coffee brewing in the air that she'd hoped would help her drink her one allowed cup of decaf. The pot that should have been full was empty.

"No," she moaned just as her coffeemaker emitted a strange gurgling sound. An even more alarming death rattle sounded before falling completely silent.

There would be no coffee for Mark to drink this morning. No coffee fragrance for her to savor as a very sad second.

"Um." A sleepy-eyed Mark stumbled into the kitchen. Bright orange boxers adorned with smiling yellow suns and a very masculine bare chest greeted Nora. He snagged a coffee mug from the cabinet then headed for the coffeemaker.

"The coffeemaker died," she announced.

Mark frowned. He peered closely at the unit. "Did you forget to program it?" His voice was scratchy.

"It's dead," she repeated in a louder voice.

Still not understanding her, Mark first jiggled the unit then picked up the pot, holding it eye level. "Shouldn't it have water in it?"

"I said, it's dead!"

Mark winced at her strident voice. "Okay, okay, you don't need to shout." He looked dumbly at the coffeemaker. "So it's not working?"

Nora threw up her hands and walked out of the room.

"I swear if the man had a brain he'd be dangerous," she muttered.

Mark looked around the kitchen. "Where's breakfast?"

"Two blocks away at IHOP!"

"Boy, she's cranky in the morning," he muttered, blindly searching the kitchen for breakfast makings.

"I heard that!"

THE DEAD COFFEEMAKER was merely the first obstacle Nora had to deal with that day. She burst into tears when she slid into her car. At least, she *tried* to slide behind the wheel. It was as if overnight she'd grown so much that she couldn't fit.

"Hey, it's okay." Mark crouched down beside her. He was unshaven, his hair sticking out in all directions, and dammit, he'd come outside without pulling on clothing over his wild boxer shorts. "Sweetie, whatever it is, we can fix it."

"I can't drive my car!" she wailed. "I can't fit behind the wheel!"

"What if you slide the seat back more?" he asked, adding, "although I'd feel better if you were driving, say, a Mack truck."

Her eyes shimmered a deep emerald with her tears. "Then I wouldn't be able to reach the pedals."

"Where are you going?"

Her lower lip trembled. "I'm going to work."

Mark shook his head. "Let me get dressed and we'll go out to breakfast. I'll drive you to the salon." He straightened up

'Damn, it's cold out here." He easily pulled her out of the seat.

Mark kept his promise. They went out to breakfast then he drove her to work.

"Last night was only the beginning," he told her once he stopped the truck in the parking lot near the salon's rear door.

"You just don't like sharing your apartment with Jeff," she teased.

"You're much better." He leaned over and kissed her.

Nora leaned into his kiss, savoring the heat of his mouth that promised so much more. She moaned softly when he pulled back a little.

"I didn't pamper you last night just to get you into bed," he wanted her to know as he nibbled on her lower lip. "Damn, I am so addicted to that champagne-flavored lip gloss," he murmured, nipping the corner of her lips.

Nora made a mental note to pick up a couple extra tubes that day.

"What time is your last appointment?" he asked.

It took her a moment to think coherently. The man's mouth alone was a lethal weapon. "I should be finished by seven."

"I'll be here before seven then. We'll go out to dinner." He climbed out of the truck and walked around to the door, helping her down. He didn't leave until she was safely inside the door.

Nora had just finished fixing herself a cup of lemon herb tea when Ginna breezed in.

"And how's my little niece?" Ginna asked, patting Nora's tummy. "My, my, we're active this morning."

Nora curled her lip at her friend.

"I hate people who don't have a tummy," she muttered, sipping her tea and hating every drop of it. She really missed her coffee!

Ginna turned and gazed at her. She grabbed her friend's shoulders and moved her around to fully face her. She peered closely at her face then screamed.

"Nora Summers, I am shocked! I want details," she ordered, shaking her gently.

"And I want caffeine, but since I can't have it, I guess yo don't get whatever you're looking for."

Ginna refused to release her. Nora looked into eyes the sam blazing blue as the man's she'd looked into not long ago.

"If my brother can put that kind of color in your cheeks an a smile on your lips that I haven't seen in a long time, I sa terrific," she said softly. "You and my niece deserve the best.

Nora hated her rock-and-roll emotions that struck her at an time. She could feel the tears threatening to fall at any secon

"I don't know," she admitted in a whisper.

Ginna cocked her head to one side. "Oh, honey, it hit yo hard, didn't it?"

Nora's head bobbed up and down. She was doing everythin she could not to cry, but a lone tear still made its way dow her cheek.

"Tell me this crying is a good thing," Ginna said, releasin Nora long enough to snag a tissue from the box on the counte "That you're not crying because he's done something stupid.

Nora shook her head. "He hasn't done anything stupid, she replied. "But I could be doing something stupid."

"And what would that be?"

"Falling in love with him."

MARK HAD NEVER FELT so out of place. He stood just insid the main door of a store that took up an entire block. Lookin at the wide variety of merchandise, he could understand wh He swore the place must hold just about anything a baby woul require.

He looked from right to left, seeing an array of bassinet cribs, strollers, chests of drawers, changing tables and ca safety seats set along one wall. He walked past them and foun racks of tiny clothing that he couldn't imagine fitting any hu man, along with shelves holding pastel-colored blankets an just about any style of mobile imaginable to hang over the crib and bassinets. He checked out a corner set up with paint an rolls of wallpaper fit for the newest arrival. Mark lingered b a lamp designed to re-create a castle straight out of a fairy tal

He touched a mobile of animated Disney stars that rotated to a selection of popular songs.

All around him women in various stages of pregnancy were studying furniture or oohing and aahing over the large selection of tiny clothing.

"May I help you, sir?" A woman with a tag in the shape of a cherub that stated her name was Teri approached him. Her snowy-white hair was pulled up and back into a bun on top of her head and tiny glasses perched on an even tinier nose. She could have been someone's grandmother.

"Uh, yeah." He cleared his throat. "I'm—ah—I'm having a baby," he admitted. "And, well, your catalog was lying around." For the first time he was speechless. How did he explain he found the catalog in Nora's stack of magazines? He'd picked it up and noticed it had pages folded down and items circled. "I want to surprise her," he said finally. "And I hope she won't kill me for doing this."

"Why would she be angry?" the clerk asked. "I think what you're planning is a lovely idea." She fairly beamed at him.

"She's a redhead." Mark figured that would say it all. "And pregnant, to boot."

Teri smiled and nodded. "Do you know the sex of your child?"

Mark's grin widened. "A girl."

"Girls are much more fun to shop for than boys," she confided. "Although, I guess most fathers would prefer shopping for a son."

"Hel-ah-heck, I'm excited about shopping for a little girl," he admitted.

Teri smiled. "Have the two of you made any decisions on what theme you'd like for the nursery?"

He reached in his back pocket and took out the small catalog. He opened it to the pages Nora had folded down and handed it to the clerk.

"A lovely set," she agreed. "Your wife has excellent taste. If you'd like, we have an area where we can set up requested furniture so the prospective parents can get an idea what it would look like in their home," she suggested.

"Could you have it set up by tonight?" Mark asked, liking the idea.

Teri looked over the pages. Her eyes lit up.

"Let's get started, shall we?" With the feminine force of a battleship, she herded him toward the cribs.

Mark didn't have a chance.

NORA HAD JUST FINISHED her last client and was cleaning up her station when Mark walked into the salon.

"If you hurt her, I will not only tear out your heart, I will personally stomp on it," Ginna said in a pleasant voice as she glided past her brother.

"I love you too, much older sis."

Ginna shook her head. "If you weren't a prospective father…" Her voice trailed off.

Nora chuckled as she dumped hair clippings into the waste-basket.

"You shouldn't be doing that." Mark swooped in and took the broom from her hands.

"We're not talking something heavy-duty," she told him. "Let me get my jacket."

Mark dropped into her chair and idly swung it back and forth. He leaned forward and studied himself in the mirror.

"You need a trim." Nora appeared behind him. She ran her hands through his hair. She pressed down on his shoulders when he started to get up. She leaned down and murmured in his ear, "Don't worry, I promise not to cut off anything important." Her eyes danced with laughter as she swept a drape around him. She picked up a spray bottle and misted his hair. She combed it through then picked up her scissors.

"I didn't expect you to cut my hair," Mark said, watching her section off his hair and snip. He quickly discovered he liked having her hands in his hair. He only wished they were in a more private place while she ran her hands through his hair.

"You sit in my chair, you get your hair worked on." In no time, she had stray ends neatly trimmed. She used the hair dryer to style it into order.

"Wow." Mark peered at his reflection. "Don't tell Gin, but you're better."

She grinned back. "I give great haircuts. And no. Do not insult me that way." She stopped his action when he pulled out his wallet.

"Okay, but that means I better take you to someplace fancier than Mickey D's," He used the popular slang for McDonald's.

"Darn straight. I expect to be given a menu, not have to read my choices off a wall." She looped her purse over her shoulder.

"Syd's Place?" Mark asked as he helped her into his truck.

"Coconut shrimp? Oh yes," she practically purred, settling back in the seat.

Mark switched on the heater immediately.

"I stopped by the house and fed the Brumb, so you don't have to worry about him," he told her.

Nora looked surprised he'd thought to check on her dog, although she knew, contrary to his jokes about her beloved bulldog, he did care about him. "Thank you."

"After dinner, if you don't feel too tired, I thought we could stop and check something out," Mark said.

"Check what out?"

He grinned. "You'll see."

Nora believed in not allowing curiosity ever to overtake her life. She blamed it on hormones that curiosity about Mark's cryptic statement was eating her alive. For the first time she didn't fully enjoy her favorite meal. Any question she directed to Mark about their next destination was met with nothing more than a mysterious smile and a murmured "you'll see." By the time they finished dinner and were back in the truck, Nora felt ready to burst.

"Are we there yet?" She sang out the age-old question given by many children on a road trip. "Are we there yet?" She kept repeating the words.

"No wonder my parents hated having all of us in one vehicle," Mark muttered. He clicked the turn signal and slowed down for a right turn.

Nora turned her head in the same direction. "Why are we at All For Baby?" she murmured.

Mark parked the truck and hopped out. He helped Nora down.

"Because we're having a baby," he replied, guiding her toward the door. "And they have everything a baby needs."

The minute they stepped inside, Nora cocked her head and sniffed.

"Baby powder," Mark murmured in her ear. "Cute, huh?"

"I still want to know why we're here." She allowed him to lead her toward a sales desk. She wondered what exactly he was up to.

"Hi, I'm Mark Walker. We're for the viewing," he told the clerk who Nora was convinced was all of twelve. Her cherub's badge proclaimed her name was Tiffany.

Her eyes lit up. "Oh yes! Teri spent all afternoon making sure it would be perfect," she confided. She looked past him at Nora and fairly beamed. "You have such a wonderful husband." She walked around the counter to them. "Right back here."

Nora started to follow her, but Mark stopped her. He whipped out a bandana and tied it around her eyes.

"Mark!" She reached up, but he lightly slapped her hands.

"Wait for the surprise," he told her. "Don't worry. It's clean."

Not able to see a thing, she took his hand as he guided her through the store.

"What is going on?" she asked.

"Just another minute," he promised.

He stopped her then turned her slowly to one side. "Okay." She pulled off the bandana and then just stared.

"Well?"

Nora looked at the three walls with each painted a different pastel color. She saw the crib she'd looked at in the baby catalog along with the changing table, chest of drawers, a baby swing in one corner and a playpen in another. Even a rocking chair sat under the faux window.

"Feel free to go in," Tiffany told her. "Did your husband do a great job or what?"

Nora slowly stepped into the display and ran her hand along the top of the crib. She picked up a dainty crocheted pillow. She turned her head to look at Mark.

"You chose all this?" she asked in a small voice. She held the pillow against her breasts. She didn't miss the wary expression in his eyes. She couldn't remember ever seeing him look unsure of himself. Mark was the most self-assured man she knew.

"Just the night-light," he admitted, walking over to the chest of drawers and fingering the castle that emitted a soft light. He shrugged. "I thought it was kinda cool."

"If you approve, Mrs. Walker, we can deliver it all tomorrow," Tiffany explained with a perky smile.

Nora shot Mark a look filled with panic.

"Do you like it?" he asked.

"Yes, but—"

He didn't take his eyes off Nora's face as he pulled out his wallet and extracted his credit card. He handed it to the clerk.

Nora walked over to him and grabbed his shirtfront. "What are you doing? Do you realize how much this all costs?"

"No arguments, woman. I want to do this."

She tried to blink the tears back, but they trailed down her cheeks anyway. She cupped his face with her hands and kissed him with every ounce of feeling inside her. He reacted instantly and wrapped his arms around her.

They were so lost in each other it took a minute for them to realize applause was in the background. They broke apart and looked to one side. A small group of couples stood there with smiles on their faces.

"Why can't you do something romantic like that?" One woman smacked her husband lightly on the chest.

"So I did good?" Mark asked, his breath warm against her ear.

Nora's smile wobbled dangerously. "Oh yes."

Nora kept her hand on Mark's thigh all the way back to her house.

"It's still too much money," she protested, but it sounded a little faint. "I heard the total, Mark."

"I think I just sent Teri's kids through college," he joked. When he stopped at a stop sign, he turned to her. "I wanted to do something special for you, Nora."

"You did."

At the house, Mark followed Nora inside. Brumby greeted them with rumbling barks.

"Do you want something to drink?" Mark headed for the kitchen.

"I'm pregnant. I seem to spend half my time in the bathroom and you ask me if I want something to drink," she chuckled, walking down the hall.

Mark rummaged through a dog-shaped cookie jar and pulled out a rawhide stick that he handed to a happy Brumby. He waited until he heard the bathroom door open.

Nora walked into the kitchen. Mark handed her a glass of sparkling water.

She started yawning.

"I'm sorry," she apologized, laughing. "I'm needing more sleep lately."

"That's because you're sleeping for two." He took the glass out of her hand and turned her around. "Time for bed for you." He gently pushed her back into the bedroom.

"I still can't believe you bought all that," she marveled. "How did you know?"

"I saw the catalog and what you marked," he explained. "I went by the store after I dropped you off at the salon. They were only too happy to set up everything you'd marked so you'd see what the pieces would look like together."

"I don't have the room painted yet," she argued.

"I have the next couple of days off, so all you have to do is pick out the paint and I'll do the work. I can tell the store to hold off delivering everything until the room is ready."

She blinked away her tears. "If I'm not in the bathroom I'm crying," she said, making fun of herself.

Mark pulled her into his arms and cradled her face against his chest.

''Then it's a good thing I'm so absorbent,'' he said gently. ''I can't help out by carrying the baby or going through all that, so I'll do what I can.'' He dropped a kiss on the top of her head. ''You're not going to make me go home, are you?'' he whispered in her ear. He breathed in the unique scent of her perfume. ''Did I tell you Jeff snores? The first time I heard him I thought a freight train was going through the apartment. We won't even talk about him staying up all night channel surfing for Michelle Pfeiffer movies because she's Abby's favorite actress. If you let me stay I'll even let you put your cold feet on me.''

She chuckled. ''How can I refuse such a generous offer?''

Chapter Sixteen

Mom always made it look so easy.

Mark winced as he glanced around the kitchen that looked like the center of an avant-garde painting.

He'd woken up early and thought he'd surprise Nora with breakfast. His idea of breakfast at home was a couple of power bars and coffee or a stop at the closest coffee shop.

But he'd seen his mother make omelettes a lot of times and Sean whipped up breakfast at the station. How hard could it be? When he discovered there were only a couple of eggs in the refrigerator, he decided to make waffles instead. Now he was afraid he might have used too much milk in the batter because it was running over the sides of her waffle iron and onto the counter.

"Damn!" He been so busy trying to mop up the mess on the counter, he hadn't realized it was dripping onto the floor. Brumby headed straight for what he thought was an extra treat. He carefully nudged Brumby to one side with his foot. When the bulldog protested, Mark opened the back door and pushed him outside. He ignored his howl.

"What are you doing?"

This howl was human. And feminine.

Mark spun around but one foot landed in the batter puddle on the floor. He started sliding and ran into the table. Like the domino theory, the chair he tried to grab so he could keep his balance tipped to one side and he fell to the other side.

A pungent curse escaped his lips as the back of his head connected with the tile floor.

"Are you all right?"

When he opened his eyes, he found Nora standing over him. A look of concern darkened her eyes. She held out her hand, but he shook his head then wished he hadn't.

"I was making breakfast." He sat up then grabbed hold of the table to pull himself up the rest of the way.

Nora turned in a slow circle.

"Really?" She didn't sound convinced.

Mark snagged a couple of dish towels and dropped them onto the floor. He used his foot to tamp them down. At a slight sound that could have been distress, he looked up.

"I'm cleaning up," he hurriedly assured her.

"That's what paper towels are for," she choked out, staring at the mess on the floor.

"Let me get the kitchen cleaned up and I'll take you out to breakfast," Mark promised.

Nora started to say more, when she turned her head. She looked toward one of the counters. "What is that?"

Mark turned around and pretended surprise. "It looks like a box." He walked over and examined the top. He held up a large tag with Nora's name printed on it. "It's for you."

She shook her head. "Will I be seeing a miniature of what I saw last night?"

He grinned. "Beats me. Open it and find out."

Nora walked over and tore the brightly patterned paper away from the box. She laughed as the box revealed that it held a coffeemaker.

"We're talking state-of-the-art here," Mark announced with the theatrics of a game show host. "It does everything but serve you coffee in bed, so I guess I'll have to stick around for that. Once you're allowed coffee again, that is." He grinned at the bright color dotting her cheeks. "And here you thought all you were getting was a nursery."

She kept shaking her head. "You must have maxed out your credit card with the nursery alone. And now this."

"Call it selfish. As you must have seen yesterday morning,

I'm not exactly myself when I haven't had my morning co
fee." He surveyed the mess around him. "I guess that mear
today too."

Nora threw her arms around him. "You are a crazy man!"

"Then save me from insanity by marrying me."

She dropped her arms.

Mark smiled faintly. "I'm serious, Nora. Marry me."

Nora stepped back. "You said something about going out t
breakfast," she said. "I'm afraid you'll have to use the mo
to clean up the batter. Just dump everything else in the sin
and I'll take care of it later. I don't have any appointment
today."

Mark froze. "Maybe you didn't hear me. I asked you t
marry me."

She didn't look at him. "I'm going to get dressed." She le
the kitchen.

A baffled Mark stared after her.

"You're supposed to scream and say yes," he muttered
looking for the mop.

Mark didn't miss that all through breakfast, Nora touche
on every subject but his proposal. He also didn't miss that sh
pushed her food around on her plate and only nibbled at he
scrambled eggs. He wasn't sure he had much appetite for hi
ranch house scramble that had peppers and cheese in his scram
bled eggs served on top of crispy hash-browned potatoes. Bu
when he looked down, his plate was clean, so either Nora ha
been sneaking bites of his food or he'd been hungrier than h
thought.

He'd wisely not said another word about his proposal. He'
wait until they were alone.

"I called the store and asked if they could hold off delivering
the furniture for a week," he announced. "That will give me
time to paint the room."

"I can paint it."

He shook his head. "Not a good idea in your condition. It'
not just the paint fumes. You'd have to do a lot of bending
and stretching. I'll get Jeff to help me. You just pick out the
paint."

She arched an eyebrow. "How magnanimous of you."

He grinned. He was glad to see a spark of color in her cheeks and glimmer in her eyes that hadn't been there a few minutes ago. He was even happier when Nora picked up her fork and began eating instead of just pushing her food around.

Now all he had to do is jolt her into giving him a positive answer to his question.

"I REMEMBER PAINTING the nursery when we were expecting the twins." Jeff held the paint roller in one hand, now forgotten.

"Funny, what I remember is Mark and I painting the nursery while you and Abby argued about how much longer she should be working," Brian recalled.

"Yeah, Abby said she'd keep on working until the babies were ready to pop out, and you wanted her to stay home and take it easy," Mark said, picking up the conversational ball. He turned to Brian. "Didn't Abby go straight to the hospital from work?"

"The girls came early," Jeff protested, not thinking as he waved the roller in their faces. Both brothers jumped backward but still ended up with flecks of creamy-yellow paint on their faces and hair.

"Hey!" Mark yelled. "I promised Nora we'd have the room finished today. Once it dries I've got to figure out how to put up the wallpaper border."

"I can't believe it," Brian chuckled. "Baby brother putting together a nursery. Did you really go into that mega baby store and pretty much buy it out?"

Mark's face reddened. He returned to carefully painting the molding. "I only got a few things. Mom said Grandma's knitting an afghan for the baby."

"She always knits an afghan for a new baby," Jeff said. His trademark blue eyes turned dreamy. "The girls still sleep with theirs." His shoulders moved up and down with a sigh that was as heavy as the expression on his face. "I miss them all so much."

Mark and Brian looked at each other.

"I can't believe you thought he'd be useful," Brian muttere to his brother. "All he's done here today is moan and groa about Abby and the kids."

"It's better than his staying in my apartment and moanin and groaning about them." Mark surveyed the work that wa already finished. What should have amounted to half a day work tops had taken just about all day.

Mark and Jeff had arrived early with the intention of clearin the furniture out of the guest room Nora had earmarked for th nursery. By the time Brian arrived, the two brothers had ev erything moved into the garage, the closet doors taken off th track and propped against the hallway wall and a tarp laid ou on the carpet. After the windowsills and molding were covere with masking tape, the three brothers got busy stirring the pain and painting the walls.

Mark looked upward. "Wouldn't it look cool if the ceilin had glittering stars on it that glowed in the dark? I found really neat lamp that looks like a castle out of a fairy tale. we painted the ceiling to look like a sky with stars we'd hav the perfect surroundings for the lamp and the wallpaper bo der."

Brian looked at Jeff. "This is downright scary. He's sound ing more and more like us."

"It had to happen sooner or later," Jeff agreed.

"Then you'll help me paint the ceiling?" Mark asked.

"Not on your life. It may look great, but it can be a hass to do. I found that out when I did it to Jennifer's room," Bria groaned. "Besides, you need to do that kind of job before yo paint the walls. You said you want to put up the wallpape border tomorrow afternoon if the paint's thoroughly dried b then. Wallpaper border, that I understand, not Nora, but yo chose." He looked at his brother with disbelief.

"It went with the lamp," Mark defended his choice.

"Abby and I chose the wallpaper for Seth's room together," Jeff whispered. His handsome face was grave with sorrow. " had all those little trains on it."

Mark and Brian exchanged glances.

"I have never seen anything so pathetic," Brian murmure

"Pathetic? This is downright cheerful for him since he moved in with me," Mark grumbled. "I'm talking two weeks of pure misery for me. I'm ready to pay Abby big money to take him back."

"I thought you said you'd be finished by now." Nora stood in the room's doorway.

"We're almost done. I'm finishing up the windowsills," Mark told her. "Why don't you take a nice relaxing bath while we get this cleaned up in here?"

She shot him a look that clearly conveyed he was an idiot. "If I tried to get into the tub I would not get back out without the help of a crane. I'm going to take a nap."

"Okay, honey! We'll make sure to keep the noise down," Mark called after her.

"I bet you rub her feet too," Brian kidded.

"She's on them a lot," Mark defended himself as he still stood in the nursery's doorway. "I asked her to marry me." When he turned around he found his brothers staring at him with equal amounts of shock.

Brian smacked the side of his head with his open palm. "Excuse me, I don't think I heard you correctly. What did you just say?"

"You're kidding," Jeff threw in his opinion.

Mark set down his paintbrush. "I said I asked Nora to marry me."

"Since you don't have that goofy 'I'm getting married' look on your face I gather she said no," Jeff said.

"She didn't say anything. She won't even talk about it. She acts as if I didn't ask her," he said morosely.

"Hey, don't worry about it. Gail kept saying no in the beginning too," Brian said. "Everything turned out fine for us."

"But Nora didn't turn me down," Mark argued. "She just refuses to talk about it."

"Then you'll just have to get her to talk about it, won't you?" Jeff advised. "While you're at it, maybe you can find out why Abby still won't talk to me. I called her this morning and she hung up on me."

Brian glanced at his watch. "We're talking world record

here, big brother. Only two minutes since the last time you mentioned her name.'' He slung an arm around Mark's shoulder. ''We'll finish up the trim and clean up. You go in there and rub the lady's back. They love that kind of attention. I'll drop Jeff back at your apartment.''

''You're more than welcome to take him to your house for a few months,'' Mark muttered.

''Nah, he's your problem,'' Brian said cheerfully.

Mark left him and Jeff to their duties and walked to the room next door. He found Nora stretched out on her side, sound asleep. Brumby lay on the floor next to the bed. The dog lifted his head then resumed his nap.

Mark went into the bathroom to wash up and exchange his paint-splattered T-shirt for a clean one.

When he went back into the bedroom, he leaned over and adjusted the blanket to cover Nora's shoulders. He toed off his shoes, sitting down on the other side of the bed and stretching out next to her. He lay on his side facing her.

''You may have the red hair, babe, but I'm just as stubborn as you are,'' he whispered. ''Which means I intend for our daughter to have a pair of happily married parents by the time she's born.'' He smiled when Nora murmured in her sleep and edged closer to him. He slipped his arm under her neck and carefully pulled her against him.

When Mark later opened his eyes, he found Nora awake and looking at him.

''Hi,'' he whispered.

She smiled. ''It's very quiet.''

''Brian said he'd take Jeff home. Trouble is, he's taking him to my place and not his.'' He rolled over and switched on the lamp, sending a soft glow throughout the room that had darkened with evening dusk. ''Want anything special for dinner?''

''Do you ever think about anything but food?'' she teased.

''You.'' The sincerity of the one word startled her.

Nora slowly rolled over onto her other side and carefully maneuvered herself up off the bed.

''Have you ever seen those toys that were inflated clowns on these big cardboard feet?'' she asked. ''The ones you hit,

...ey bounce backward then bounce back up. That's how I ...el.''

Mark was instantly on his feet and around to her side of the ...ed. He grasped her hands and pulled her upright.

"You need to eat," he said. "I'll get anything you want."

"Coconut shrimp from Syd's Place?"

He shook his head. "How many times have you had that in ...e past few weeks? I'm surprised you haven't turned into a ...rimp by now.''

"I've heard some women say that after their pregnancy they ...dn't even want to look at the food they craved during it. I ...ink I even dream about Syd's shrimp," she confessed. "This ...w of dancing shrimp.''

Mark ran his hands through his hair. Obviously not pleased ...ith his method, Nora picked up a comb off the night table ...nd fixed it herself.

"Would you also see if they have any of their key lime ...ie?" she asked.

"I guess I should be grateful you're not going for anything ...eird," he muttered, finding his shoes.

"Putting chunky peanut butter on key lime pie is not ...trange," she protested. "In fact, it's really good." She burst ...ut laughing at his look of horror. "Gotcha!''

Mark rubbed his face with his hands. "You've effectively ...uined my appetite. You call the restaurant and order the food ...o it will be ready when I get there," he told her. "I'll take ...he teriyaki chicken with rice.''

After Nora heard the front door open and close, she went ...nto the bathroom to wash her face. Moaning in horror at hair ...ticking out every which way after her nap, she applied a brush ...o it and added blush and lipstick.

Marry me.

She determinedly ignored the voice going through her head.

Marry me.

She closed her eyes as if that would stop the seductive voice ...hat could offer so much. Or take away even more.

"I refuse to end up like my mother," she whispered to her- ...elf. "I won't do that to my daughter.''

She opened her eyes and looked at her reflection in the mirror. She picked up her washcloth and dampened it under the faucet. She wiped away every trace of blush and lipstick.

When Mark returned with their dinner, Nora had plates set on the kitchen table and Brumby's face was buried in his bowl.

"I took a peek in the nursery. The walls look beautiful," she told Mark.

"Wait until the wallpaper border goes up," he told her. "I thought it would be neat to have glow-in-the-dark stars on the ceiling, but Brian said we should have done it before painting the walls."

Nora unpacked the food containers and laid everything out.

"I should have thanked Jeff and Brian for their help," she told him as they dug into their meals.

"Don't worry about it. They'll talk me into helping them on something. It all evens out." He shrugged.

She picked up a slice of melon that came with her food and nibbled on it.

"How is Jeff doing?"

"He has to be the most miserable human being in existence. I'd say he's ready to beg Abby to just shoot him and put him out of his misery. And if she won't do it, I'm almost ready to volunteer for the job." He offered a piece of chicken to Brumby, who didn't hesitate in accepting the gift. "I know you've seen her. Ah-ah-ah, no giving me that innocent look." He waved his fork at her. "She had to have told you why she kicked him out."

"It's something he has to figure out for himself," she replied.

Mark made a face. "Great. That means I'll never get rid of him."

Once finished, he helped her clean up the kitchen and carried out the trash. Mark turned on Nora's stereo and scanned channels until he found music to his liking. He smiled when he heard the mellow tones of the Righteous Brothers flow out of the speakers. He turned off all the lights except one, before walking over to the couch where Nora was seated. He pulled her to her feet.

"Dance with me," he coaxed.

"Dancing isn't all that easy," she protested.

"Sure it is." He looped her arms around his neck while wrapping his own around her now nonexistent waist. He swayed back and forth, his hips bumping gently against her. He cradled her face against his chest so he could rest his chin on the top of her head. "Our daughter might come out dancing."

"More like doing handsprings," she said softly.

When the song ended and another started, they didn't pull apart but kept on dancing.

Nora could hear the steady thump of Mark's heartbeat under her ear as they slowly moved from side to side. If she opened her eyes, she knew she'd see hula girls dancing under palm trees adorning Mark's shirt. But she preferred keeping her eyes closed and inhaling the familiar scent of his skin with the warmth of his arms around her.

When had things changed?

Was it the first time they made love?

When he didn't run in the other direction when he learned he was going to be a father?

She knew she was in love with him, but she feared it wasn't enough. It hadn't been enough for her father to stay with her and her mother. Not when there were so many women out there to charm.

She hadn't missed the way the clerk at the baby store had looked Mark up and down. Or that smile of his directed at her.

What if he got tired of her and the baby the way her father had gotten tired of her and her mother?

Except your father didn't surprise your mother with an entire room of baby furniture or paint your bedroom. He never went out and got anything she wanted. He never thought of her well-being the way Mark has.

Nora frowned. *All right, Grammy Fran, you've made your point!*

He'd also surprised her with the new coffeemaker. And no matter how much he jokingly complained about Jeff staying with him, he hadn't kicked his brother out.

"What are you thinking about?" he murmured in her ear.

"Nothing important," she said, not even realizing that s[he] was speaking the truth. She started to feel that Mark wasn't much like her father as she had feared he was.

"Then think about something important." His breath tickle[d] her ear. "Think about marrying me. Think how happy you['d] make my mother if you made an honest man of me."

His arms tightened around her when she would have pulle[d] away.

"No more ignoring me, Nora," he ordered. "All it takes [is] a yes or no. Preferably yes," he joked. His smile disappeare[d] when she refused to look at him.

This time she was successful when she pulled awa[y.] "There's more to it than just one word," she pointed out.

"Such as?" He kept hold of her forearms. "Dammit, Nor[a,] tell me! Tell me why you won't marry me."

"It's not a good idea," she mumbled.

"Oh no, I want more of a reason than that," he persiste[d.] "We're good together. I'm in love with you."

Nora's head snapped upward. "No, you're not," s[he] breathed.

"Yes, I am. Dammit, Nora, look at me!" He shook h[er] gently. "I don't know when it happened. Just that it did and [I] refuse to believe you don't have feelings for me."

"I can't." She stepped back.

"Can't, not won't." He jumped on her word choice. "Mea[n]ing something's holding you back. What?"

"Nothing!" She could feel her respiration increase. Agit[a]tion rose inside her.

"What?" He pursued her. "Tell me why."

"Because in some ways you're like my father. I'm afra[id] the day will come when you'll grow bored with me and wit[h] the baby and you'll look for women who offer a new challeng[e.] And I'll be left behind. I refuse to end up a pathetic victim lik[e] my mother!" She pressed her fingertips against her lips. Sh[e] was horrified the words had come out so easily.

Mark froze. "After everything you still believe that?"

She nodded. "The baby wasn't planned. My dad left m[y] mother and I years ago because he hated to be tied down. H[e]

er bothered with us again.'' She walked over to one of the
irs and sat down. ''My mother said he always liked to flirt.
liked to have women's attention centered on him. He wasn't
py unless he was charming a woman. He couldn't have it
easily when we were around. So he left us instead.'' The
words were a faint whisper.

Mark stood in the middle of the room, his hands hanging at
sides.

'Sometimes when we were out, you'd suddenly change.
u'd become distant, almost cold. Now that I think about it,
happened back when we were dating,'' he muttered. His
ehead creased in thought. ''Is that why you broke up with
back then, Nora? Because you thought I'd grow bored with
the way your dad did with your mother? Did you ever
ik to just talk to me about it? To tell me how you felt?''

Nora shook her head. ''Wouldn't that have been a good
gh? You would have thought I was using it as an excuse,
you would have said it was my imagination. Except, we'd
out and you'd smile and joke with our waitress. Those
men would practically fall all over you. How many slipped
i their phone numbers?''

'I was never unfaithful to you.'' He raked his fingers
ough his hair. ''As for phone numbers, I always threw them
ay. I didn't want to be with anyone but you.'' He spun
und in a tight circle. ''I drove myself crazy trying to figure
why you broke up with me so abruptly.'' He muttered a
se and stalked over to her. He leaned over, bracing his hands
the chair arms. Mark lowered his head until his face was a
ath away from Nora's. ''I thought we had something spe-
l. Instead, all we have is a lack of faith on your part. You
ver gave me a chance.'' His eyes bored into hers. She
ıldn't remember ever seeing them so cold. He shook his
id as if he was shaking something off. He pushed himself
ay. Mark paced the length of the room for a moment. Instead
his usual athletic grace, his movements were jerky. ''I can't
this right now,'' he muttered. ''I can't.'' He walked out of
room.

Nora remained in the chair. She heard faint sounds from her

bedroom then Mark's footsteps in the hall. He appeared in archway.

"You've got Ginna and my mom if you need anything," said in a quiet voice. "Since they're women, I'm sure the no reason why you can't trust them."

A moment later, she heard the front door open and c with a soft click. The neighborhood was so quiet she heard sounds of Mark's truck as he drove away.

Nora was still in the chair an hour later. One thing that st in her mind was the look of sorrow on his face and especia his eyes. There was anger in them but even more unsettl were the hint of tears. She knew he wouldn't be back.

For months, she'd told herself she was better off alone.

Now that she was alone, she realized it was the last th she wanted.

Chapter Seventeen

One Walker down in the dumps is bad enough. Two is way
st pathetic.'' Brian snagged a nearby chair and turned it
ound, straddling the seat as he rested his arms on the back
the chair. He looked from Mark to Jeff and back to Mark.
oth men were sprawled on the couch staring at the television
t. The only problem was, the set wasn't turned on. ''We've
ways had an upbeat station here, guys. And now…'' He
used. ''Well, now it's pretty depressing around here. Which
why I've been chosen by our comrades—'' he indicated the
en standing around in the large kitchen acting as if they
eren't eavesdropping ''—to find out what we need to do to
eer things up. Jeff, we already know.'' He held up his hand
halt his brother's outpouring. ''Mark, we're not sure, but we
ve a pretty good idea it has to do with Nora.''

Mark continued staring at the dark television screen. ''She
inks I'm like her low-life dad. She's positive I'll leave her
r another woman, or women, like her dad did.'' He spoke in
monotone. ''That's why she broke up with me before. She
esn't believe I can be faithful.'' His jaw worked furiously.
I never gave her any reason to doubt me. None.''

''Whoa,'' Brian whispered. He shook his head. ''Nora
esn't seem like the paranoid type. And, yeah, no matter what,
u've never been unfaithful to any woman you've dated.
u've never given any woman cause to doubt you. We've
en you look at Nora as if she's the most incredible woman

in the world. I can't believe she doesn't know how you f
about her.''

"She knows. I told her," Mark said in a wooden voi
"She just didn't believe me." His somber gaze swung fr
Brian to Jeff. "So what do I do now? How do I convince N
we're perfect together?"

"Don't ask me," Jeff muttered. "At least Nora told y
what was wrong. Not like Abby who's acting as if I sho
have a clue."

Brian exhaled a deep breath. "You honestly and truly lo
her?" He zeroed in on Mark. "You want to make a life an
home with her? Take on everything it entails?"

He met his brother's gaze unflinchingly. "With every fib
of my being."

Brian searched Mark's face and must have liked what
saw. He glanced at Jeff. "You've always had good ide
Where are they now?"

"At home. With Abby."

Brian glanced over his shoulder at their friends and c
workers. "Any ideas, guys?"

"You need to put your priorities in order," Eric advise
walking back into the room.

"Figure out a way to make Nora believe the two of y
belong together," Rick chimed in, following him in.

"Send her little love tokens," Gary, one of the firefighte
advised. "Not flowers. Something different."

"Zach sent Ginna a license-plate frame and new hea
lights," Mark recalled.

"I once sent a girlfriend a singing telegram," Dan, anoth
firefighter, brought up. "Except she broke up with me a
started dating the guy who sang the telegram to her. May
not such a great idea, after all," he murmured.

Mark closed his eyes in an attempt to block out the sugge
tions that came from all sides.

"I'm sorry I asked."

"I DON'T WANT A PEDICURE!"

"Yes, you do." Ginna practically dragged Nora out of h

the way she'd dragged Nora out of her bed and out of her ouse. Nora argued she was tired and napping, but Ginna was ving none of it. She bullied Nora into clothing and paused ng enough to make sure Nora didn't leave the house without touch of makeup.

"Why does it matter? I can't see my feet," Nora grumbled.

"It will make you feel better," Ginna was relentless as she shed and prodded her toward the salon's rear door. "Maybe oebe can give you a facial too."

"I want to go back home!" Nora whined.

"Cheryl has you scheduled for a pedicure and you are get-g a pedicure." Ginna opened the door and pushed Nora in-de. "Come to think of it, you need your hair trimmed too."

Since it was Monday, the salon and day spa was closed and lent, but the employees were allowed to make use of the cilities.

Nora put her hand up to her head. "It's fine."

The moment they stepped into the darkened waiting area for e day-spa clients, lights came on.

"Surprise!"

"Happy baby, Nora!"

Nora knew her mouth hung open, but she was unable to ose it as she looked at the room filled with her friends, co-orkers and even many of her regular clients. Pink and yellow reamers along with balloons in the same color hung from the iling. A table had been set up in one corner with a large eet cake and a variety of finger foods. Nora smiled at the d-fashioned baby carriage that decorated the cake along with border of frosting alphabet blocks. Another table was piled gh with brightly wrapped gifts. A stroller decorated with a rge bow stood next to the table.

"I see we have truly surprised you, my dear." CeCe brushed light kiss against both her cheeks.

"I guess this means no pedicure," she said numbly, unable take it all in.

"Tomorrow," Cheryl promised, hugging her.

Nora turned to Ginna.

"I can't take all the blame," Ginna said. "We all did [our] part."

CeCe slipped her arm around Nora's waist and guided [her] toward a nearby chair. "We wanted to show you how mu[ch] you are loved here," she told her.

"I don't know what to say." Nora smiled shakily wh[en] CeCe pulled an embroidered handkerchief out of her poc[ket] and gently dabbed at her eyes. "Perhaps this afternoon will [put] a smile on your lips," the older woman said.

"So what threats did my daughter use to get you here[?]" Cathy walked up and hugged Nora tightly.

"Just the usual. Get up or I'll take pictures of you looki[ng] your worst," she replied. "It is so good to see you."

"No matter what goes on between you and my son, I s[till] consider you one of my own," Cathy whispered before kissi[ng] her on the cheek. She laughed softly. "Don't cry, sweethe[art,] Mark will come around."

"Come around?"

Cathy nodded. "Sometimes it's like a delayed reaction. [It's] as if they wake up in the morning and suddenly realize they'[re] going to be a father. It's a frightening feeling for them. It w[as] for his father. Lou scared himself so badly he was afraid [to] hold Jeff after he was born for fear he'd drop him." She patt[ed] her shoulder. "Mark will realize all his fears are for nothing[."] She moved off when someone called her name.

Nora looked at Ginna who had appeared at her side the m[o]ment Cathy came up.

"I didn't tell her a thing," Ginna whispered.

"And neither did Mark," she murmured back. "It's as [if] he's letting her think it's all his fault when it's really mine."

Ginna arched an eyebrow. "Does Mark know this?"

Nora shook her head. "I still have a lot of things to wo[rk] out in my mind."

"Just don't wait too long," she advised.

The next few hours were a daze for Nora as she nibbl[ed] food, made a point of speaking to everyone, laughed at Ginna[']s ideas for baby shower games and opened gifts.

"I don't think the baby will be wearing any outfit more th[an] once," she commented, staring at the piles of baby clothes, blankets and any other necessity a baby would require. She noticed some of the clothes were in a larger size so the baby had something to grow into. The stroller proved to be a group gift from all the hairdressers, while some of the other women gave her everything else the baby might need. She even received baby-sitting gift certificates from her friends.

"Emma's not a happy camper that she isn't old enough to baby-sit," Ginna told her.

"It will take me days to write all these thank-you notes," Nora murmured. She frowned at her friend. "I can't believe you kept all this from me."

"Considering your mood lately, we could have planned the shower right in front of you and you wouldn't have noticed." She touched her friend's hand. "You haven't said one word," she said softly. "What did my idiot brother do to you?"

Nora blinked back the tears that appeared at the mention of Mark's name. She'd been hurting inside since the moment he'd walked out of her house. It had been more than two weeks and he hadn't called once, although Cathy called her just about every day. After today's conversation, Nora realized that Cathy thought the split was due to Mark, when it had been Nora who had been the one to practically push him out of the house.

Nora tried hard not to think about that night. She hadn't even looked at a piece of coconut shrimp or key lime pie since then.

"Don't forget you're coming out for Theo's birthday party. The only allowable excuse will be if you go into labor early," Cathy told her.

"I'll be there." Nora smiled. She'd come up with an acceptable excuse before then.

Cathy studied her closely. "I'll see you then." She shared a secret look with her daughter before she left.

"Zach is coming over and will load the big items in his SUV," Ginna told Nora as they stacked the gifts together. "He'll drop them off at your house."

"I appreciate this so much," Nora told her, meaning it. "Thank you."

"We all love you and wanted to show it," Ginna replied.

She chuckled. "Just the expression on your face was thank
enough."

"Then I hope I can do just as good a job when it's you
turn."

"I don't know. I've been told my having a baby could be a
scary thing," she said lightly. "Zach's still adjusting to sharing
a bathroom with me."

"You just sit there and let us do the heavy work," Chery
ordered, picking up a stack of boxes and following Ginna out
side to her car. "And come in tomorrow at ten for your ped
icure." She glanced down at Nora's hands. "We better do a
manicure while we're at it."

Nora frowned at her friend. "Were you always this bossy?"

"None of those, dear." CeCe's fingers floated across Nora's
forehead. "They cause lines. Since you have tomorrow morning free, we'll see about an aromatherapy facial for you."

"And a hair trim," Ginna threw over her shoulder as she
walked out the door, her arms loaded with gifts.

Nora had already cut slices of cake for Cathy to take home
to Lou, and Ginna to take home to Zach, Emma and Trey.

"So I'm forgiven for manhandling you out of the house
today?" Ginna asked when they returned to Nora's house with
Zach following with the rest of Nora's gifts.

"You made sure there was chocolate cake with raspberry
filling. Of course you're forgiven." Nora thought of the three
tiny caps and three pairs of matching booties Mrs. Crockett had
knitted for her. Since the woman suffered from arthritis, Nora
knew she would cherish the items even more. She placed her
hand over her protruding tummy and felt a reassuring kick.

Zach carried in the packages.

"Just call me the pack animal." He grinned at Nora as he
set the stroller down in the nursery.

Ginna explored the room with great delight.

"It's adorable!" she exclaimed, stopping to inspect the castle lamp. "And to think Mark chose this." She shook her head
in wonderment. "I'm impressed."

"It all goes in perfectly," Nora agreed, feeling that now-
familiar pang at the sound of his name.

"Are you going to be all right?"

Nora smiled at her friend. "Of course I am. Thank you so much for the shower and everything."

Ginna quickly hugged her. "And you are very welcome." She stepped back and held her at arm's length. "Do what's right," she whispered before hugging her again.

Nora felt the air slam out of her chest at words she only remembered hearing her grandmother speak.

"Tomorrow is Make Nora Feel Beautiful Day, so don't be late," Ginna reminded Nora as she followed her husband out of the house.

"For a morning of pampering? I'll be early."

Later, as Nora carefully folded and put everything away, she realized something was missing. Mark wasn't there to see each item. Sharing it with Brumby wasn't the same.

But there was still that tiny hint of fear deep within her that if she accepted Mark's proposal, she could end up like her mother.

If there was to be any kind of future with Mark, she would have to banish that fear.

"WHAT DO YOU MEAN you can't make it to my birthday party?" Theo Walker's growl boomed so loud out of the telephone receiver Nora winced.

She knew she couldn't lie to this man. Especially since he would easily shoot down any lie she gave.

"It's my party and I can have anyone I want there. And I want you there," he informed her in his brusque voice. "You shouldn't be driving that distance in your condition, so I'll have someone pick you up. And no getting out of it," he warned her before hanging up without waiting for her reply. Or even hearing her excuse.

Nora had a long list of excuses she would have used to say why she couldn't come to Theo's party, but she knew the older man would ignore every one of them.

She looked downward. She couldn't remember the last time she'd seen her feet. She knew her toes were polished the same coral shade as her fingernails, courtesy of Cheryl. And her face

was creamed and soothed with various lotions and toners after
her facial. She had even been treated to a shoulder massage
with a fragrant mint cream.

"It's a conspiracy," she told her stomach.

It didn't stop her from thinking about what to wear to the
party.

NORA DIDN'T NEED a psychic to tell her who Theo would send
to drive her to his party. But she was surprised when Mark
showed up in the same Jaguar sedan he'd driven that night so
many months ago. For a second she'd experienced a sense of
déjà vu.

"Gramps asked me to pick you up for the party," he explained when she opened the door. He looked unsure of his
welcome.

"He said he didn't think I should be driving." She stepped
back to allow him to enter. "I just need to get Theo's gift."

"Hey, guy." Mark crouched down and scratched behind
Brumby's ears. He slipped a rawhide chew stick to the happy
bulldog, who trotted off with his prize secured between his
jaws.

When Nora returned, she carried a brightly wrapped box in
one hand and her coat in the other.

"Are you feeling okay?" Mark stared at her stomach. "You
look…bigger."

"I can't see my feet and pretty soon I don't think I'll be
able to see the ground at all," she confessed. "Sleeping has
turned into a sport, since athletics seem to go on all night. I'm
convinced once she's in school she'll go out for every sport."

He helped her on with her coat.

"Can we at least be friends?" he asked quietly.

She looked over her shoulder. His serious voice and the look
on his face was a surprise to her. She noticed he'd traded in
his trademark Hawaiian shirt for a brick-red polo shirt tucked
into tan khakis that even sported a razor-sharp crease. She
reached over her shoulder and covered his hand with hers.

"I didn't think it ever stopped," she told him. "I just need
to work things out in my mind."

He smiled and nodded. "Are you ready to go out and celebrate? It seems Theo's parties get wilder every year. You'd think for an old guy he'd want to do something a little less crazy, but that doesn't seem to happen." They walked outside to the car.

"I don't think Theo would ever be any other way." Nora slid onto the buttery-soft leather seat.

Mark set the gift on the floor of the back seat and walked around to the driver's side. Once he was settled behind the wheel, he turned his head to look at her.

"Seems like years ago, doesn't it?"

She didn't need a further explanation to know he was talking about the night he'd picked her up at the airport.

"Another lifetime," she murmured, tucking her coat around her.

Mark switched on the heater and adjusted the vents so the warm air would be directed at Nora.

"Have you thought of names yet?" Mark asked.

"I received something like six baby-name books at the shower at the salon," Nora replied. "Some say choose the name with your baby's personality in mind. Others suggest you consider the child's astrological sign. Then there are the parents' astrological signs, their personalities, what you hope your child will grow up to be. I was thinking about writing names on slips of paper and just tossing them up into the air and see what comes down first. Or wait until she's old enough to choose her own name."

Mark chuckled. "We used to have neighbors who were children of the sixties. They believed their kids should be named according to the weather on the day they were born. So there was Sunny, Rainbow, Raine and Earthquake." He could barely keep a straight face as he recited the names.

"Earthquake?" Nora giggled. "Are we talking boy or girl?"

"Boy, but it was Rainbow that had it the hardest since he was another boy. Earthquake insisted on changing his name, which really upset his parents, so he compromised on Rich for Richter," he explained, naming the method of registering an earthquake's strength. "Rainbow settled for being known as

Bow. That he could handle.'' He was quiet for a moment. ''I've always liked the name Sara without the h.''

''Old girlfriend?'' she teased.

He shook his head. ''My kindergarten teacher. The day I painted my desk purple Miss Sara predicted I'd be a colorful character. I asked her to marry me, but she said by the time I was old enough for us to get married, I'd consider her too old for me.'' He heaved a theatrical sigh. ''I was in love with her from then on.''

''And have you seen Miss Sara since then?'' Nora asked, amused by his story that she was convinced was true. Only a young Mark would paint his desk purple.

''Actually, I have. She still teaches kindergarten. But she broke my heart when she married the principal,'' he said. ''You haven't told me what your idea for a name is.''

''Evelyne that ends with an e,'' she explained. ''I went to school with someone with that name and I thought the spelling was very elegant. Maybe an elegant name will give her good luck.''

''She'll have two great parents, fantastic grandparents, an ornery great-grandfather and the perfect great-grandmother. That's the best luck any kid can get.''

''True,'' Nora murmured, thinking of her grandmother.

As if he sensed the direction of her thoughts, Mark reached over and briefly covered her hand with his.

''She knows,'' he said quietly.

Even after he took his hand away, Nora felt the warmth against her skin for the balance of the drive.

She smiled when twinkling lights suddenly appeared in the distance.

''Your parents' house could double as an airplane landing strip,'' she commented as he parked the car.

'':You weren't the one risking his life on the roof while being told where the lights had to go,'' he grumbled good-naturedly. ''Jeff only had to put lights in the trees, while Brian got lucky and was given the patio. Me, they put on the roof,'' he said, helping her out of the car.

''That's because you bounce better than we do. Hey there,

gorgeous,'' Jeff said as he walked up to them. He bent down and kissed Nora on the cheek.

She kissed him back. ''You look better.''

He smiled sadly as he shook his head. ''Still trying to figure out the meaning of life.''

''I have faith in you.''

''Here, be useful for once.'' Mark stole Nora's hand from Jeff's and handed him Nora's gift for Theo.

The house's interior was filled with people. Music that Nora was convinced sounded more like bells and whistles rolled out of the stereo's speakers. She winced at one clanging sound.

''Gramps loves the Spike Jones band as much as Dad does.'' Mark raised his voice to be heard. ''And they call our music insane.''

''About time you got here!'' Brian kissed Nora on the cheek and handed her a filled glass. ''Mom said you'd probably need this,'' he told her.

''Where's the birthday boy?''

''In the family room.''

''Then we better head that way.'' Mark eyed his brothers, who remained on their heels. ''Thanks for the offer, but we don't need an escort. I grew up here.'' He waved them off.

The two men ignored him as they made their way through the crowd.

Nora smiled and greeted those she knew as Mark led the way, keeping his hand tightly clasped around hers. She appreciated his way of protecting her from the crowd.

Nora noticed Theo sat in an easy chair looking like a king surveying his kingdom. She smiled at the thought that fit the man.

The older man looked up and noticed the small group heading his way. His face broke into a broad smile as he stood up and gathered Nora in his arms.

''Happy birthday,'' she said, caught up in his hug.

''Did he drive carefully?'' He looked over her head and glared at his youngest grandson. ''You didn't hit any bumps and jostle this precious package, did you?''

''Like we were going to church,'' Mark intoned, setting the

gift on the table near the chair that was already piled high with gift-wrapped packages.

"It was a lovely drive." Nora smiled.

"Good to hear. Now come with me." Theo took her hand and led her away. Nora looked startled at the abrupt kidnapping. She glanced over her shoulder. "He doesn't need to come."

"Maybe I want to," Mark called.

"Don't worry, I'll bring her back safely," the older man growled.

Nora found herself outside as Theo guided her down the path leading to the garage where he and Lou worked their magic on classic cars.

"You're not going to show me a flattened Beetle, are you?" she asked, once recalling his teasing threat to show her what her car would look like as a pancake.

"This is much better," he said mysteriously. Once they reached the first building, he switched on a light and gestured for her to go inside.

Nora had only been in the garage a few times. Tonight, all the tools were put away in their proper places and a vehicle was covered with a tarp. What caught her eye was what sat on the workbench.

"Oh, my," she breathed, walking toward the object. She tentatively touched the highly polished wood. "It's beautiful." She couldn't resist stroking the curves of the old-fashioned cradle.

"My grandfather made it for his firstborn," Theo explained. "It's been passed down to every generation and now to you."

"No!" Nora shook her head. "That wouldn't be right."

He placed his hands on her shoulders. "You're family, Nora. You're having my great-granddaughter," Theo said gently. "Abby and Jeff and Gail and Brian have a family heirloom and it's only fair you have one. I wanted you to have this. I didn't mean to make you cry." He pulled out his handkerchief and handed it to her.

"I call them hormonal tears," she sniffed, hugging him

tightly. "I don't know what to say. It's your birthday. You're supposed to receive gifts, not give them."

"That's right, it's my birthday, which means I can do anything I want. And what I want is to give you this cradle."

"But it's your family's cradle," she protested through her tears. "It needs to stay in your family."

"And it is. I consider you part of my family."

His words brought out more tears.

Theo chuckled as he hugged her. "You love my rascal of a grandson, don't you?"

Unable to speak, she settled for a jerky nod of the head.

"But what if it isn't enough?" she asked.

"I've seen the two of you together and you've got a lot more going for you than love, but let me tell you, love's a pretty powerful beginning. I've seen my grandson look at you as if you're the center of his world. And I've seen the way you look at him, which is pretty much the same. You know what you can do for me?"

She dabbed at her nose. "What?"

"You can give me the perfect birthday present by finally putting the boy out of his misery."

Chapter Eighteen

"What are they doing out there?" Mark pushed aside the curtain and peered outside although he couldn't see much past the patio.

"Maybe he's showing her the Duesenberg he and Dad are working on," Jeff said absently while he looked around the room. "Are you sure she said she was going to be here?" he asked Brian.

"For the millionth time, yes," Brian groaned. "Abby told Gail she might be a little late, but she'd be here."

Mark looked at Jeff. "I thought you talked to Abby last night?"

He shook his head. "Just to the answering machine. I asked her if we could meet somewhere and talk. She didn't call me back."

"I don't know what you did, but you better fix it fast," Mark advised. "If I can't get Nora, I'd at least like my apartment back." He looked out the window again. "There they are."

Jeff and Brian looked out also.

"I'll make a deal with you. You make things right with Nora and I'll do whatever I have to do with Abby," Jeff vowed. "Hopefully, I'll know what I'll have to do by the end of the evening. Oh, man," he sighed.

When Mark turned around, he saw what his oldest brother saw. Abby walked into the room looking like a bright ray of sunshine. She'd pulled her hair up into an array of loose curls with one left to dangle down her neck. Her black knit top sparkled with silver lights and her black velvet pants hugged her trim body like a glove.

Mark couldn't miss his brother's hangdog expression as he gazed at his wife, and that for all the sparkle on her clothing, Abby didn't look all that perky. He'd even hazard a guess that the smile she directed at Ginna was more forced than natural.

"Did you hear that Lucie bought the McDaniels' property?" Brian asked.

"I heard she got a hefty settlement from the airline and even the airplane manufacturer for that engine crashing through her house," Mark replied. 'I don't blame her for wanting to move. I probably would too, but why all the way out here?"

"The move was made more for Nick than herself." Jeff mentioned Lucie's son. "His school won't take him back. Seems they didn't like the way he redesigned the school's Web site. Thanks to Dad, she got him into Fieldcrest." He named a local private school well known for its academics.

"If nothing else, they'll teach him how to hack into more secure computer systems than he does now," Brian commented.

"Take a look at that." Jeff gestured with his beer bottle. 'Someone's got Lucie on their radar."

"I thought Logan was seeing Trish Carson," Mark said, watching the local veterinarian who in turn was watching Lucie as she talked to Ginna.

"Trish went to Las Vegas for the weekend and came back with a bronc rider." Lou walked up. "Which you have to admit is pretty funny since she hates horses. You boys take care of your granddad's gift?"

"We stuck a bow on it," Jeff replied. "I'm sure you'd understand we weren't going to go through the hell of gift wrapping an engine for a 1938 Packard Sport Coupe Six. You know, most people his age would be happy with a tie or a sweater."

"Abby gave him a studio portrait of the kids," Lou said.

Jeff looked over his shoulder. "She's not happy."

Lou sighed. "I thought we'd raised you boys to have more

sense.'' He patted Brian's shoulder. ''Thank God you got i
right.''

''Dear brothers.'' Ginna slid in between Mark and Jeff. Sh
lifted her wineglass in a toast. ''Is this exclusive to the XY
chromosome set or can we double Xs intrude?''

''It depends on what you have to offer the group,'' Mark
told her. ''Where's Zach?''

''Discussing his latest column with some of the guys.'' Sh
lifted her glass to her lips. ''I must say, except for Brian, you
men look extremely pathetic.''

''Has Abby said anything about me?'' Jeff asked his sister

She shot him a pitying look. ''Why don't you ask her di
rectly, Jeff? Go up to the woman and just ask her. As fo
you—'' she turned her attention to Mark ''—I honestly thin
you've got a good chance to add Nora to our family before th
baby's born.''

''Why can't you women share with us?'' Mark demanded
''Why do you have to make everything like some state secret
If we do something wrong, why can't you just tell us?''

Ginna smiled. ''But you do know everything, Mark. It's jus
that the male brain comes to the same conclusion from a dif
ferent direction than the female brain does.''

''Since my wife is still speaking to me, I think I'll opt ou
of the lecture.'' Brian gave his sister a one-armed hug an
walked toward Gail, who gave him a dazzling smile and kiss

Mark looked around the room that was filled with famil
and friends. He saw his grandfather and grandmother were talk
ing to Gail and Brian. His parents were over by the fireplac
while his dad was obviously talking cars to Eric while Eric'
girlfriend and Mark's mother chatted about what Mark alway
called girl stuff. Ginna and Zach were across the room talkin
to Abby and a couple of the guys from the station. He notice
something else along the way. Abby covertly kept an eye o
Jeff even though his thickheaded brother didn't seem to know
it. Mark noticed that baby sister Nikki was a little too coz
with one of the new firefighters who'd recently joined th
station.

"Jeff," he said quietly, then inclined his head in Nikki's direction.

"She's over eighteen."

"But does he know she's our sister and what could happen to him if he tries anything?" Mark asked.

"My money's on Nikki. The last guy who tried to go too far got a broken nose."

Mark let out a low whistle. "Way to go, Nik." He grinned.

"So, Mark, what are you going to do about Nora?"

"Persuade her to marry me," he said without hesitation.

"And how exactly do you intend to do that?" Jeff asked.

Mark kept his gaze focused on Nora who entered the room with Theo. She kissed the elderly man on the cheek then moved over to a group of women who gestured her over toward them.

"I don't have a clue," he murmured.

All of a sudden the room was darkened and Cathy walked in pushing a serving cart bearing a large sheet cake decorated with several miniature antique cars. Tiny candles blazed around the perimeter of the cake. Everyone began singing "Happy Birthday."

"Good thing I still have a good set of lungs!" Theo boomed as he was urged to make a wish and blow out the candles.

Martha cut squares from the cake while several women passed out the pieces.

"A corner piece." Nora smiled at him as she handed him a paper plate.

Mark smiled back. He was touched she remembered he always liked the corner piece of a cake.

"Did I tell you how beautiful you look tonight?" he asked, taking a bite of his cake.

She brightened. "No, but it's always nice to hear."

He looked around. He found a miserable-looking Jeff in one corner, Abby in another. He watched his mother hand a piece of cake to Jeff then pause long enough to say something to him. She must not have liked what he said because she shook her head and moved on. Mark looked back at Abby then swung back to Jeff.

"Would you hold this, please?" He didn't wait for a reply

as he handed Nora his plate. He walked over to Jeff and too
his arm.

Jeff looked over at him. "What are you doing?"

"What should have been done long ago," Mark said griml
pulling his brother with him. He alternately pushed and pulle
his brother until they reached Abby. "Abby." Mark nodded
his sister-in-law before grabbing her hand and pulling her alor
with Jeff.

"What are you doing?" Abby exclaimed, digging in h
heels, but Mark was a man on a mission. He didn't stop un
he'd reached the middle of the room. He kept a tight grip c
the couple.

"Maybe it should have been done this way in the begi
ning," he told them. "Abby, Jeff did something stupid on yo
anniversary so you threw him out. And now he either mope
around the station or he mopes around my apartment. We a
talking pathetic with a capital P." He didn't care that he wa
attracting attention. He was even hoping the public displa
might help. "And I doubt you're doing any better." He ignore
her killing gaze. "So do us all a favor. *Give the man a clu*
Give all of us a clue! What can I say? We're men. We're n
perfect. We'll all probably figure out the meaning of life a h
of a lot sooner than we'll figure out what goes on in a woman
mind." His intensity rang out in the quiet room. "We don
always know when we say something wrong. You want t
know how bad it's become? Just look at your husband." H
waved his hand toward Jeff. "He loves you so much he can
think straight and he loves the kids. Will you put him out c
his misery?"

"Is there a reason why you have to do this so publicly?"
Abby asked in a low voice.

Mark grinned. "Yes, there is. But that's something you'
have to figure out for yourself."

Abby buried her face in her hands. She took a deep breat
and looked up. She turned to Jeff. "I swear, if you ever agai
give me a household item for an anniversary gift I will shoc
you."

"This was all because of what I gave you?" he asked.

She nodded jerkily.

"But what about the necklace?"

She looked blank. "What necklace?"

"The one I slipped in the envelope that held the paperwork or the vacuum unit," Jeff explained.

Abby looked stunned. "I didn't open the envelope. It said held the warranty so I didn't bother looking inside. I'm not ure whether to kiss you or kill you right now," she declared.

Jeff grinned. "I'll choose for you then." He pulled her into is arms.

Mark grinned too. "Just call me Cupid." He turned around nd zeroed in on Nora. He moved her way with everyone staying out of his path while they enjoyed the impromptu entertainment.

"Don't do this, Mark," Nora said in a low voice.

"Did you hear everything I said to Abby?" he asked, waiting for her nod. "It goes double for you and me. Nora, I love ou so much I can't think straight. I'm not perfect. I've done ome stupid things where you and I were concerned, but I think ne of the best things between us, is, well, between us." He ently laid his palm on her tummy. "I know with you beside ne, I can be about as normal a guy as you can get and hopeully, be as good a dad as the other men in my family." His aze was solemn as he stared at her. "The best day of my life vas the day I met you. The problem was I just didn't know it. Oh baby, please, don't cry." He used his thumb to wipe away he tears from the corners of her eyes.

"I don't want you normal," she whispered. "I like you just he way you are."

Mark was afraid to hope. "Does this mean you'll marry me vithin the next week, because I don't want to wait any longer."

Nora nodded.

He let out a loud "wahoo!" as he picked her up and spun er around.

"Mark, I'm getting dizzy!" she protested, gripping his houlders. "Besides, I'm too heavy for you."

He put her down but refused to release her. He dipped his

head and kissed her. He wished they were alone so he cou
kiss her the way he wanted.

"Get a room, you two!" Eric shouted over the applause.

Mark lifted his head. "I can't wait until our daughter
born," he whispered.

Nora laughed. "Why?"

"Because I've got it all worked out. When she starts datin
I'll just say to the boy, 'Let me show you my gun collection'

Mark kept grinning. "Now things feel right."

"The best birthday gift I could have gotten." Theo mov
in for the first hug.

Ginna made sure she was second.

"Much better," she told her friend.

Nora nodded. "Grammy Fran was right. She said somethi
was missing from my life. That something was Mark. Beside
how can I resist a man who was willing to admit what he d
in front of his family and friends."

Ginna hugged her brother. "So what's next on your agend
master matchmaker?"

Mark looked over where Jeff and Abby were in a corn
having a conversation that he hazarded was going the way
should. It didn't matter anymore that Jeff wouldn't be goir
back to Mark's apartment that night because Mark wouldn't t
there either.

Mark shook his head. "Are you kidding? I'm quitting whi
I'm ahead."

Epilogue

'One more push, Nora, and your daughter will be here to greet you.''

"Easy for you to say!" she growled at her doctor, who merely grinned.

"You can do it, honey," Mark encouraged cheerfully. He stood behind her, bracing her up each time she needed to push.

She shot him a look that should have turned him into ashes on the spot.

"You think so? Then you do it." She sounded a growl worthy of a horror film. "And stop acting so damn cheerful." She geared herself up.

"Okay, a little more. And now." The doctor grinned.

A mewling cry sounded.

The doctor held up a tiny wiggling body and gently placed the baby on Nora's stomach.

"Mr. and Mrs. Walker, I'd like you to meet your daughter."

Nora burst out crying as she cradled the baby. "She's so beautiful, isn't she, Mark? Mark?" She looked around.

The nurse chuckled. "I'd say our new father is out cold. I'll get an ammonia capsule," she told the doctor.

Nora looked down at the floor where Mark lay. The nurse crouched down, broke an ammonia capsule under his nose and waited as he came to.

Mark immediately jumped to his feet and bent over the tiny bundle Nora held.

"So beautiful," he murmured, kissing Nora deeply. "Both of you are so beautiful."

"Are you all right?" she asked, amused.

"Just a little light-headed," he explained. He looked at Nora. "Any delivery I've assisted was because the baby was ready then and there to come out. But I have to say the last seventeen hours was more than anyone should go through. I'm not sure I can go through this again."

Nora patted his cheek. "We'll discuss it later, sweetheart. For now, say hello to Sara Evelyne Walker."

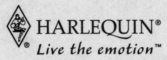

Your opinion is important to us! Please take a few moments to share your thoughts with us about your experiences with Harlequin and Silhouette books. Your comments will be very useful in ensuring that we deliver books you love to read. ***Please take a few minutes to complete the questionnaire, then send it to us at the address below.***

Send your completed questionnaires to:
Harlequin/Silhouette Reader Survey, P.O. Box 9046, Buffalo, NY 14269-9046

1. As you may know, there are many different lines under the Harlequin and Silhouette brands. Each of the lines is listed below. Please check the box that most represents your reading habit for each line.

Line	Currently read this line	Do not read this line	Not sure if I read this line
Harlequin American Romance	❑	❑	❑
Harlequin Duets	❑	❑	❑
Harlequin Romance	❑	❑	❑
Harlequin Historicals	❑	❑	❑
Harlequin Superromance	❑	❑	❑
Harlequin Intrigue	❑	❑	❑
Harlequin Presents	❑	❑	❑
Harlequin Temptation	❑	❑	❑
Harlequin Blaze	❑	❑	❑
Silhouette Special Edition	❑	❑	❑
Silhouette Romance	❑	❑	❑
Silhouette Intimate Moments	❑	❑	❑
Silhouette Desire	❑	❑	❑

2. Which of the following best describes why you bought *this book?* One answer only, please.

the picture on the cover	❑	the title	❑
the author	❑	the line is one I read often	❑
part of a miniseries	❑	saw an ad in another book	❑
saw an ad in a magazine/newsletter	❑	a friend told me about it	❑
I borrowed/was given this book	❑	other: _____	

3. Where did you buy *this book?* One answer only, please.

at Barnes & Noble	❑	at a grocery store	❑
at Waldenbooks	❑	at a drugstore	❑
at Borders	❑	on eHarlequin.com Web site	❑
at another bookstore	❑	from another Web site	❑
at Wal-Mart	❑	Harlequin/Silhouette Reader	
at Target	❑	Service/through the mail	❑
at Kmart	❑	used books from anywhere	❑
at another department store or mass merchandiser	❑	I borrowed/was given this book	❑

4. On average, how many Harlequin and Silhouette books do you buy at one time?

I buy _____ books at one time	❑
I rarely buy a book	❑

MRQ403HAR-1A

5. How many times per month do you shop for any *Harlequin and/or Silhouette* books?
One answer only, please.

1 or more times a week	❑	a few times per year	❑
1 to 3 times per month	❑	less often than once a year	❑
1 to 2 times every 3 months	❑	never	❑

6. When you think of your ideal heroine, which *one* statement describes her the best?
One answer only, please.

She's a woman who is strong-willed	❑	She's a desirable woman	❑
She's a woman who is needed by others	❑	She's a powerful woman	❑
She's a woman who is taken care of	❑	She's a passionate woman	❑
She's an adventurous woman	❑	She's a sensitive woman	❑

7. The following statements describe types or genres of books that you may be
interested in reading. Pick *up to 2 types* of books that you are most interested in.

I like to read about truly romantic relationships	❑
I like to read stories that are sexy romances	❑
I like to read romantic comedies	❑
I like to read a romantic mystery/suspense	❑
I like to read about romantic adventures	❑
I like to read romance stories that involve family	❑
I like to read about a romance in times or places that I have never seen	❑
Other: _____	❑

*The following questions help us to group your answers with those readers who are
similar to you. Your answers will remain confidential.*

8. Please record your year of birth below.

19 _____

9. What is your marital status?

single ❑   married ❑   common-law ❑   widowed ❑
divorced/separated ❑

10. Do you have children 18 years of age or younger currently living at home?

yes ❑   no ❑

11. Which of the following best describes your employment status?

employed full-time or part-time ❑   homemaker ❑   student ❑
retired ❑   unemployed ❑

12. Do you have access to the Internet from either home or work?

yes ❑   no ❑

13. Have you ever visited eHarlequin.com?

yes ❑   no ❑

14. What state do you live in?

_____

15. Are you a member of Harlequin/Silhouette Reader Service?

yes ❑   Account # _____   no ❑   MRQ403HAR-1B

If you enjoyed what you just read,
then we've got an offer you can't resist!

Take 2 bestselling
love stories FREE!
Plus get a FREE surprise gift!

Clip this page and mail it to Harlequin Reader Service®

IN U.S.A.	IN CANADA
3010 Walden Ave.	P.O. Box 609
P.O. Box 1867	Fort Erie, Ontario
Buffalo, N.Y. 14240-1867	L2A 5X3

YES! Please send me 2 free Harlequin American Romance® novels and my free surprise gift. After receiving them, if I don't wish to receive anymore, I can return the shipping statement marked cancel. If I don't cancel, I will receive 4 brand-new novels every month, before they're available in stores! In the U.S.A., bill me at the bargain price of $3.99 plus 25¢ shipping & handling per book and applicable sales tax, if any*. In Canada, bill me at the bargain price of $4.74 plus 25¢ shipping & handling per book and applicable taxes**. That's the complete price and a savings of at least 10% off the cover prices—what a great deal! I understand that accepting the 2 free books and gift places me under no obligation ever to buy any books. I can always return a shipment and cancel at any time. Even if I never buy another book from Harlequin, the 2 free books and gift are mine to keep forever.

154 HDN DNT7
354 HDN DNT9

Name	(PLEASE PRINT)	
Address	Apt.#	
City	State/Prov.	Zip/Postal Code

* Terms and prices subject to change without notice. Sales tax applicable in N.Y.
** Canadian residents will be charged applicable provincial taxes and GST.
  All orders subject to approval. Offer limited to one per household and not valid to
  current Harlequin American Romance® subscribers.
  ® are registered trademarks of Harlequin Enterprises Limited.

AMER02   ©2001 Harlequin Enterprises Limited

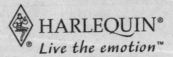